"... I came up here to Get Involved. Think I haven't missed you, sexpot? And come to think, I did come to relieve you, in a way. Need relief, Quindy?"

She rolled her eyes. "Why do I put up with this man—love him, even?"

Because I know what you need, he thought, *and love to provide it. That's wonderful for us both—doing well by doing good!* He said: "Because we're both sensual animals who love to screw and love it rough and besides I think you're the most beautiful and the sexiest ship-handling genius along the spaceways. And besides tha—"

"Oh, talk talk talk. That's enough talk. Come down here."

SPACEWAYS

SPACEWAYS #9

IN QUEST OF QALARA
JOHN CLEVE

PLAYBOY
PAPERBACKS

SPACEWAYS #9: IN QUEST OF QALARA

Copyright © 1983 by John Cleve
Cover illustration copyright © 1983 by PBJ Books, Inc., formerly PEI Books, Inc.

Published simultaneously in the United States and Canada by PBJ Books, Inc., formerly PEI Books, Inc., 200 Madison Avenue, New York, New York 10016. Printed in the United States of America.

The poem *Scarlet Hills* copyright © 1982 by Ann Morris; used by permission of the author.

ISBN: 0-867-21236-5

First printing January 1983

for Sharon Jarvis,
for seventy mental reasons

*If at first you do not succeed, Sunmother counsels,
then try again. Only thus can one be worthy of the
spaceways.*

—Captain Janjaglaya

*If at first you don't succeed, it's been said, try and
try again. Noble words, to which I would add these:
If you try again and still don't succeed—whistle and
pretend you were doing something else all along.*

—Trafalgar Cuw

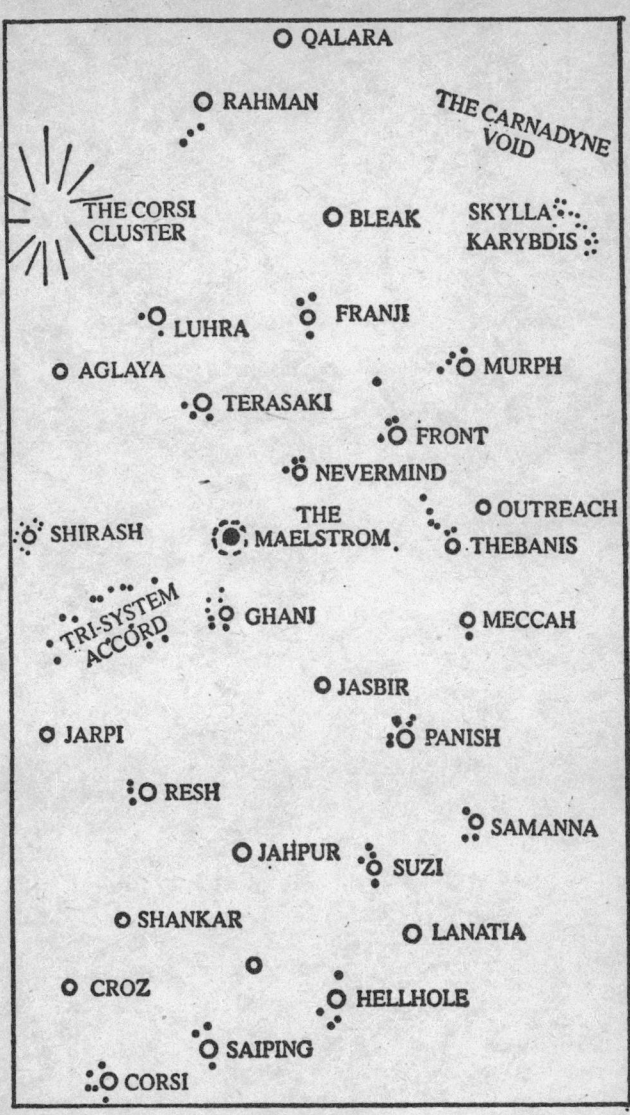

O QALARA

O RAHMAN

THE CARNADYNE
VOID

THE CORSI
CLUSTER

O BLEAK

SKYLLA
KARYBDIS

O LUHRA

O FRANJI

O AGLAYA

O MURPH

O TERASAKI

O FRONT

O NEVERMIND

O SHIRASH

THE
MAELSTROM

O OUTREACH

O THEBANIS

TRI-SYSTEM
ACCORD

O GHANJ

O MECCAH

O JASBIR

O JARPI

O PANISH

O RESH

O SAMANNA

O JAHPUR

O SUZI

O SHANKAR

O LANATIA

O CROZ

O HELLHOLE

O SAIPING

O CORSI

A: All planets are not shown.
B: Map is not to scale, because of
   the vast distances between stars.

SCARLET HILLS

Alas, fair ones, my time has come.
I must depart your lovely home—
Seek the bounds of this galaxy
To find what lies beyond.

(chorus)
Scarlet hills and amber skies,
Gentlebeings with loving eyes;
All these I leave to search for a dream
That will cure the wand'rer in me.

You say it must be glamorous
For those who travel out through space.
You know not the dark, endless night
Nor the solitude we face.

(reprise chorus)

I know not of my journey's end
Nor the time nor toll it will have me spend.
But I must see what I've never seen
And know what I've never known.

Scarlet hills and amber skies,
Gentlebeings with loving eyes;
All these I leave to search for a dream
That will cure the wand'rer in me.

—Ann Morris

Prologue

The four men hand-carried each of the seven big crates down the umbilical tunnel from the ship and onto Franjistation Two. That was unusual, but hardly sinister. All the crates were checked past station scanners and thermosensors. Only one person on the big wheel-shaped space station noted aloud that the boxes resembled coffins. They were not.

Oddly, all seven were several times wrapped with hollow tubing of a bright canary color. Apparently it served as cord or cable. Who knew why those crazies on Terasaki used hollow duraples rather than stiktite binding or even plain old fashioned carbon ropes?

One end of each yellow tube swung loosely down. A station securityman made a lewd remark about the appearance of that. So did a spacefarer off another ship, and a stevedore.

She was one of the two who paced importantly along, orange-coveralled and yellow-hardhatted, beside the four green-clad handlers of those nuttily wrapped big crates.

Neither stevedore was doing a thing aside from walking, although the station was busy with incoming traffic and cargo to be moved. Too, there was outbound cargo, and some of it was waiting while cargo-handlers played escort to seven big long boxes.

A whole load of Bose, a Franjese wine popular on a number of other worlds, languished awaiting the attention of this very pair of stevedores. Both were members of Cargo Carriers Crosscontinental, which of course was part of LPAF—Laboring Persons of All Franji. CCC/LPAF rules demanded that at least two stevedores unload cargo of over six pieces with a weight of over 500 kilos, and the combined weight of the seven boxes was 577.886.

If these green-clad baggy-pantsed fobbers off spaceship *Hot Squid* insisted on carrying their own precious crates of Hojatocorp Duasonik insect repellors, that was not the fault of LPAF or CCC or two smug Franjese cargo-handlers. If they couldn't handle the cargo, then by damn they could slicin' well accompany it!

"Every single person deserves whatever break they can get," stevedore Sashah said with smug austerity and dropout grammar, and her companion nodded with smug austerity.

And so they importantly accompanied the incoming cargo off spacer *Hot Squid* out of Terasaki, and drew their pay. Security watched without particular interest. Other spacefarers off other ships took note without paying much attention. They had more important things to do. They were on their way to the station's bar, mostly.

One man openly stared. He was the master of merchant spacer *Nakaret*, and he was less than patiently awaiting the loading of the last of his cargo. One hundred twenty cases of Bose.

"No wonder most of this planet is in the grip of an impossibility," he muttered; "an ugly recession *and* highflying inflation all at once! No wonder its swinish president, that jowly demagogue Mujazia, is trying to blame all Franji's problems on its people, *and* TMSMCo—*and* for pissake, on Murph!"

Beside the captain his First Mate grunted. Planet Murph was Franji's nearest "neighbor," and pretty much ruled by T.M.S. Mining Co.

"This dam' planet's run by demagogues—union bosses

and their puppet politicians—and naturally they put Mujazia in office, once he dam' near ruined Velynda by caving in to every union demand! Now he seems to be workin' to save his fat ass by preachin' hate—*war*, for pissake!—on Murph!''

"Uh," his First Mate grunted agreeably. Velynda was planetary capital of Franji, third planet of hot, red-orange Chandrasekhar, and the Mate of *Nakaret* well remembered Velynda under Mujazia. A mess. Now the planet was. And *Nakaret* was long since ready to redshift. If Mujazia wanted to blame his failures and problems on TMSMCo and Murph, *Nakaret* might as well blame its current problem on Mujazia!

"Oh well," the captain muttered on, glowering after the little parade of four green-clad *Hot Squid* crewmembers and two orange-clad stevedores. Cargo *Un*-handlers, he thought. "Could be worse. If somebody doesn't Do Something about that maniac on Shankar, General Filatravia, *they're* going to have a planetary war, for pissake! (No no—make that Filatravia's sake!) Half the sisterslicin' planets along the spaceways are in the hands of idiots and TGO ner nobodyelse's doin' a dam' thing about it. If it wasn't for us honest and long-sufferin' merchanters, the whole universe'd fall apart!''

"Firm," his Mate agreed, idly rubbing her cheek.

"On the other hand, you do have to wonder why those baggy-pantsed rot-rectums off *Hot Squid* have to carry their own stupid bug killers!''

"Yeah," his Mate snarled, thinking that the four crew carrying the crates, followed by two do-nothings, looked like a funeral procession on Jorinne.

The four greensuits off *Hot Squid* did carry their seven boxes around the station rim to the shuttle terminal, one by one.

Only when the last of the big crates was on the cargo shuttle-pod and en route down to Franji did the two cargo-handlers amble over to the stack of wine cases. They were ricked up before the umbilical tunnel that connected the outer perimeter of Franjistation Two to docking berth G-1. Outside the station, electromagnetically coupled to it with airlock sealed to umbilical, awaited *Nakaret* with an empty hold, expensively temp-controlled to accommodate the wine.

Sashah and her buddy at last went back to work.

Wait until *Nakaret*'s sour-faced captain found out they were due for mandatory break in eleven and a half mins!

Neither they nor anyone else had noticed that the bright yellow tube around the fifth Terasak crate was really two; or that the other end of the trailing length of tubing fed into the crate.

That arrangement was the sole reason the seven cases were so strangely wrapped.

The reason for that was the sole reason they were personally borne by crewmembers of *Hot Squid* rather than by unimaginative but ever-nosy stevedores—or that there were seven of the big boxes, rather than only one.

The other six really did house Hojatocorp insect repellors.

One of the baggy-pantsed greensuits insisted on accompanying the boxes—*inside* the shuttle-pod's cargo hold. That was against the rules. The Terasak greensuit was insistent, and then raised so much hell that at last a wise clerk decided to look the other way. At least the dumb Terasak flainer had a breather! It wasn't as if anyone bothered to provide atmosphere inside a pod. The clerk hoped the crates floated up and crushed the sisterslicin' son of a Terasak bug en route down to Franji.

On the other hand, she didn't, really. If the greensuit got himself killed in the pod by gravity-less, airless cargo shifting, the clerk would be held responsible. She'd be in a lot of trouble until the union bailed her out.

•   •   •

The moment the shuttle settled onto Franji's surface and was clutched close by the planet's .73 gravity, the greensuited spacefarer in the hold dragged off his breathing mask and popped open the side—not the lid but the spring-hinged *side*—of the special crate off *Hot Squid*. The fifth. That revealed the fact that most of the big box's interior was occupied by a semi-soft silver bag.

Squatting, the spacefarer broke the hardened foam around the top of the silver bag's zipper pull. A hand the color of old gold drew down the zipper. Heat gushed out. A moment later, the very *very* latest state-of-the-art spacesuit rolled out. It was silver, and it was occupied.

The air-conditioned spacesuit had fed its occupant's heat—body and breath—out to be trapped by the silver bag. The bag, 97 percent thermo-retentive, had bled some of that heat out through the yellow tube. Meanwhile it had baffled Franjistation's scanners and heat-sensors.

Each of the other six crates gave off a heat-reading that varied by no more than one degree Celsius from each other, including the fifth crate. No one had thought to scan the dangling ends of the finger-thick tubes of yellow duraplas. Why bother?

The Terasak spacefarer began stripping off his baggy green two-piece.

The spacesuit sat up, stood. Its owner began removing it.

The Terasak saw an astonishingly homely woman with old-gold skin, in a blue skintite that molded her angular leanness from neck to toes. The spacefarer said nothing, but he did turn away. This was his first view of the person they had smuggled onto Franji, and he could live quite well without seeing another.

What even he didn't know was that the spacesuit's wearer was a decent-looking if not quite handsome man with deep tan skin. A not at all angular man, though he was rangily well-muscled. He wore a pair of tights in a drab gray. And nothing else, except the holographic projector that made him seem to be an astonishingly homely woman of Terasak coloration, with an angularly lean body snugly encased in medium blue.

The holoproj that cloaked him with that false aura was so advanced that even Kislar Jonuta was unaware of its existence.

Neither man spoke a single word. Talk was not part of the drill, but there was a time limit. Shuttle pods were too important to be allowed to sit around unloaded. Too bad Franji couldn't make its own sonic insect repellors, but once a growing conglomerate got hold of one of the only two companies, the unions really did a job on the conglomerate and despite two government bail-outs, Franji's SoundKil Co. had collapsed.

The real Terasak got into the spacesuit. It fitted him, naturally, because that was the way the operation had been planned. The other man donned the green two-piece and stuffed the pants into the green boots so that the full legs bloused baggily.

The newly spacesuited man got down and got himself into the thermo-retentive bag, the other man helping. He zipped the bag to within two sems of its closure, where the little airtight lid would clamp it.

"You all right?"

"Pos," the silver-bagged man said, very grateful for the human contact and the concern but hardly charmed by the other's unfeminine voice. Maybe she could earn enough on this mission to get her face and voice fixed, he thought, and was zipped in.

The bag's former occupant detached the sealant spray from where it had been attached, to the inside end of the crate. He gave the zip-lock two puffs and set the little sprayer down beside him, on the shuttle-pod's padded floor. He patted a little sticker into place on the silver bag. All with careful swiftness. Everything so far had been practiced, rehearsed again and again. (Not on Terasaki, where *Hot Squid* had not come from. As a matter of fact the ship's name was not *Hot Squid*, either.)

The man in the loose greens re-closed the crate, and tested it. He nodded his satisfaction. There had been this sealed crate and a man in a green suit, beardless and jet-haired. There still was. The only added factor was the spray-can of sealant. The spacer crewman's breather still lay on the floor where he had dropped it. The holoprojector was off.

The man in the loose greens paused to listen. Good. Here came the unloaders, and their machinery.

Squatting, he picked up the sprayer and the end of the yellow tube whose other end entered the crate and then the bag, that point of entry long ago meticulously sealed.

Pulling up the mini-sprayer's red top until it made a little snicking sound, he gave it a one-eighty turn, counted five, pressed the top down into its proper position though reversed, and counted off four seconds. Only then did he insert its little snout into the end of the yellow tube.

He had given it the required three-second burst just as the cargo door was opened from outside. The ruddy light of Franji rushed into the pod, along with city-sounds.

The green-clad man picked up the other man's breathing mask and popped in the sprayer. He kept it there with his left thumb. He rose to greet the Franjese workers who had come to unload the shuttle. Both wore orange helmets and yellow CCC patches on their coveralls, which were orange.

The shuttle-pod's "pilot" was just behind them, looking anxious.

Actually she was a highly paid watcher of the con, the green-clad man knew, since the shuttle piloted itself. But unions were unions. The word "featherbedding" was lost in the upheavals and linguistic reforms of the past, but the practice remained on Franji.

"Ah," she said. "Are you all right?"

"Firm," the man in the cargo hold told her, and looked at the cargo handlers. "I am to accompany the seven crates from Terasaki to their destination. In your truck's cargo hold, I mean."

"That's against the rules, Terasak," he was told, with a xenophobic sound highly unusual along the spaceways.

"Can't letcha do it," another said.

"I'll be riding in the back of the truck with the crates," the man in green said, and he moved toward them.

"Uh—but it's against the—"

A sharper stevedore said, "You unload it if you ride with it."

The green-clad man ignored the truculence. "Right. I'll unload it at the other end."

The cargo-handlers looked at each other, shrugged with a "humor the dumb offplanet fobber" look and stepped back while the dumb offplanet fobber came down out of the pod. Then they went to work.

He watched, unobtrusively testing his muscles against their planet's gravity, which was twenty percent lower than the galactic standard but only .07 lower than the usual shipboard G. He also noted that blue-dyed hair and blue wigs were still popular in Velynda.

He rode in the back of the truck, which had to detour around the parade of a few thousand welfare recipients on strike. Somewhere between the shuttle station and the cargo's destination, he vanished.

The cargo-handlers' attitude was natural enough: Who gave a shit?

(By that time his adjusted holoprojector made him seem a Franjese in a "standard" Franjese suit, blue-haired and surly-looking. The stevedores probably wouldn't have given a shit about that, either. It didn't have anything to do with their job and wasn't their responsibility.)

They weren't around when the crates were opened, of course. By that time, several days later, Velynda and much of Franji were in quite an uproar. Planetary president Mujazia had been murdered by an unknown assailant.

The conservative running mate Mujazia had put up with only in order to be elected had been sworn in. As a matter of fact he had already replaced Mujazia's personal bodyguard with a dozen dedicated career professionals, and had already accepted the resignation of every cabinet officer but one. He set about trying to get the planet into shape again, without mentioning TMSMCo and Murph. As a matter of fact, TMSMCo soon signed contracts with two separate Franjese companies, which was a more than welcome boost to the staggered economy.

The new president would not have to put up with that demagogue who headed the LPAF for life, because that life had ended abruptly on the evening of the same day as Mujazia's.

Mujazia's death was called an ''assassination''; an unduly pleasant-sounding euphemism for the murder of someone important. The presidor-for-life of the LPAF appeared to have been slain by his mistress who then, still naked in bed with him, had suicided.

Only one man on Franji knew otherwise, and he was not on Franji for long.

He was the man who had killed them both. All three; he had also ''assassinated'' Mujazia. He had come a long way in the discomfort of a big packing crate to carry out the double mission, for his employer. His employer was opposed to wars, interplanetary or otherwise.

He had long since departed Franji, along with the ship whose name was not *Hot Squid*. Now it and he were en route to Shankar, where General Filatravia was scheduled to be stopped. That is, murdered. That is, assassinated. ''Musla's Lion'' Filatravia was just one more small-country fundamentalist religious bigot and zealot who thought it would be a wonderful idea to plunge his planet into war for the glory of his god—and himself.

In such enormously important galactic missions, spear-carriers could not be considered important. They had to be considered loose ends. There had been one real witness to the advent on Franji of the professional killer—who went through six disguises before he left, in peace. That witness was inside a spacesuit inside a silver bag that bore a small sticker showing a familiar symbol and the three letters "TGO."

The chemical in the adjusted sealant spraycan had reacted with the powder awaiting it in the yellow tube—and his own body heat—as planned. The Terasak had been dead before his coffin was removed from the shuttle pod.

1

Thomas Carlyle, as he looked up at the stars (c. 1850, Old Style): "A sad spectacle. If they be inhabited, what a scope for misery and folly. If they be not inhabited, what a waste of space."

The planet called Bleak receded in the distance behind spaceship *Coronet*. And then its sun was only a reddish spot of light, and none too soon for *Coronet*'s master and crew.

Spacer *Coronet*'s master was Kislar Jonuta. The crew were Kenowa, Sakyo, and Shiganu of Terasaki; and the recent additions who were part crew, part passengers: HRadem and HReenee of HRalix. Four were Galactics—the human word for humans, now—and two were not. The furry feline people—felinoprimates—from HRalix were not the first non-Galactics to ship with Captain Jonuta, but Sweetface of Jarpi had long since departed his crew. Their leavetaking was not friendly.

Jonuta and HReenee the HRal were very friendly indeed.

So were Jonuta's long-time *companion*, Kenowa, and HReenee's "step-sib" brother, HRadem. Dem, he was called.

Those onboard pairings left out Sakyo and Shiganu. Unfortunately, both were male and each was entirely heterosexual. What Shig and Sak were was horny.

Still, there was unity on *Coronet*. Their "Captain Cau-

23

tious'' was not a military or militaristic man and while he
was not so stupid as to try to run a spaceship as a democ-
racy, he was no tyrant. He was also demonstrably superi-
or. The feeling onboard was almost a family one, with
Jonuta the respected patriarch—although he was hardly old
enough for that role.

Too, they had been through a lot, dared and attempted
and survived a lot, in triumph. Profits were looking good,
too. Besides, they were unified in their delight at putting
Bleak behind them, along with its bleak capital, Zero, and
its homely sun.

Of *Coronet*'s crew, only HReenee had gone down onto
Bleak's bleak surface with the captain. She was only
recently off her planet, whose people were not spacefarers
until a Galactic ship stumbled upon their world, and a
"new race" was "discovered." Already she had experienced travel on four spaceships, rape, a pirate attack,
personal killing—which was even more a thrill for the
HRal than for Galactics—a hand-to-hand fight in freefall,
the hours-long stressful agony of a duel in space with
spaceship *Firedancer* of Captain Corundum, and Jonuta's
lovemaking.

All in all, she preferred the last two, in reverse order.

"Of *course* I shall go down onto this planet you demean
so," she had said, in the perfect diction her people brought
to Erts, the language of the Galactics. She wore a loose
smock-like garment in burnt orange spattered with diamond-
shaped outlines the color of old wine, and trousers of that
fine old wine hue. "I want to see everything!"

"Even *Bleak*?" Shig had demanded, incredulously.

"Even Bleak," HReenee had assured the smallish man
with the shining jet hair.

"You'd see as much of interest and get just as big a
thrill spending ten hours in the sitter," Sak assured her.
He used the spacefarers' current dodge-word for that facil-
ity variously called the head, the can, the john, the crap-

per, the *pissoir*, the yahya, the bathroom, and more coyly, the rest room or powder room.

The lean, seemingly boneless HReenee had laughed at that picturesque warning, and she had gone down onplanet with Jonuta. There was doubtless some truth in Kenowa's unspoken thought that the sensuous HRal just wanted to be wherever Jonuta was.

She and the others never left Bleak's small spacecraft docking-and-loading station in space.

At that, Kenowa and Dem returned pretty quickly to the ship. It hung in space, electromagnetically docked to Bleakerstation. Its outer airlock was joined and sealed to the station's exterior and connected with its interior, the rim of the wheel, by Bleakerstation's sealable umbilical tunnel.

Coronet's inner airlock hatch remained closed. On Bleak or its station, even security personnel were suspect.

Shig and Sak spent most of their time in the station's smallish bar.

Since Bleakerstation had little traffic—as little as possible, by spacefarers' choice, but at that it received more visitors than the planet below—the bar grandiosely named the Golden Citadel was never full. On the other hand, there were lots of other spacefarers, when Sak and Shig entered. That was eminently understandable. Who in its right mind wanted to go down onto Bleak?

They indulged in a wee bit of the relaxer and head-changer called repsonal and quite a bit of beer. They waited until they had a damned good buzz on before they decided it was time to pop a red, too. Even then each man dropped the antintoxicant pill—citromine, or "a red"—directly into the Bleaker beaker of beer currently in use.

They didn't get laid or even try to. Booda only knew what you might pick up from a Bleaker!

They merely sat quietly, elbows on the table, drinking and cracking jokes about Bleak, Bleakerstation, the Golden Citadel, and Bleakers. Until their waiter, a human (more or less, anyhow; he was a Bleaker) objected and expressed offense taken. Sak snapped something unkind, urging an impossible act, and the incredibly rude waiter "accidentally" poured beer in his lap and Shig got up and knocked the Bleaker down. Then a chair overturned across the smallish room and here came a spacefarer in a hurry and looking mean. He wore the chest-dagger and armored left glove that marked him as a spacegoing Bleaker. They did that, probably just to let others along the spaceways know that they were ready to dispute any snot about their home planet.

"You'd think that flainer'd be so happy to be off that cesspool of a planet for good, farin' in space," spacefarer Shiganu later said darkly, "that he'd be too proud to stick up for a *waiter*, just because he, she, or it also happened to be a Bleaker!"

Instead, the spacefaring Bleaker hurried right over and punched Shig down.

Immediately Sak hurried to his feet and punched the Bleaker one, if not down. As the fellow staggered back, the waiter rolled up onto his knees and bit Sak in the leg. And Sak yelled and kicked him, backwards. And as Shig turned a questioning look on all that racket, the other spacefarer punched him. With his left fist, the one in the armored glove.

After that it was pretty raggedy-andy in the Golden Citadel, with the two Terasaks off *Coronet* beating the snot out of the two Bleakers. Then the spacefaring Bleaker's crewmates—two men and a woman built like a man with hips—sort of hurried over to help their Bleaker buddy. And they weren't even Bleakers!

Fortunately two station securitymen arrived soon after that broadening of the brawl. They took one look at the melée and intelligently decided to use their stoppers to restore order or at least a cessation of hostile activity. Having thus got the attention of the combatants, they forced every one to pop a red and one of the mild tranks carried by Bleakerstation securitymen. With the hostilities ended and the combatants both sobered and softened up, the two securitymen escorted the pair off *Coronet* and the other four to their respective ships. They took the time to see them on their way up the inclined tunnel called umbilical, and left them with stern warnings. They also made quiet assurances to Shiganu and Sakyo that the waiter would be dealt with sternly.

When one asked after their captain, Sak told him the captain was down onplanet, selling some merchandise.

"What sort of merchandise?"

Sak and Shig exchanged a look, and shrugged. Sak said, "It walks."

"Really!" The securityman brightened visibly. "How many?"

"Four. Wanted pirates."

"The very best kind!" the Bleaker enthused.

"Four more warm bodies to help take up the work load," his companion enthused.

"Right, and since they're wanted by policers they got nobody looking for them and nobody who cares! We've got 'em for life!" Having enthused that, the first securityman looked again at the two *Coronet* crewmembers, and he was beaming. "You boys pop on into your ship and be good now, all right? Hope we wasn't too rough with you, but we can't have fighting now, can we, spacefarers?"

"Oh my no," Sak said, and went on into *Coronet* in quest of a microgram or two of endorphinol.

"Nah," Shig said, wagging his head and wincing because that armored fist-blow to the rearward side of his neck *hurt*. "Just a few long-deprived spacefarers letting off a little steam. 'Night, guys."

"Uh-huh."

Shig went on up the tunnelway and into *Coronet* in quest of a few micrograms of endorphinol and some antiseptic for his scratches. That woman had landed proper punches, but the dam' waiter had kept biting and scratching.

The waiter was being dealt with sternly, meanwhile. Not by the Bleakerstation Securitymen. His boss held him responsible for the loss of business of six easy-spending and freely-drinking spacefarers, and fired him, cut lip and newly acquired limp and all. The poor fellow went back down onplanet, where the only job he could find was out in Snailslime Gulch. He lived unhappily ever after, or nearly.

Kenowa and Dem of HRalix, meanwhile, had been onboard *Coronet* all along. HRadem was in Kenowa's cabin, where he had been spending a lot of time, once again watching an Akima Mars holomelodrama. The things done to that extraordinarily famous fictional masochistic secret agent acted as a sexual spur to Dem. Where he came from, this sort of cruelty was known as "play-with" and "toy-with" and was pretty standard behavior. The HRal didn't bother denying their love of it, as Galactics had always done. Tormenting was fun, anybody knew that.

It was also sexy, and soon Dem was responding. Kenowa liked that, and soon the holomeller was playing to a disinterested audience of two. Neither watched. Dem's people possessed eight breasts or "breasts"—not much more than nipples, really—and not all eight of any given HRal, female or otherwise, massed as much as Kenowa's two. They were not "The Biggest Pair In The Universe" as Akima Mars's were advertised to be, but Kenowa was amply cushioned and upholstered between collarbones and waist. She and Dem had long since discovered that her un-HRal plentitude did not disgust or disturb him, or even put off the felino-man in the least. As a matter of fact, their effect on Dem was quite the opposite. The HRal were as fascinated with the exotic and variously erotic as humans. He was entranced by her breasts and her strange inner coolth, just as she was both fascinated by and delighted with the extreme warmth of him, beside her and inside her. The normal body temperature of a HRal was forty degrees, which was feverishly high to a Galactic.

Onscreen, actress Setsuyo Puma as Akima Mars was once again enduring the shredding from her of her skimpy, skin-tight clothing by a rapacious badguy captor, who showed his enjoyment in tourniqueting both her meaty thighs. And leered as he took up his electrowhip while staring fixedly at what he had just bared: The Biggest Pair In The Universe.

Onbed, the Pongida-anthroprimate Kenowa was not acting. It was she who made purring noises as her alien lover forgot the movie. Both hands clamping while he chewed away at her superb superstructure, felinoprimate HRadem was soon deeply into interracial relations, and Kenowa.

The holomeller played on, to a disinterested audience of two. The sounds of panting and gasping emanating from the movie joined those from the bed.

Captain Jonuta and HReenee, meanwhile, took a shuttle down. Jonuta, a romantic with a fine sense of drama, was attired as usual: He wore a piratically long coat of dark red, flashing up the front with two rows of brassy prass buttons, pale laurel-green tights, and gleaming boots into which the pants vanished without a trace of rumple or wrinkle. His stopper, slung at his side, was not disguised. Its holster trailed two strands of rawhide-imitating equhyde.

With them went four others, as prisoners. They wore pants and nothing else; their boots were in a duffel-bag on the seat beside Jonuta, who was their captor. Captives, he had observed, tended not to run so fast or so far, barefoot.

The four were Menekris, captain of *Satyagraha* until he had attacked the merchantship bearing HReenee and had been captured by Jonuta-to-the-rescue; and his three surviving crewmen. Pirates, all. Ex-pirates, now.

They had become what Jonuta called walking cargo. Jonuta was an independent businessman. His business was the selling and buying of people—which aided both his personal economy and that of the worlds of the spaceways. He sold more "walking cargo" than he bought. Certainly four murderous pirates were better off earning their keep as slaves on Bleak than receiving that form of public welfare called imprisonment.

In two hours on Bleak he and a happy mines manager struck a bargain. Menekris and crew became slaves to expiate their sins; Jonuta received enough for them to pay for his trouble in capturing them and conveying them here. Since Bleak always needed more warm bodies of the working type and these four were able-bodied, strong, and beloved by no one (meaning they were stuck on Bleak for life and good riddance), Jonuta received his price. Expenses and then some.

He was offered an amount equivalent to the price of all four men for the fascinating exotic woman accompanying him. She continued to look proud and serene while he affected minor insult at the offer.

That brought them both an apology from mines manager Chiranalli, followed by exaggerated politeness and niceties.

That was that, on Bleak. HReenee wanted to tarry and look around; to observe as a tourist of another race. Jonuta wanted to take the next shuttle up to *Coronet*.

"That was a rich offer you turned down, my love," she said. "Are you sure you don't want to sell me?"

Jonuta's cultivated basso rumbled up from his chest: "I am not even smiling, HReenee."

She took his arm with both hands and pressed against him, unconsciously moving with the sensuous rubbing of her kind. Men stared, swallowed, and tried to keep their minds on their business.

Jonuta and HReenee took the next shuttle up to *Coronet*.

A short time later they were onboard ship, zipped up, cleared, and easing away from Bleakerstation with the aid of a reversed magnetic repulsion.

Then they were hot-tailing it out of that solar system.

"Up" toward the double star Payne-Humason and their six planets (including the single really inhabited one, Jorinne), and on "up" and out toward the star named Galileo. One of its planets was Qalara, and Qalara was Jonuta's home.

(The four pair of boots he had kindly given to Chiranalli on Bleak. In addition to the cred-exchange, Jonuta bore away with him his duffel-bag. In it were four stoppers of the Outer Planets type, unregistered and not signed for. Their second setting was frowned upon by most planets here toward Galaxy Center—the area long ago misnamed the Outer Reaches because the original settlers of space came from the Sol system, way out at the edge of the galaxy—although those same governments did not frown on the third setting, which was death by complete disintegration.)

Past the canary yellow FO Payne and its blue dwarf companion, *Coronet* and all onboard would convert to tachyons and thumb their noses at light-speed and Einstein. In terms of time, Qalara was not all that distant, across the surrealistic arabesques of stars in all their colors.

A few million kloms out from Bleak and its fading sun, Jonuta called Sak to the con. Sak came, to find his captain standing as was his wont. The captain was also staring at the shiner on that old-copper face with its high, sharply etched cheekbones.

"What's the other guy look like?" he rumbled.

Sak heaved a sigh and affected a bowed head. "Not too bad, Cap'n. There were five of them."

The reply was silence, and Sakyo looked at the console. Anywhere but at Jonuta. At last the latter spoke.

"How clever of you! Five of them! What kind of shape is Shig in?"

"He's all right too. A few cuts and bruises."

"No broken bones, no stab-wounds."

"Neg, Captain," Sak said quietly, addressing the console with its multicolored lights.

"Two against five and only a few cuts and bruises! What were they, children?"

"Negative, Captain. The, uh, station security got there before they had time to do a better job on us."

Jonuta snorted, but grinned inwardly. One thing about Sak—the man was honest even when it hurt! "Umm. Just sittin' in the bar, sippin' a few and making remarks about Bleak?"

"Pos," Sakyo nodding, almost swallowing the word and showing great interest in the sensor readouts. He added, "Cap'n."

"Anything serious, Sak?"

The Terasak shook his head. "Neg, Captain. Nothing serious at all. We're sorry, Captain."

"But you've kept the black eye rather than cover it up. Can you see all right? Ready to take the con?"

Sakyo abandoned the self-denigrating posture that was part of the ancient culture of his people—Terasaki having been settled by two ships full of people from a Homeworld district called Nippon, centuries ago—and adopted a military pose.

"Firm, Captain! Ready to take the con, Captain!"

Jonuta nodded and headed for the hatchway. There he paused to look back.

"Damn your ass, Sak, a fight in a saloon! That was flainin' stupid!"

"This pitiful person absolutely knows it, Captain sir." Suddenly Sak turned to look at him, and both assumed postures were gone. "Captain . . ." he said, in a normal voice.

Jonuta remained where he was with one eyebrow lifted. It was reply enough: Let's hear it.

"Uh—Shig and I are both horny up to here, and especially since there's plenty of sexual activity onboard." All that came in a rush, Sakyo relieving himself of the words in the way of a nervous youngster saying his first public "piece." And before Jonuta could answer the shorter man went on: "That's neither gripe nor excuse, Captain. But Shig and I are worried, too."

"Worried." Implied criticism was taken, and Jonuta was captain. He had to be noncommittal, but could not walk away.

Meanwhile Sakyo was having trouble meeting his captain's eyes. "Pos, Captain. You and Kenowa are . . . you go 'way back. She was with you before Shig and me—uh, before Shig and I were. You two make us feel good and so *Coronet* has always felt good. Lovers and friends, I mean. Then we took the HRal onboard and you—they've come between you and Kenowa. And the ship is *different*. Feels different I mean. Captain."

Jonuta was Jonuta, and he was captain. He had to put a good face on it, a captain's face. At last he said, "Spacefarer Sakyo, you're so far out of line you're talking sideways. You have the con." And the captain redshifted.

He thought about it as he went along the ship's corridor called "tunnel." This one was tan with the hint of yellow. He considered what the other man had said, and not with anger.

"The poor bastard's right on every count," he muttered, and he was not a man given to muttering to himself. *There's nothing military about* Coronet, *but it's Kenowa and I who are out of line. We aren't being fair to Shig and Sak. We gave him that black eye— I did, not some fight-happy spacefarers in a bar!*

Damn it!

It's just that I've done it again. I've fallen into infatuation—again. So has Dem, and either Kenowa has or she's compensating very well for my . . . abandoning her, for HReenee.

On the other hand, that's the way it is. I've done it many times before, just not on the ship. Fortunately. Thought I was iron disciplined, didn't you, ole loverboy Jone! But this is the way it is. I'm hot for HReenee right now, and now at all interested in bedding down with Kenny. It's always been that way, and then I come back and it's over, with whoever-she-was, and it's better with Kenny and me.

Do Sak and Shig know that? They certainly know that Kenowa and I have an agreement, just as she and I both know I'm not the sort who possibly could remain either celibate or monogamous! Hmm—whether Sak and Shig know that or not doesn't much matter. It doesn't help their bad case of swollen balls, and it doesn't excuse me for breaking my own shipboard rules!

He passed a side tunnel, pale blue. *Coronet* was hardly enormous, but even a "small" spacer wasn't small. The engines worked on, stealing matter from space and turning it into energy that kept the ship hurtling on at a velocity that not even Jonuta could grasp, with all his intelligence and after all his years on the spaceways. Axial spin provided centrifugal force, which was gravity's twin brother. On *Coronet* it was maintained at .8 standard G. That was standard operating procedure in spacecraft. Since their next stop would be Qalara and Qalara's gravity was .82, it was also perfect preparation for Jonuta's next homecoming. He walked easily.

"The trouble is," he muttered, and broke off to keep his thoughts to himself, *is Kenny only taking care of herself with the (very!) warm body at hand, that fobby Dem, or is she really interested in him? (Whatever "interested in" means!) If that's the case, we could be in trouble, after all these years—and so could Coronet!*

Could we all survive it, if Kenowa and I parted?

How about if we were onboard the same ship?!

He paused at the blue door to his own cabin. Another thought had come skidding in on a tangential course.

Can we all survive if Kenowa and I don't part, but try to continue this way?

For all I know HReenee and Dem are inseparable. For

*all I know they are even more fickle than I (am). There's
more I don't know about her than about* . . *bop-ball!*

And Jonuta, who had never played bop-ball or watched
a game, entered his cabin.

A reddish, gold-dotted plain ran out to lavender moun-
tains that reared spikily under a pinkish sky. From behind
the leftward peaks emanated a warm, coppery-gold glow.
This was not a mural, or any sort of painting; it was the
illusion of spacious reality provided by the holoprojection
that was a hobby and a love of Kislar Jonuta of Qalara. On
the plain stretching away before him, red-and-tan animals,
ruminants, fed peacefully. Across the sky away out there
in the simulated distance a white cloud sprawled, like spilt
buttermilk.

By the time he walked in he had decided what he should
do, like it or not.

HReenee was disappointed, of course, but tried to understand when he said he had lots to do and thought she
needed and would welcome some time on the con, anyhow.
She straightened the clothing she had deliberately disar-
rayed for him, and went to join Sak.

That accomplished little positive purpose save in Jonuta's
mind. He felt Sak would appreciate it, too. It did little for
Jonuta's mental state, or HReenee's, or of the horny
Terasak she sat beside in the con-cabin.

2

An exhaustive 1977–1981 [Old Style] study of twenty-seven women of widely varying ages showed the women superior to males in adapting to the physical and psychological rigors of those tests. A spokesman for N.A.S.A. [Homeworld], in response to the query why the U.S. had put no women into space by 1980, said, "A lot of reasons were tossed around, but the main one was that until the shuttle came along, there was no way to manage women's waste."

"On the far lower right hand corner of a living room wall," the wise-looking computer program told Janja of Aglaya, "make a firm thumbprint and draw a circle around it. Call that Thebanis, only planet of the double star Janski. Basing distance on the same scale as Thebanis's size on the wall, take five paces to its left and, on tiptoe, make another thumbprint. Circle that and call it Jorinne, fourth planet of the double star Payne."

The program blinked at her from the screen and quirked his mouth into an expression that was not quite a smile. "Now you have some concept of the size of just this central area of our galaxy, and the distance between its suns and their planets."

Janja nodded, sighing. She understood—in a way.

It didn't seem so, whizzing along in a spaceship that

could also slip into that nonentity called "subspace" purely for the sake of convenience, mental and linguistic—and cover distance even faster than whizzing. Hard enough to accept that the person she was looking at was not a person at all, but had been and was dead, and was now wholly an electronic simulation.

"Time is a distance," it/he said, "and distance must be measured by time. This remains so even with our ability to convert into tachyons and travel faster than light, seemingly in contravention of the ancient al-Einstein postulation and yet entirely in accord with it—when we include the few little *adjustments* made in arriving at the Grand Unified Theory. Time is a distance, and distance is vast, because the galaxy is vast."

"Yes, yes," Janja said, impatiently drumming her fingers. "My question concerned Qalara, not catch-phrases and GUT and al-Einstein."

The highly sophisticated computer readjusted and responded without so much as a blip or a pause.

"Return to the representation of Thebanis at the far lower rightward corner of the wall of a good-sized living room. There is not space enough on the wall to show Qalara as well as Thebanis. Both would have to be reduced to mere dots."

"Damn," Janja muttered uncharacteristically. "I knew it, but damn anyhow. It's been a year now. Will I never reach Qalara? I have gone from ignorant 'barbarian' and slave to captain of my own ship in a year-ess. Must I wait a lifetime to find Jonuta?"

Presumably recognizing a rhetorical question when it "heard" one, the computer made no reply.

Janja stared at the waiting image and its carefully designed friendly, receptive face. She wore no such expression. She had never lost sight of her goal since her kidnap off her idyllic, non-technological and pre-industrial planet, Aglaya. The kidnappers were Captain Jonuta's men. Slavers, off the slaver Jonuta's slaver-ship. One of them had murdered her lover and affianced, Tarkij, without necessity. She had been sold—by Jonuta—and had suffered and fought and killed and tricked her way to freedom, and had been tricked by Corundum, and had joined Hellfire almost on a whim, and with Hellfire she had been enslaved again, on Knor.

Still she knew that she was no slave and still she did not feel truly a part of this culture. *Their* culture, these arrogant colonizers and enslavers she called *them* because they were not her people, these Thingmakers. *They* were humans who arrogantly called themselves Galactics, the race of the galaxy, as if they were alone in it or other races were of no importance. *They* looked upon Jarps and Aglayans and others as inferior peoples and enslaved them.

Janja knew better. She possessed an ability *they* did not, and thus could not be called a human. Not inhuman or subhuman, but more than human. *They* devoted much attention to their physical selves and appearance and they made Things. They had done very very little to get to know themselves, to improve their inner selves (save in the cases of a few individuals), for millenia.

She was among them, because they had dragged her off Aglaya and thrown her among them. Still, she was not *of* them; merely among them. As a person named Byron had put it, time out of mind, she was often wrapped "In a shroud of thoughts which were not/Their thoughts."

And for a year she had sustained herself by holding one goal, by never forgetting the one driving intent that gave her purpose. It had a name, and the name was Jonuta.

She would remove Jonuta from the spaceways his presence soiled.

That was her vow. She was worthy of Sunmother and worthy of Aglii and Aglaya. She would be worthy of the spaceways and thought that she was. She would kill Jonuta, who was not.

For a year now she had considered herself as being on a quest. In quest of Qalara.

And still I cannot rush there, to find and confront and slay Jonuta!

Instead, she must go to Thebanis. To go to Thebanis she must avoid one of the largest collapstars—a dead star or "black hole in space"—in the galaxy. The Demonhole.

It was an inconceivably huge magnet that once had been a star. Now it lurked invisibly in space, emitting absolutely no light and doing its best to suck in anything that passed. Should anything, whether a mote of interstellar dust or a spaceborne pebble or stone or a ship or even a comet, dare pass too close—the Demonhole succeeded. It made that object part of itself and increased its own power by a tiny fraction. Its newly captured component it tucked away out of sight, forever. For the gravity of any collapstar was greater than the escape velocity even of light, and nothing could be seen of the Demonhole or its prey beyond its suction perimeter, its Blue Event Horizon.

Not until spacer *Satana* had pursued a course— "swerved"— to avoid that horrid lurking eater of matter and energy could the ship and all onboard be converted to the faster-than-light particles called tachyons. Only after *Satana* avoided becoming a part of the Demonhole could it defeat Einstein and jump in close to the Janski system and Thebanis.

Janja wanted to go to Qalara; was compelled to go to Qalara. And first she had to go to Thebanis.

Qalara* was still months away.

But I am on my way, Janja thought, and her teeth were compressed with purpose. A small blond, paler than any Galactic, slave no longer and full of purpose and confi-

---

*No letter exists to represent the soft-*k* sound of Qalara's first letter, in the alphabet of Erts. The easiest course is to think *Khalara* and say "Kuh-LAIR-uh."

dence and the ancient desire for what she considered justice: revenge. *For this is my ship now, and soon, oh soon
on Thebanis I will trade it for a better one! And then . . .
outbound, outbound to Qalara and Jonuta!—as* Captain
Janjaglaya, *by Aglii and Sunmother!*

She rose then from the superb "Spacefarers' Aide" on
Soljer, docking station of planet Jorinne, and hurried to
where the ship—*her* ship, *Satana*—awaited. Captain Janja,
on her way.

Graborn and Laleemis were gone, down onto Jorinne
with Mehdi-daktari for tests and learning and, the "Satana
Coalition" hoped, happiness. Hellfire, Cinnabar, and Quindy
were onboard and waiting. Quindy lounged at con with
seeming calm and patience, a jet black woman with hair
the color of sunflowers (both colors by choice) who wore
an extremely revealing, extremely pale blue bandeau-with-
cutouts above and a pair of pale, hotly pink pants below.
Soon after Janja was onboard, here came their companion
who was not quite part of the crew and yet who was friend
and advisor and savior and . . . definitely part of what
they had dubbed the Satana Coalition. Dashing Trafalgar
Cuw, dashing now to join them, in his rainbow clothing
and big broad-brimmed hat.

They zipped up the ship, breaking contact with Soljer-
station's umbilical.

Hellfire grinned. "Let's blow this joint!"

Cinnabar looked around all huge-eyed and pursed the
lips of its small roundish mouth. "The whole damned
joint?" it asked with exaggerated interest, and Hellfire
swatted the Jarp.

"The whole furbaggin' planet, by Shaitan's balls!"
Hellfire snapped. "Let's just get me to someplace where I
can start practicing being rich!" She clapped her hands
together, a tall, angularly lean woman with tan skin and
hair the color of prass—by choice.

"It will have to be yours and Quindy's authority, Janja,"

Trafalgar Cuw of Outreach said. He gave Hellfire a big blandly innocent look—one of his best affectations. Maddeningly, disgustingly boyish. "Cap—I mean Hellf, I regret to say that you died, down on Jorinne."

She stared at him. She was less volatile now than she had been before some particularly unpleasant experiences,* but still a woman who had been ship's master for several years, and a pirate besides.

"I did *what*?"

He flipped his fingers. "You died. The pirate Hellfire is dead. We will have a document recording her transferring ownership of her *Satana* to one Janjaglaya Jee, of Outreach. Sorry, Janja—you had to be from somewhere, and you don't have any official ID or numbers *yet*. We'll worry about your new ID once we reach Thebanis, uh, whatever-your-name-is, ma'am."

"Oh, Tra-*Fal*-garr! And to think that I once hated your guts and called you Trafalgar Pew."

He shrugged. "Ah, that was only because I'm a man, bigot."

The Satana Coalition laughed, including the (former) captain. True, she no longer quite hated all men, and Trafalgar was partly responsible, along with her experiences on Knor and Jorinne. On the other hand, she was still strictly lesbian.

Abruptly, as she stared smiling at him, seemingly poised, Trafalgar raised both hands in a fending-off gesture and backed a step. "No no, don't even think of hugging me—people will talk!"

"Oh God," Hellfire cried, and broke up again.

"I think I'm going to throw up," Quindy observed, in her quiet voice.

"Not till we've redshifted station Soljer and the whole

Payne-Humason system, *please*!'' Janja said, smiling. Yes, she could smile and enjoy their camaraderie, she who had not laughed or smiled for the better part of a year, and then only wanly, as if it were an effort. "Trafalgar—you really did that?''

He flipped five and tried to look self-denigrating. "Oh, I had some help. We have a couple of friends or ten on Jorinne, you know. It is officially registered, though. The wanted pirate Captain Hellfire was slain on Jorinne— by other outlaws, not policers—and transferred her ship, with witnesses, just before she died." He clapped a hand over his heart and rolled his eyes upward.

"Who—who were the witnesses?''

"Oh, no less than the renowned Caldera-clan Mehdi-daktari, respected all along the spaceways, and the Director of Station Soljer Security, Cosi—*Prefect* Cosi." He rolled his eyes. They knew about his and Cosi's . . . coziness.

"I'll be damned," Hellfire said, shaking her head, leaning against the closed airlock hatch and looking very serious.

"Oh, without doubt," Cinnabar told her, and ducked a flying elbow.

"Hellfire," Trafalgar said, noting her very serious expression and becoming just as sober, "you are wanted on more planets than you've ever visited. We are your friends, and we've been through more than one hell together. We can't possibly see you step off onto Thebanis and be arrested and hauled away, or knocked off by some TGO assas—uh, eliminator. We know you've changed, partly because of mental scar tissue or something like. We all heard you give—well, almost—*Satana* to Janja, now that you're rich—''

"Now that we are *all* rich!" Cinnabar practically shouted.

"—and of course now there's the business arrangement with those people down on Jorinne, and the banker on Thebanis." Trafalgar paused to shake his head. "Knorese gemstone jewelry, Jorinne 'cataract' pearls, and spaceships, too! What a complicated trade! I will tell you this, though, citizen!'' He leveled a finger at her. ''I am charging you an obligation, a service rendered should ever I need one and call on you. And right now I am saying that everyone else onboard—the Satana Coalition, no less—should demand the same.''

''Not me!'' Janja said. ''I have *Satana* and I will have . . . whatever the name of the new ship is!''

''You've got it,'' Hellfire said, her glance sweeping them all, and they saw something they had never seen before, any of them—the liquid glint of tears in the eyes of the vicious pirate Hellfire.

''And come to think, I am thinking *Tarkij* as the name for my ship, and you others had probably better try talking me out of it,'' Janja was continuing.

''I've got an ob on you, Cap'n-I-mean-citizen,'' Cinnabar said, and poked a long, thin, orange finger into Hellfire's breast—or the place where one would have been if she had breasts, at any rate. ''And I'll take it. You'll never be free of me, you sexy Galactic!—*ouch*!''

Trafalgar had casually swatted Cinnabar in one rounded breast; at almost the same instant Hellfire gave the Jarp a finger-flick in the crotch, where its penis nestled in a pair of horribly blue trunks.

Quindy came to Hellfire and set both hands on her shoulders. She looked into those moist mahogany-colored eyes.

''I take no favor and demand no obligation, Hellfire. Just that if ever I set down on a planet where you are, I want you, and you know how.''

Hellfire nodded, and tears spilled down her cheeks bright and glistening as rolling pearls. She knew. She and Quindy had long been lovers, and their relationship was master and slave—the consummately competent ship-handler and computrician Quindy as slave. There was no masochism gene for bioengineering to remove, and Quindaridi of Ghanji was most definitely masochistic.

There followed some hugging, which was followed by an awkward silence.

"All right Quindy," Janja said at last, "let's go get ourselves spaceborne!"

3

"An ancient writer, I understand, once asked 'What's in a name?' He wouldn't have asked that if he'd been called 60640329a0!"

—Trafalgar Cuw

Cinnabar suggested "Ellfira" or "Elphira," but Hellfire turned up her nose and besides Trafalgar said it sounded too much like "Hellfire" anyhow. Janja suggested her nickname for Hellfire: "Prasstop" could be used as a name. No it couldn't, Hellfire said; "Prasstop" wasn't any sort of name and besides the color of her hair really should be changed. As a matter of fact she was wondering if raggedy-pixieish black bangs mightn't soften the long angular lines of her face.

He would come up with a name she could not resist, Trafalgar told her, and have it registered into reality on Outreach before they reached Thebanis. As a matter of fact they could easily stop off at the Outreach docking station, at least; it was a mere four light-years from Thebanis's star, Janski.

(The ship was falling through starlit indigo and gray, past Bleak now and rushing on, on. Spacedust caressed them, fitfully lit by starfire in blue and yellow, ruddy orange and greenwhite as they hurtled faster than meteors through a domain never meant for their kind.)

45

Hellfire said, "Outreach?"

Trafalgar Cuw nodded. He was positively scintillant in a prismatically colored Joser robe that made him look like the priest of some chromohedonistic cult. He wore his ingenuous boy expression, which he did well.

"Pos. I can arrange identities, you see, on Outreach. I have a lot of influence, on Outreach." Suddenly he jerked his head toward Janja and his eyes were bright with the excitement of discovery. "Janjaglaya Wye! W-Y-E."

Janja looked at him. Eyebrows up, head on one side as she considered, briefly. "I . . . can live with that."

"Thought you could," he said, beaming.

"I love it," Cinnabar said or rather its translation helmet did. "Captain Janjaglaya Wye."

Rather plaintively Janja said, "I don't know anything about Outreach."

"SIPACUM does. So study."

"I don't either, dammit," Hellfire said.

"So study," Trafalgar repeated, in the same bland tone. "What was your name before? I mean, you weren't *named* Hellfire at birth, were you?"

"None of your business. I hate that name. How do you have influence, on Outreach?"

"Oh—" (He gestured, robe's polychromatic sleeve streaming, flapping so that its colors flowed in a beautiful blur.)"—family. You know. It's not important. A person gains influence. Consider—we all have some on Jorinne now, for instance. Anyhow, would you rather whisper your old name to me, let me see if I can make anything out of it? Another name, I mean."

He evades questions better than anyone in the Galaxy, Janja mused. *Now there's something I want to learn to do!*

Hellfire made a face. She sat on the edge of her bed in her cabin—the captain's cabin of spacer *Satana*. "No." She was looking down at her tight blue shimmerfabric pants, idly scratching at the metallic glint on her thigh with a close-trimmed fingernail. "Oh, Tao's balls, all right! My birth-name was Aljareh. And a string of numbers. I really believe I've managed to forget them."

"That's not so terrible," Janja said. She was already tap-tapping the cabin's SIPACUM link, initiating a computer scan for planet Outreach.

"It is to me," Hellfire said petulantly. "I never liked it and besides you don't have my memories, Cloud-top. Besides, it won't do, anyhow. It's known too, that name. I mean—more than one policer organization's records have my real name in the banks. And description."

"And *all* of them have the names Hellfire and *Satana* on file," Trafalgar said rather quietly, feeling her moroseness.

She shot him only the briefest of dark glances. Those almost-black eyes were hardly soft, but they were a lot less hard and mean, these days. In a way Hellfire really was dead.

"*Hellfire's* real name, not yours," Cinnabar corrected her lightly with a pretense at solemnity, but Hellfire didn't smile.

She sat on the edge of the luxurious bed she had caused to be installed on *Satana* for her comfort and her sexuality, and she stared at her hand at its idle work on her thigh. Her friends were trying to help. Her *friends*! Friends were new to her, and the acceptance of them. So were the concepts of wealth, and retirement, and identity-change with disguise. Her pensive dolor was an aura that stretched out to darken the thoughts and faces of her companions. Her friends. A vicious space pirate, with friends!

Cinnabar bit its lip. With its orange skin and carmiana-red hair, the Jarp knew how good it looked in the skin-hugging red jumpsuit Janja had bought for it, back in Komodi on Jorinne.

It matched the one Janja wore, sitting hunched forward toward the little terminal. The viewscreen, small but equipped with a holomagnifier, was full of a beautiful big swirl of luminous blue and indigo and lavender all traced through with ribbons of true black. The remnants of a long-dead star, richly decorative. Now that it was dead, it could be looked at and enjoyed as natural art.

Gas and dust, sprawling majestically off to their "left." Way off to their left. Janja wondered idly what color the nebula had been when it was aflame, a living hydrogen furnace among billions, but she was not sufficiently interested to ask SIPACUM for readings and analysis.

(SIPACUM was running the ship as well as monitoring constantly, inside and out in space, close to hand and long range. For it to detach a portion of its microcircuitry to access every Outreach reference it held was less trouble than for Janja to scratch her nose while reading.)

Janja was calling up peripheral/ancillary refs to Outreach and Outies, before bringing up the main entry onto the screen.

"Rich," Cinnabar murmured for the nth time, nervous in the silence laden with dark thoughts. It stared at nothing at all with its great big round, soft eyes.

SHONDEKAYAN EPH, SIPACUM printed, "first Insarch of reunified Outreach," and followed with a date two hundred years old. Staring, Janja was thinking about the patterned oddness of Outreacher names when she heard the voice of one called Trafalgar Cuw:

"Once, on Outreach, I had a friend named Varnalgeran Yuw. We . . . went to school together. And I have a cousin named Calcutta Kay, did you know that? We don't get much on Outreach, but we Outies get good names. Varnalgeran Yuw, and Calcutta Kay, and Trafalgar Cuw and Janjaglaya Wye. And"—abruptly, happy-faced and triumphant, he pointed at Hellfire—"not Aljerah, but *Kalahari Kay*!"

"That's *beautiful*," Cinnabar said, whose Jarp name was of course unpronounceable by any but Jarps and who had been Raunchy before it decided that was no proper name at all, and Janja had come up with "Cinnabar."

Hellfire had twitched her head up to stare at the Outie just as Janja had done. She glanced at the blond.

Janja had looked around; she smiled. "I like it, Prasstop."

" 'Kalahari Kay,' " Hellfire said, tasting the sound of it, testing the feel of it on her lips. "Kalahari. Pretty enough, I guess. Does it mean something?"

Trafalgar shook his head. "A very ancient word, we're sure of that."

"Kalahari," she said again. "What about 'Kalahari Cuw'?"

"Merciless Theba! You want to be *my relative*?"

Cinnabar and Janja laughed. Oddly Hellfire, who had once scornfully called him "Trafalgar Pew," did not.

"I could do worse, Traf. Could you?"

"Oh, I might have to think about that a little!" Trafalgar said. "Particularly with Corundum gone. But—" He made an extravagant gesture—a Trafalgarish gesture—smiling ingenuously.

Hellfire snatched up an empty drinking plass and threw it at him.

It was both empty and lightweight. Its lip caught air and it drifted for a moment, then fell leisurely. Trafalgar's smile became a grin.

"I'll go to con and get us patched through to Outreach," he said. "My cousin Saratoga Jee."

"To Outreach! That'll cost a fortune!"

"We have a fortune, my dears! So—Janjaglaya Wye and Kalahari Cuw?"

Hellfire smiled a little. "I like it. Unless . . . Janjy wants to be sisters."

The orange non-human looked from short, pale-skinned blond with bluegray eyes to tall, lean, deeply tan Hellfire with the mahogany-hued eyes.

"I don't think you'd pass," Cinnabar said, and both Janjaglaya and Kalahari broke up.

Trafalgar grinned, made a sleeve-flutteringly deep bow, and headed for the con. He moved like a breeze; like lazily trickling water. Easily, unself-consciously. That was Trafalgar Cuw of Outreach, who was both enigma and hero and who blithely denied both.

The others gazed after him, each wondering, none voicing its thoughts and emotions about him.

"Trafalgar," Janja called when he was in the hatchway called doorway, "the head of government on Outreach is called an 'Insarch.' Why Insarch?"

He looked back at her, eyebrows up. He blinked, then spread both hands. "Who wants to be governed by an Outsarch?" And he left.

"Fascinating," Janja said in an unfascinated voice.

"Logical, too," Cinnabar said, and they exchanged a glance and chuckled.

"Well," Hellfire a.k.a. Kalahari said, "I guess that's that. Please to try to call me by my new name. And . . . with Traf and Quindy in the con-cabin, let's be kind and leave them alone for an hour."

"Shall we synchronize chrons for this operation?" Cinnabar asked, and they chuckled, all three. Maybe it was a giggle.

The ship fled past a triad of stars that took no note. A family of suns, sullen ruby and flaring golden topaz and tired old slate-blue, strung all about with their little satellites that flashed in the fiery light of the triple primaries like jewels hung upon space. Six planets, all to close; three, little more than cinders. All were baked and lifeless and their shining glory was reflection, like the dead eyes of those who knew they were mere chattel.

The only life was on the passing spacecraft. One bubbled and belched; it was a stiglul and its name was Stillwell.

Three sat in the captain's cabin, researching the planet named Outreach. Another sat at con, idly playing at working out the complicated pattern the three stars wove about each other.

She was one of the best ship-handlers and creators of guidance control cassettes along the spaceways, fleet-trained and piracy-experienced, long Captain Hellfire's First Mate/Second, friend, sometime lover, stabilizing influence when possible, and right hand. Her name was or had been Quindaridi something-or-other and she had held the rank of lieutenant on spacer *Poulander*, but for some years she had been simply Quindy. Disgraced and self-exiled Quindy, who seldom left the ship.

"Pee-yeep," a ridiculous travesty of a ship's whistle came from behind her; "Permission to come onto the con, First. Pee-yeeep."

Seated in the captain's chair, she smiled without turning to peer around its tall back. "Hello, handsome. Your bosun's whistle needs fixing."

He whistled two perfect notes as he moved into the cabin and between the two chairs before the console with its multicolored panels, toggles, keys, and lighted displays, readouts, and telits.

"Just to prove I can do it," he said.

"Show-off," she said, and lifted her face as he bent, beside her.

He kissed her and eased his butt down onto the arm of the Mate's chair.

"H'lo sexy lady. Wanna drink? Wanna play games?"

"Hmp. Did you get laid on Jorinne?"

"Firm," he said, which was the same as saying "sure."

"Hmp. At least you're honest—about that, I mean."

"Whew—you sound rough. Jealous?"

"No, I'm not. Maybe I'm delighted. Maybe you learned something new in the way of technique from that . . . Cozy?"

"Cosi," he said, "right. What's the matter with my technique?"

"Probably nothing. I can't remember that far back."

"Aha. Not jealous or rough, then. Just in œstrus. Or horny, if you prefer."

"Did you come oncon to relieve me, get involved, or just play steward?"

"None of the above." He sipped one of the drinks he bore. "Umm. That li'l creature just sits back there happily eating table-scraps and uh, cess, and keeps excreting good booz."

She smiled, glancing over her console because she was conscientious. "I've an idea Stillwell's the most valuable member of this ship's crew."

"Or any other. We can make a fortune off Stillwell." He sipped.

"Let me have a taste," she said, and reminded him: "We already have a fortune."

"Two or three more then," he said, and handed her the second drink he had brought. "I left our shipmates in the cap'n's cabin, with new names and IDs. Came up here to contact Outreach and make them official. Legal, even."

She gave him a look. "You can accomplish that, too?"

He nodded.

Quindy shrugged. Maybe he was a TGO man masquerading as a sub-deepcover agent for TMSMCo, the mining giant—and maybe he was an agent for TMSMCo as he said, with an invented TGO ID. He was a lot older than he looked, this man "on his second time around," and had had plenty of time to cultivate and plant various pieces of false information in various places, including computer memory banks. There wasn't much about Trafalgar Cuw that one could be sure of, except that he was awfully talented and versatile and awesomely competent at a lot of things. And that he sneered at heroism while vigorously being a hero, with consistency.

"Well you can't do it *now*!" she told him. "Because of our route, you won't be able to get a link with Outreach for nearly an hour, Trafalgar. And even then it will cost a fortune!"

"What'd you say about that before?" he said, grinning.

"Oh. We already have a fortune. But—"

"And I know I can't do it now, Quin-dee. I hope the others haven't thought about that. I came up here to Get Involved. Think I haven't missed you, sexpot? And come to think, I did come to relieve you, in a way. Need relief, Quindy?"

She rolled her eyes. "Why do I put up with this man—love him, even?"

Because I know what you need, he thought, *and love to provide it. That's wonderful for us both—doing well by doing good!* He said:

"Because we're both sensual animals who love to screw and love it rough and besides I think you're the most beautiful and the sexiest ship-handling genius along the spaceways. And besides tha—"

"Oh, talk talk talk. That's enough talk. Come down here."

He stood and this time he bent way over. Her hands slid up into his hair while his moved over the outer swells of her breasts. On Quindy, they really were shaped like warheads. This time their kiss was longer and more loving. And more intimate. This time they groped each other with a shameless salacious delight. When she chewed his tongue enough to hurt, he clamped her in the armpits and tried to push his thumbs through the outswelling sides of her breasts.

Then he straightened, swiveled, stepped, and plopped down into the other chair before the con. He sipped his drink. Tilted it higher, to drain the plass.

"It'll be a lot easier if you come down here," he said.

With a jerky nod she tapped a few keys—jerkily—to put SIPACUM in full control. In her excitement she made an error, groaned and corrected and re-tapped, thought just a moment and added another command, waited for onscreen affirmation from Ship's Inboard Processing and Computing Unit (Modular), and released herself from the big chair.

She stood, in the same black-sashed red jumpsuit that Cinnabar wore. It looked a lot better on Quindy, who was constructed with a brain for the con and a body for bed.

With her back to the console and her eyes on Trafalgar's, she broke the snug suit's closing field. It separated all down the front—and under, and halfway up the back—to show him an enticing vertical line of gleaming skin. Black, true black, dyed at the cellular level and broken from chin to crotch now only by the scarlet of her bandeau. And the sash.

"An old-fashioned bra? You? Theba's pectorals Quindy—why?"

"The ring's outline shows right through the jumpsuit," she said, in a quiet voice.

She put her hands to the knot of her sash. He leaned up enough to catch one of its dangling ends. He hung on while he leaned back.

Because she was willing, she was pulled forward into a controlled fall. Onto him. He let go the sash in time to get his hands on this and that, all Quindaridi of Ghanj.

"*Uh*!" she grunted. "Brute!" she added, in a small and entirely artificial voice. She had put on a pitiful look, gazing up into his face.

"Uh-huh," he murmured, and slapped his hands onto the rounds of her backside to urge her against him.

She was tugged up along his seated body until their mouths came together. His hands clamped, kneading. Hers were more restless on him, and just as busy. So were her lips and tongue, alive and warm and seeking. Fine strands of yellow hair slid, separating, on her shoulders and back.

The roughness, the slapping of those hands onto her and now their firm and possessive palpating of her rearward cheeks; these were a part of her sexuality which he was more than willing to accommodate. After that time of her disgrace, she had denied herself men and joined Hellfire both as ship's second and as lover. Their sexuality had been that of Hellfire as domina, always in firm control, usually rough and sometimes brutal. The relationship had pleased both Quindy and her volatile captain, for Hellfire was or had been admittedly and unashamedly cruel by temperament.

With Trafalgar, it was still a matter of the domination, the illusion of use needed by Quindy's crippled confidence and old feelings of guilt. With him it was less rough, however, and never cruel or brutal.

The "old Hellfire" had left stripes and toothmarks and occasionally worse, breaking the skin with her whip or leaving bitten nipples or labia bruised for a week. Trafalgar left only fingerprints, an occasional bruise, and a satiated glow. He had sustained a few bruises, too, in coping with this woman's passionate responses. Even within the framework of submission she wanted and needed, she was an aggressive lover.

She was now. Tugging at him hungrily, her hands ever amove; making a sound between a hum and low growl. He called it her sex-purr. It was more, because of its urgency. She was also imitating pelvic thrusts with her tongue in his mouth while grinding her body almost ruthlessly into his in an apparent attempt to meld them both into one body, one person, one glowing unit.

The ancient violence of their race underrode the rising passion of them both. They were breathing hard in seconds and panting in a minute. Heat and need raced upward like the color of a thermometer dipped in boiling oil.

Grinding, her breath steamy against his face, she lost control of her hands. They clawed greedily, trying to hurt without wanting to. He brought a hand down onto one partially-clothed hemisphere of her butt, hard.

"Stop clawing, woman!"

Eventually they had to rearrange themselves. This was the Mate's chair, not a bed or even a couch or floor, and both of them were clothed.

She didn't remove the jumpsuit. She got it the hell out of the way by widening its long opening. It still clung to the arms and legs and back it covered. He smiled, because he liked that. This way she was lewdly revealed and that was more sexy than nakedness.

They didn't remove his robe, either. Instead they got it up and the hell out of the way. The staff of his sex stood tall in tribute to her.

Then she was on him, astride his legs, feeding the hard heat of him up into herself while he wiped her bandeau down to bare quivering breasts the color of shining egg-plants. He clamped a hand onto each of those thrusts as if it was a handle for his convenience, a knob provided for his fingers.

Her face writhed as she jogged on thick erection, twisting and bouncing with her eyes fixed on his face. Gliding up and down his slicer as if on a living piston.

"You're . . . hitting my cervix!"

"I can feel it. Does it hurt?"

"Yesss!" she told him, and kept right on posting on him. Deliberately twisting her hips, bouncing and jiggling to increase both his pleasure and her own.

Between the fingers of his left hand jutted the perma-nently erect crest of her breast. Her movements made it seem to flaunt the slender ring of rutilated quartz that pierced it, a souvenir of her enslavement on Knor. Sanded and polished to the smoothness of metal, transparent with gold flecks, it caught the cabin's light enticingly.

The obscene sounds of united genitals accompanied their movements while the odor of sex rose about them. Sounds and smell were beautiful to woman and man.

He watched delighted while she rode him, while she shook and moaned in a blissful passion that grew ever more urgent. His hands slid free of her breasts so that he could watch the way they jumped, ring flashing, catapulted by her movements so that they became wildly mobile ornaments of glossily gleaming black.

"Oh," she groaned, hair flying and face working, "oh, lover!"

"God but you're beautiful on the bounce, sweetheart," he murmured with a grin, and she smiled back.

"Grab 'em again, you with the flagpole!" And she ground down hard.

He did, grasping both breasts and flexing. His motions were those of a puppet master. Lifting and lowering in rhythm with her own movements in skewering herself up the middle. All about them trinkled a billion billion burning lights, suns all in blue and yellow and blinding white, and neither of them noticed or cared.

At the same time that a groan was torn from him, she began whipping her head back and forth in a frenzy of gamic pleasure. Hair flew in a yellow cloud. Spasms rocked them both. Their voluptuous joy with each other, with themselves filled the cabin like a hot-pink mist.

Abruptly his hands clamped harder. With a surging strength that popped her eyes wide, he propelled his loins up at her, into her. That blatant use of strength tired him but was exciting, gratifying. It gave them both an erotic pleasure that was overwhelming in its intensity and her delighted, impressed reaction made him proud. Atop him she writhed under the carnal stimulus of their burning mutual need, pumping and panting, biting her lip, moaning with the joy of it. So was he, now, working toward an explosion.

They lunged and plunged at each other while the ship plunged through the parsec abyss. Spaceship *Satana* in dull orange and pink, a streak whose 0.19 albedo must have been raised a point by the glow in its con-cabin where the temperature rose along with the smell of sexuality and the noise level and rapidity of movement.

4

Jaded? Bored?
want ADVENTURE?
Try the Chateau d'If.
                                        —Jack Vance

Kislar Jonuta came smiling out of Hakimit Medical Center on his own planet of Qalara wearing a small smile and a loosely cut white suit indifferently enhanced with touches of nothing-beige. The suit bagged on him and somehow made him look shorter, as well as considerably less imposing. That was deliberate; his intention was to make himself overlookable in a crowd of three. The soft white cap, worn without style or panache, added to that effect. The v-topped tunic's plainness was broken only by the beige touches and by the strap—beige webbing—that ran across his chest and back to his right hip. It supported an ordinary eyecorder case there. A beige case.

There was no eyecorder and no case. The holoprojection disguised his holstered stopper. A prominent citizen of Norcross and indeed of the rest of the planet of which Norcross was capital, Jonuta was licensed to carry concealed or disguised armament.

He had just visited with Fumiko Kita-daktari and one of her assistants, inspected himself and the monitors, and passed on another million memories. They were electroni-

59

cally recorded, like stellar purchasing units in the bank vault of Hakimit's holographic store-against-need-for-recall systemry.

Jonuta, who had read long-ago writings that few others had so much as heard of, smiled a small smile.

Hakimit Med center indeed! he mused. *Chateau d'If, this place!*

He stood politely back for other pedestrians, ignoring the glidewalk until he could step over and pace along beside it. How stupid to use only lifts and glideways and transportation and neglect the legs that needed work!

Since some others were as sensible and many were dressed in white, his walking in preference to being conveyed while standing was hardly noticed. Already he was thinking about matters neither literary, medical, nor genetic. His thoughts did involve Fumiko Kita-daktari.

He could hardly wait until dinner, to see how Miko and HReenee got on and behaved in each other's company. Would HReenee feel challenged and try to be possessive, display a proprietary attitude? Would the two women compete? He hoped not.

His and Miko Kita's relationship had long ago passed beyond the purely professional, on those few occasions when he visited Qalara openly and the fewer ones when he came here secretly. Last time she had shown her fascination with another concept. Discussion of it was brief, and he and she and Kenowa had quietly agreed to enter into that concept. They were just about to get together in Miko's nice bed in her nice home forty kloms and less than six minutes from Norcross, when an emergency called her back to HMC.

Surely it had been intended as a hint, her mention a few minutes ago of her theory-unto-assumption that all persons were born bisexual and were intended to function so.

Now we'll see about bisexual and *biracial*, he thought,

curbing his smile as he stepped into the public transport depot.

Then he tried to put that out of his mind, settling back to be rushed into the center of Norcross. He let his mind wander to a remark made long ago, about his being "Captain Cautious" with a back-up everything except a back-up Jonuta.

Unfortunately that reminded him that it was Kenowa who had put that thought in his mind, and now he was helpless not to frown and reflect on her, and their years together. And HReenee, and HRadem. Right now Kenowa was with both of them, on one of her beloved shopsprees. Jonuta could not help wondering whether she was giving him a thought at all. He was sure HReenee was.

Kalahari Cuw walked out of the umbilical tunnel connecting her ship to Thebanistation. Her goal was to test both her disguise and her ID through the docking station and then down onplanet.

Just now she was quite busty, which Hellfire had never been—and neither was Kalahari, without the stuffing. A new plumpness in her stomach, hips, and butt made her appear shorter and about one meal away from being dumpy. Her short cap of hair made her face appear fuller. Besides, it was black. Nearly all her brassy mane was gone forever, snipped off onboard *Satana* and poofed. A minor adjustment to ship's daktari or shipdoc—*Satana*'s almost standard cylindrical, mostly automatic medical care chamber—had persuaded it to darken her skin almost to blackness. Both skin- and hair-color were temporary, not at the cellular or even subcutaneous level. And she was Kalahari Cuw, now. ID lost but bearing a puterfax from her native Outreach to prove her identity.

She had always attracted attention and tried not to worry about it now. Besides, the looks she was getting showed more interest than in the past. Interest in her as an attractive woman. She was even working to walk, rather than use her customary leggy stride.

She went straight through the station, straight through its security and ID-check, and straight down onplanet. Kalahari Cuw had no apparent connection with *Satana*. As a matter of fact she was assumed to have come off *Tritonian Ring*, a passenger-carrying spacer berthed near *Satana*.

An hour later she wore typically Thebanian paint-on jewelry and side-split pants of the sexy local wetcloth. The matching shoes of royal blue forced her not to stride, though she was hardly in love with the ten-centimeter heels of stylus-thinness.

She hoped the off-white blouson tunic made her look shorter and fuller. Maybe the shoes were a mistake, she mused nervously, but at least this way she wasn't about to forget herself and stride out!

She passed up the Thebanis Mahal Hotel and, gaining pleasant attention once she had showed her credaccount, took a suite in the Grand Khan. Then she went out again, to get a drink and buy just a few more clothes.

Just in case, her fellow members of the Satana Coalition waited well over an hour before leaving the ship. Janja was cramming with SIPACUM's aid, trying to learn and remember all she could.

Then Cinnabar emerged, was passed, and went down onto the planet and its station-town capital, Raunch.

Within two hours the call came up from Raunch's Pilgrims' Hospital, seeking confirmation of the Jarp's identity. (More likely its right to all the cred it appeared to possess, in addition to free status.) ID was confirmed; wealth confirmed. Cinnabar was admitted to Pilgrims' for any Jarp's dream: a translator implant to eliminate the need for translahelm.

With Trafalgar Cuw and a reluctant Quindy, Janja left *Satana*. Since it was her ship now, she tarried to reprogram the lock. She also shared the new code with Quindy, who nodded and smiled. No one else was likely to say "Yaood Pilishishi" to the vocalock! *Satana* would open to nothing else save torches or time-consuming application of electronic genius.

Janja's hair was a deep brown and her pale eyes injected with a temporary iris-darkener that turned them the approximate shade of her hair. She, Quindy, and Trafalgar wore the jumpsuits she had bought on Jorinne. They were red, fitted to upper arms and torso and legs to the knees. Each long sleeve flared and was cut into a point behind, while the over-the-boot pants were flared at the bottoms. The sashes were black, four fingers wide and with bias-cut ends that dangled long.

None of the three was armed. That was appearance, not reality. It took a little longer to get a stopper out of an easy-open jumpsuit, but the stoppers were there.

Quindy's entire appearance was adequately changed simply by making her hair black and curly. Now she was simply a black woman with black hair. Nothing exotic about her, and they hardly expected to see anyone they knew.

Trafalgar did flaunt his eleven-gallon hat, which was called a Wayne for no particular reason; none, at least, that anyone knew.

Janjaglaya Wye, Trafalgar Cuw, and Quindarissa Gh-778328s, who had never been on Thebanis anyhow.

Shortly after their arrival onplanet both women also wore the hats favored by Outies and a few others; the store was easy to find. Next they visited the necessary offices to be certain that spaceship *Satana* was legally Janja's rather than salvage property of the deceased Captain Hellfire.

It was Trafalgar who made the call to the Grand Khan Kharavansery. Pos, Kalahari Cuw was registered. She did not answer her comm. Perhaps she was napping or had stepped out. Was there a message?

"Pos. Leave her a message that her brother called. Than kyou." And Trafalgar turned smiling to his companions. "All's well, presumably. She's here, she's registered, and when she comes in she'll know that we're in Raunch without incident. Would you beauties like to take an arm on either side?"

They would, and went directly to the Second World Bank of Thebanis. Executive Vice President Mujaz Th753650m* was delighted to see the new friends and "business associates" he had met on Jorinne. Bills of transfer of property were waiting for Janjaglaya of the Satana Coalition.

Two hours later they had enjoyed a sumptuous late luncheon with banker Mujaz, who was also a gem collector. The caloric content of all that turkey and topatoes and mushrooms, just touched with Thebonion and covered with melted cheese topped by soybakon strips—plus wine—was adjusted to allow gluttony without weight-gain. The meal provided each diner with two hundred calories. Even; not a jot more.

By the time they finished, the transfer had been effected.

From his own bank Mujaz's swiftly formed holding company had purchased a certified-superb spacecraft that had been more than half paid for before its repossession by the bank. Mujaz became the owner of one more of the magnificent Joser "pearls" called cataracts, increasing his collection to six—and of spacer *Satana*, which he assumed would be a quick sale to someone who needed a ship but whose cred was limited.

Janjaglaya Wye of Outreach received title to the repossessed spaceship. It was far more modern and handsomer than *Satana*, and slightly better equipped. The point was that it was not an ugly old ramscoop. Both ship and equipment were newer, much less-used, and less . . . weary than *Satana* and its systemry.

The unnamed ship was also worth a great deal more.

The gemstone from Jorinne, on the other hand, was a valued prize too, which was why Janja also received forty thousand stells.

Mujaz was happy. Janja was happy. She was owner of a fine swift spacer, with double-P drive and tachyon converter.

Of course she was not yet its captain.

Very late that afternoon, with Thebanis's angry red giant of a sun so low that its pale companion was gaining visibility 'way over there, the trio parted company with Mujaz.

They walked two blocks down and one ramp over to Redfern Boulevard—where they saw no ferns of any color— and up a few steps onto the gleaming blue lift. It took them up to Anytra Municipal Complex. The "mall" rose up on its mighty legs to bulk over ten square blocks of streets lined with stores and bars and offices. All were kept safely well illuminated by the glareless lights all over the AMComplex's underside. Presumably everyone working in them was happy to be out of the lurid red glare of Janski alpha.

There was no use arguing in the licensing office. Certainly there was no reasoning to be done, not with a government employee!

Licensing Bureau, she advised rather sternly and somehow almost accusingly, was nine minutes from closing. Everyone here would be happy to deal with Janjaglaya Wye and "process" her application and testing—after nine-hundred hours, tomorrow.

Disappointment became frustration, which fed anger. Janja calmed herself with a little effort and proved something: She held the guv-clerk up. Janja sat at the applications terminal inputting information about herself until the gong sounded to signal closing time.

Trafalgar leaned languidly against the burok counter, grinning. This way the clerk must leave a few minutes late, rather than as customary: at the stroke of the gong.

Angered but powerless to eject anyone before closing time, she nevertheless found a way to get even. Janja's information was "accidentally" wiped before it went into permanent electronic memory.

Janja stared at the other woman. She said nothing. Trafalgar advised that he needed to make a quick call to the Grand Khan Kharavansery.

"I'm sorry, sir. This office is closed. This is a *government* office and must close at the appointed time. There are public commsenders outside, just down the areaway."

Theba be thanked that Hellfire isn't here, Quindy thought, while Trafalgar Cuw nodded and kept nodding as he gazed at the clerk. Slowly his face eased into his most endearingly boyish smile.

"You know . . . you really should do something about your unfortunate mouth," he told her.

The trio from offplanet redshifted the Licensing Bureau then, knowing that one guv-clerk would soon be spending a lot of time peering nervously into this mirror and that, frowning, making faces, worrying about her mouth. It was unlikely that she would arrive at the conclusion that he had meant her *use* of her mouth rather than its appearance. That would require thought on her part.

"Wait," Quindy said, when the others turned left to head for the exit. "I can see the sign—the public commbooths are back this way."

Janja, working to exert the Aglayan control to calm herself, glanced at their male companion.

"Bars," Trafalgar Cuw said, "close only when you've had that last sip. And bars are happy to offer free calls to visitors."

They found a bar in the "mini-city" under the Anytra Municipal Complex. The man from Outreach was right, too.

5

You can't do a thing about death—or your birth either. All you can do is try to have fun between the one and the other.

—Trafalgar Cuw

As planned, Janja, Quindy, and Trafalgar took a room for three in the Grand Khan. They hardly used it; they spent the night with Hellfire-Kalahari in "her" suite. They talked, drank, caught up on the news or pretended to, drank, listened to music old and new, and talked. They fell asleep that way, here and there, and awoke late in disorder and disarray.

Because Janja loved the concept of uniforms for them, they took turns showering and tending the red jumpsuits in the renew-it chamber (time- and load-monitored; small extra charge For The Convenience Of Our Patrons).

Quindy had been so careless as to awake with a headache and was chided for lack of precautions. The headache was worked at with this and that while they breakfasted in the suite: hot tea for Janja and Quindy, iced tea for Trafalgar, a carbonated soft drink for Kalahari. The four chicken legs and bit of ham came from no chicken and no pig or indeed anything else faunal, and were good.

A call to Pilgrims' Hospital discovered that Cinnabar had been implanted just under an hour ago, and that "the patient is fine and resting well in a T.E.R.U."

"T-E-R-U?" Janja said.

"Patient?" Trafalgar said.

"Everyone in a hospital is called a patient," Quindy advised him. "It's ancient tradition."

"A total environment recovery unit," the sound-only comm told them in that same undauntably cheery voice. "Nothing whatever to worry about. It's a simple operation and the patient should be available for release tomorrow, or for visitation this evening between eighteen and nineteen-hundred."

"Patient?" Kalahari said, emerging rather hurriedly from the sitter.

Quindy told them that a TERU was a hyper-healer; a solution-suspension cylindrical "environment" for one individual. It was equipped with a few improvements over shipdoc, as well as one or two inferior aspects. The latter would not affect Cinnabar.

The short-haired brunette who had been Hellfire kept right on frowning.

"It's a simple operation," Trafalgar assured his fellow members of the Satana Coalition.

"Exactly what the hospital person said," Janja nodded.

"All hospital personnel lie," Kalahari said darkly. "It's ancient tradition."

"How'd you like to shower again, this time fully clothed, little sister?"

Kalahari stared at him. "Listen, you—"

"Children!" Janja briskly snapped. "You two Cuws cease this embarrassing display of standard sibling rivalry!"

That helped because it made them laugh. All had heard that a translator implant was a simple procedure; all admitted that they knew no one who'd had one. Even some Jarps on Jarpi were implanted, because Galactics could not come close to mastering the complicated whistle-trill speech. Other than by using synthesizers, of course. That led to rather painful conversations, because of delays and occasional slips.

"Well, Cinnabar has one now and it's delighted, bet on it," Trafalgar said. He scooped up his broad-brimmed hat and twirled it idly. "I have one or two little things to do in Raunch, and I know where you'll be, Janja. I'll check in at the Licensing Bureau at thirteen or so. Oh—say h'lo to my ole buddy the clerk for me."

"I'll be right there with Janja," Quindy said. "Or as near as they'll let me be, while she's taking the test and riding the simulator."

"We will deal with another clerk, too," Janja said with austerity.

She picked up her new broad-brimmed hat—black—and frowned at it. Kalahari had assured her that it looked marvelous on her. Janja had never worn a hat and certainly had reservations about starting off with eleven gallons' worth.

Trafalgar turned questioning eyes on the woman who had been Hellfire. She was examining herself in the mirror. Her clothing was new and mildly colorful, rather than the jumpsuit "uniform" she also owned.

"I have several things to do, all personal and vastly important," she said, and laughed to make certain they understood that she was joking. "None of 'em will take me anywhere near any dam' guv-office, bet on that!"

Three hours later Janja had proven that she had learned an incredible amount in only a year, and still had more to learn. She had not mastered enough to be licensed as a spaceship's master.

It was a heavy blow, and even the clerk—not yesterday's, and male, and very conscious of Janja's femaleness—was gentle in telling her. It was still a heavy blow. All her plans . . . all her studying, trying, working . . . Jonuta . . .

"I'm going down the areaway for a sip of water," she

said, and did, while both the clerk and Quindy looked sick.

Janja returned, obviously having recovered somewhat. She established that there was no recourse, not for four months at least. True, she could probably learn what she needed to know to pass within a month, with application and a little aid. But four months was the specified period between tests. It was arbitrary, oh yes, but there it was and there Janja was.

Janja paced away to stare at a wall while the clerk dealt with someone else at the counter. Once she had recovered once again, she turned. Her thoughtful look was obvious at a glance. She went over to confer with the miserable Quindy.

There turned out to be more than one way of skinning a burok test, including simulation requiring a decision or two and some fair to good ship-handling. To an experienced handler, the stress was minimal.

When they met the Cuws, Trafalgar and Kalahari, for dinner just over three hours later, it was settled.

"I failed the test," Janja announced, hardly happy and yet with a surprising lack of moroseness.

"Oh shit," Kalahari said, and put a hand on the Aglayan's shoulder.

(Hellfire-Kalahari wore different clothing again, having bought still more and having decided to wear it. Now she wore very flat "barefoot shoes" and loose pants, hot pink, under a thigh-length white dasheek trimmed in red. And a hat exactly like Trafalgar's.)

"I was afraid of that," he was saying. "Not enough real experience."

Hellfire glowered as she wheeled on him. Someone, after all, needed to be blamed. The escape-goat was an ancient tradition. "Then why didn't you warn her?"

"Tried," the Outie said, looking sheepish—boyishly

sheepish. "Didn't have the guts. I've been hoping, the same as the rest of you."

That chased the accusation from the face of his "sister" and· even brought a bit of empathic warmth in its stead. The look she bestowed upon him now was not quite one of sibling fondness, but it was not a Cap'n Hellfire look, either. Her hand was still on Janja's shoulder. She turned back to her.

"It isn't the end of everything," Kalahari said. "You can always—"

"Of course it isn't," Janja said serenely. "And we don't have to wear long faces or mope all night over poor Janja, either. Quindy passed."

"What?"

"So that's what took you so long!" Trafalgar said, instantly grasping all.

Proudly Janja patted Quindy's back. "Meet Captain Quindarissa."

"Janja owns the ship and gives the orders," Quindy told them. "She just hasn't been at it long enough to get a master's rating. I have; I just never wanted to be boss. As of tomorrow, I get master's papers. As of tomorrow, Janja 'hires' me to captain her ship. Which you just can't mean," she said, looking at the Aglayan, "to call 'Tarkij,' whatever that means!"

Kalahari's grin was bright, genuine, and almost beautiful. Trafalgar enveloped almost all three of his companions in his arms but pretended disappointment:

"Flaining hell! Then we don't get to drown our sorrows."

"Grat-shit," Kalahari said, looking sternly at a passerby who stared at their public display of hugging.

"No," Janja said, "but we can do the same thing and call it celebration, all right?"

"All right!"

"Firm!"

"Right!"

The public huggery became four-way, and passersby swung wide, staring or looking disapproving. Or envious.

"Grabbles," Quindy muttered, "we've got twenty-three minutes left of Cinnabar's visiting time, and who knows where the hospital is?"

Kalahari grinned while Trafalgar smiled. "I do," he said. "I looked it up today. It's about twenty minutes from here."

Janja's expression became one of genuine distress. "Oh, no! But we—stop *grinning,* you two!"

"There's just one thing to do now," Trafalgar said. Without quite releasing them, he half-turned and gestured with his head. "First we pop into that bar and call the hospital."

"What good will that do?"

"It will at least let me grab some booz to take to Cinnabar," Kalahari said, "while Traf calls the hospital and works some of his magic."

Quindy looked at the Outie. Her brows up, her expression dubious, her head on one side. "Surely you don't also have 'influence' at Travelers' Hospital in Raunch on Thebanis!"

"Pilgrims'," he corrected, tugging. "Pilgrims' Hospital. Come on, come on—let's see."

He swept them along on the current of his own magnetism and enthusiasm. The little place on the corner was identified by a holocube sign: A green caricature of a pig constantly saluted anyone approaching by hoisting an old-fashioned tankard and winking. A smaller sign bore the name "The Pig's Eye." At a few sems' distance the door was revealed as a holoscene with considerable depth. It was as if one could see inside the place, but the scene was impossible. At several tables sat tankard-bearing pigs, made cute by caricature, conversing with humans.

The four of the Satana Coalition approached, the faces of two showing their misgivings. The door proved to be fast shut. It opened into a mini-airlock that gave onto another door, windowed. Thus the patrons of the Pig's Eye were shielded from street-sounds—while their own noises were contained.

Kalahari opened the windowed door, which led inside. Out wafted the sounds of ancient eastern music played, paradoxically, on a spinet. It was a synther, of course, and canned as well,

"I don't really think—" Janja said, and Trafalgar pushed her almost violently into the gold-and-red-lit interior of the lounge.

She saw a medium-sized room with round red-topped tables and round-backed chairs padded in gold. Along one wall was an amber-topped red bar tended by an eye-grabbingly impossible porcine alien. Various patrons drinking and conversing; an entirely human and definitely female table-tender or waiter who was also entirely blue and appeared to be just as naked; a bit of smoke from synthesticks and perhaps marijane, not eddying but moving swiftly upward and over into the ceiling-mounted purifier; a table at which sat two Jarps, only one of which wore a translation helmet . . .

The other wore a red jumpsuit identical to Janja's.

As she stared it rose, raising its tall golden plass on high. "Cap'n Janjaglaya! In a pig's eye!" This it called jovially in a sort of anima-animus voice, neither quite male tenor nor quite female. Speaking Galactic without a translahelm.

"Cinnabar!"

She ran to it, barely avoiding collision with the waiter who tucked in one medium-blue hip smoothly without spilling a drop from any of the several plasses on her tray. (No great feat, on second look: Every plass in the Pig's Eye was bottomed with a thin strip of metal that held it fast to the table-tender's magnetized tray.)

"A dam' Sunflower," someone muttered, while Janja and Cinnabar hugged each other with obvious real affection.

"So'm I," he was told in manner surly, by the big-hatted man who was suddenly standing over him. Staring. Leaning intimately on his table. The fellow was dressed identically to the woman just sneered at with the bigot's slang phrase for Jarp-lover.

"Me too," the poor bigot was further told, this time by a totally black and black-haired woman, also in the same scarlet jumpsuit and also crowding close to him as he sat at his table. It seemed suddenly to have shrunk a lot.

"Hi, cutie," a third newcomer said, a woman with a short cap of hair like black jade and eyes like mahogny. She at least did not wear still another of the damned red one-pieces. "My name's Sunflower—what's yours?"

"Gone," the poor unfortunate replied, ducking low so as to depart the table between two of the three people crowding it so menacingly. He paused only for the door, which had to be pulled to open. He pawed it—

"Hey!" the blue waiter called. "You still owe me for two, you riser!"

—and, getting it open with a hard jerk and a swift sideward movement, he redshifted the Pig's Eye at speed.

"That's all right, little girl blue," Kalahari Cuw said, with a hand on the shoulder of the departed man's companion, who was still seated and appeared to be considering going into shock. "That bigot's crewmate here will card for the drinks, right?"

She smiled down at the stress-stiff man. So did Trafalgar Cuw. (Quindy had hurried to join Janja and Cinnabar in a three-way embrace, while the other Jarp was nervously on its feet.)

"I got nothin' against Jarps," the man under Kalahari's hand said in a low voice, and nodded to the blue waiter (who on closer approach proved not to be altogether naked). "I'll card for Fon's—uh, that riser's drinks, Shonya."

Kalahari decided that in Raunch at least, "riser" must be moving in to replace the familiar old slang expression "downer." That was a problem of the spacefarer. Language—"Erts"—remained essentially the same, while slang changed constantly from planet to planet.

Blue Shonya, meanwhile, was nodding. "Pository, then— you get the bill. Now—are you four here to drink, or you just come in to show off the red suits an' hug Jarps an' chase off my customers?"

"In that case," Kalahari was amiably telling the seated man, "*I'll* card for yours. See to that, Shonya." She patted the waiter's bare bottom while Trafalgar patted her bare shoulder. "We came to celebrate," Kalahari said—

"We'll take care of you, Blue Shonya," he said—

—and both took their hands from her and checked them. They saw no blue on palms or fingers.

"Besides," Kalahari said, "I'm not wearing a red suit, pretty thing."

The pretty blue thing gave the taller woman a sidelongish glance. It was met with only the hint of a smile, a knowing and flirtatious one.

"Looks as if we'll need a table for six," Kalahari said. "That Jarp getting all the hugging just got out of Pilgrims' Hospital and set it up with the two of us to wait in here and surprise those two. All crewmates, you see. That is one happy Jarp—"

"Oh, I've noticed that!" Shonya said. She glanced around the room. A man against the wall had two fingers up, and she nodded. "Two more Starflare Green Circles, Haj," she told the bartender.

"—and our black friend just passed her exams—she gets her master's license tomorrow."

"Master's license?"

"You mean *ship*'s master?" the impossible alien called from behind the bar, in an impressed voice. He clicked two just filled plasses on the bar while Shonya glanced at

Quindy with an expression that matched his tone. "A spaceship captain?!"

"Wow," Shonya said fervently. "Grabbles! And her so sexy, too."

"You like sexy women, sexy woman?" Kalahari asked quietly.

"Right," Trafalgar was telling the bartender, moving that way to look more closely at the long, pink muzzle with its blunt tip, the reddish eyes and floppy ears that looked almost naked.

A pig's head on what appeared to be a normal primate, ten fingers and all—and it was not a mask. Impossible! It resembled the ridiculous concepts of those old cover artists who didn't understand simple genetics and species development. A canine or porcine animal might become intelligent, bipedal, dominant, but it certainly wouldn't be a human with a standard dog- or pig-head.

"Where're you from, Haj?"

"Piganis," Shonya said, and giggled as she left the bar to deliver the two beers to the table over against the wall. "Table for six over here," she called without being too noisy about it, "or you six can try pulling a table up to that one. Leave space for me, now!" She indicated the table of Cinnabar and friend with a nod.

"Vulcan," the bartender told Trafalgar coolly. He named no planet, but a town about ninety kloms northeast.

"Uh. Of course; should've known." And Trafalgar Cuw laughed aloud. "You mental disaster—that's a holoprojection, isn't it!—with an aurasuit and a holographic projector with—what? A TP helmet over your real head?"

"Well, ain't you the smart one, Outreacher! How about hushin' up about it though, hmm? This get-up's good for business."

"Uh-huh—like Shonya's nice coat of paint." Trafalgar glanced at one of the signs behind the bar: PIGS UNITE! You have NOTHING TO LOSE but your HACKLES! and the one nearby: ALL THAT SNORTS IS NOT PIG. "Oh-Oh—looks like trouble among my friends."

He wheeled from the bar to move to the visibly tense scene involving Janja, Cinnabar, and the latter's fellow Jarp. Quindy had moved back a pace, looking nervous. Ready for trouble. Trafalgar knew the pose and the look. He was aware too that his companions wore their stoppers inside those sexy one-pieces they wore.

"Something the matter, Janjaglaya?" Trafalgar asked, easing between her and the unknown Jarp in one swift sideward movement. "Couple of paces leftward, Quin, so you can cover the jacko behind me. Can we all be cool?"

"But that's my new friend," Cinnabar protested.

Janja had been staring at that new friend as if she were ready to try chewing on its nose. She shot Trafalgar a dark look. Tension radiated from her. The couple at the nearest table moved to another one, 'way over there.

"Cinnabar's new *friend* is Sweetface, crewmember on a spacer named *Coronet*," Janja said, in a brittle voice.

6

If you want anything, just whistle.

—old Jarp saying

"Jan-ja . . ." Cinnabar said, almost pleading. Janja did not glance its way.

"*Coronet, Coronet,*" Trafalgar Cuw said, playing dumb. "An old friend's ship?"

"Definitely not. Will you get out of the way?"

"Don't think I will. Your name Sweetface, spacefarer behind me?"

"Firm," the Jarp's translation helmet said, just behind him.

"How about saying a few carefully chosen words over my shoulder, Sweetface? The kind that maybe don't lead to fights."

"It's firm that I know this Janjaglaya," the Jarp's translahelm said quietly, "though I'd never have recognized her. Cinnabar and I just met and have been talking a bit. Told me who it was waiting for. I should have redshifted right then. It is also firm that I *used* to crew on *Coronet.*"

"Uh. Did you quit, Sweetface, or—"

"Say there spacefarers, we sure don't want any trouble in here, got it?"

That voice pulled their glances barward, to see that Haj of the pig's face had laid a dark and nasty-looking sonic

78

interferencer on the bar's top. It was aimed their way. Not quite pointed; Haj was maintaining his cool, or trying to look that way.

"No trouble, Haj," Trafalgar assured, laying a hand on Janja's arm with full confidence that Quindy was ready for the one called Sweetface behind him. He was reasonably certain that the unnoticed Kalahari would by now be ready for the bartender, too.

Trafalgar wished now that he weren't standing where he was. *On the other hand, I don't dare move. Clever, oh clever, Traf me lad—heroes are killed, not born, remember?*

Janja was saying, "Used to be? Used to? Jonuta throw you off *Coronet*, Sweetface?"

"Neg," the Jarp's translahelm said over the Outie's shoulder. "I left on my own accord. Jonuta and I are definitely not friends."

"Oh, my. A falling out among slavers? Surely not a disagreement over philosophy, slaver."

Cinnabar tried again. "*Jan*-ja . . ."

"Why don't we try untensing," Trafalgar said, keeping his voice steady when it wanted to wiggle, "and sit down to discuss this over a drink. No use getting thrown out of this sty without accomplishing a flainin' thing. Celebration, remember?"

"If you lot don't care to setcher butts down and have a drink," Haj the bartender said, "you better find somewheres else to pass mean looks back and forth."

Janja's face did not change, but she nodded agreement. Sweetface shrugged. They were refused the farther table now, because Haj and Shonya wanted them right here where they could be watched until it was certain that they were mellow, and friends. The second table was drawn up, and a couple of chairs. The round tables hardly matched up, but such matters were of little concern to bar-fans. Cinnabar spoke briefly and privately to Janja, then sat between her and Sweetface.

Shonya took their order. Trafalgar Cuw kept Janja and Sweetface from talking by launching into a joke. He stretched the opening, trying to retain control until they had wetted their throats. The laugh his punch line got wasn't much, but that had not been his purpose anyhow.

Meanwhile Janja was quietly exerting her own brand of control, over her self. Heart- and pulse-rate went down, and so did her temperature. She leaned back and gazed at Sweetface. Just then Shonya brought their drinks; the hard stuff, not beer. Tension and its relief dictated a general movement among them to hoist plasses and drink.

"Did you hear about the ten priests of Gri who left Resh and went to Bleak?" Trafalgar said, almost hurriedly, and paused to sip, hoping the others would follow suit. "Their departure raised the IQ level ten points—on both planets."

Kalahari laughed, and Cinnabar (and Trafalgar), and Quindy, and a big man at a nearby table. Sweetface didn't laugh. Unsmiling, Janja spoke.

"All of you know that it was that slaver Jonuta of Qalara," she said, gazing at Sweetface, "who murdered my intended life-mate and stole me off Aglaya, a year ago. Neither Tarkij nor I had ever known real violence. Our people were not as you, and certainly nothing like Jonuta—and his crew. Of the two who came down onto Aglaya and actually did the murdering and grabbing for their master Jonuta, one is dead and the other is Sweetface. I killed Srih, Sweetface. On Franji."

The Jarp nodded. "We thought it was Corundum. Good for you. Srih was hardly a worthwhile specimen of any race. Wait," it said, as she started to speak. "You could not understand Erts then, of course, but see if any of this sounds familiar. 'You idiot sisterslicer! You had the setting on *Three*! You Fried him, Srih! Jonuta will have your ear!' " It paused to gaze at Janja for a moment, then said, "Well?"

"Am I supposed to recognize those words?" Janja's

tone was sarcastic and her face mocking. "Of course not."

"It is what I said to Srih that day on Aglaya. I can only swear, and I have an idea how much that would mean to you."

"Right. *If* that is what you said to Srih that day you two ended my life and Tarkij's life, it was mere gibberish to me. I actually thought you two were demons, back then! Barbarians, remember? Aglayans are *barbarians*. It must be true—Universal Edutapes says so!"

"I can tell you precisely how we were standing and what you did, along with every word we said," Sweetface told her. "My memory is . . . unusual. And yours? Do you remember which of us used the weapon on your man, and which of us seemed horrified?"

Staring, Janja drew a long, long breath and let it hiss out slowly.

"Horrified, no. I could not read your face or know your emotions. All I—" She stopped herself, about to refer to her ability to *cherm*. "All I saw were two horrid menaces. As to who murdered Tarkij—pos, I remember. It was Srih."

"And Srih is dead," Cinnabar said with an almost pathetic urgency. "Is that not justice? Has vengeance not been served? And justice?"

Neither Sweetface nor Janja glanced at the other Jarp; to Janja, Sweetface nodded. "I was horrified, Janja. And I did say what I told you I said. More, I prevented Srih from stripping and raping you before we took you up to *Coronet*."

"Now you speak of when I was unconscious. As well tell me you have spoken with Sunmother, god of that *barbarian* planet. You can't prove either and I can't disprove either." Janja was dull of voice and cold of eye. "Do not bother sounding the words you used then. I was unconscious—or can't you remember that?"

"Of course I can. You were magnificent. You came at

Srih despite his weapon, and you were determined to kill
him. You even tore his suit.''

"Not," Janja said dully, picking up her plass, "enough.''

"The only thing I have to tell you is that I was a
member of *Coronet*'s crew. Jonuta's crew. A slaver, yes.
We went to Aglaya and Srih and I were sent down, for
what Jonuta called—calls—walking cargo. Srih killed . . .
your man. I did not. I certainly helped carry you onto the
boat and up onto *Coronet*. Later, I did what else I was
told. E—''

"I remember," Janja said, and Sweetface looked down.

What Janja remembered was rape, multiple rape. After
she had fought and slashed through to whatever sense of
honor and pride that swine Jonuta possessed, he had drugged
her and sent his crew to rape her. They had.

"Eventually," Sweetface went on, staring at the tabletop now, "Jonuta became impossible. He was ruined, or
nearly. Financially, I mean. It had to be TGO. We fell
out. I asked to be put off the ship at the first opportunity.
He put me off on Front, with a friend, months ago. I have
not seen him since. Jonuta never forgot you, and neither
did I—and obviously you never forgot us! Srih's dead and
so is Arel. You remember Arel?''

"I remember Arel," the flat voice said. "Good. Another member of that evil crew dead. Good. Was it nice
and slow?''

Sweetface shuddered. (The others sat rather stiffly, wanting to interrupt and afraid to interrupt, not knowing how.
Ready for almost anything and hoping for nothing, not
knowing how that could be. Once Quindy opened her
mouth. She closed it again without saying a word.)

That *"was it nice and slow?"* Trafalgar Cuw thought,
keeping his lids low, *was a bit much, Janja. But I suppose
Sweetface bought it—Sweetface does not know you and
your nature as we do. A woman who is opposed to violence and killing—and who goes berserk when the time is*

*right, and is more swiftly violent and good at killing than
any five others! But not now, not now, poor old Sweetface—
not when she is calm with no reason to go berserker!*

Neither Janja nor Sweetface knew that Kalahari and
Trafalgar had held hasty and quiet conference a few minutes before. Neither Aglayan nor Jarp knew that both of
them were covered, under the table. As a matter of fact
Quindy and Cinnabar didn't know, either. At least neither
Janja's nor Sweetface's weapon was handily strapped on at
the hip—assuming that Sweetface was armed.

"That is all of it," Sweetface said. "Truth. I can stay
or leave. You can try to kill me or decide not to. I
understand, and I'd rather run than defend myself, but I
won't promise!"

"Janja," Cinnabar said quietly, in a tone that was almost plaintive.

"Wait awhile, Cinnabar." Janja did not take her gaze
off the other orange face.

*I believe it, she realized. I believe Sweetface, slaver who
served the master slaver! Oh, but I hate to believe it! Now
it has made me unsure about what to do—what I should
do. Sunmother and Aglii—oh, Tarkij, Tarkij! You are
long dead and I cannot bring you back and have done so
much, so much! They have made me as gray as they are,
these Thingmakers. I have joined them, Tarkij. You were
worthy of Aglaya—am I? If I do not kill this creature, am I
worthy of you and Aglaya? But if I do—am I worthy then?*

"You sure know how to spoil a celebration, Janja,"
Cinnabar said, and pushed back its chair. "Only the greatest day of my life," it said, rising and walking away. To
the rest room, Trafalgar noted.

Janja closed her eyes slowly against the wounding words
and lowered her head just as slowly.

*It's all so hard, she thought. I hurt Cinnabar by doing
this, and so Cinnabar hurts me back. That's understandable. I understand that. Anybody can understand that. What*

I don't understand, O Sunmother . . . is what to do. So much easier to look at things Hellfire's way, and handle things her way and Corundum's way! So much easier if I had killed, the moment I knew this was Sweetface!

"I didn't learn well enough, Corundum, Hellfire," she muttered to the tabletop.

The woman called Kalahari Cuw half-heard, and recognized a name that had been hers. Without thinking she said, "What?"

Janja did not look up. She shook her head, staring at the plass she turned and turned in her hands. Just as Quindy started to cover those hands with hers, her Aglayan friend looked up. At Sweetface, whose face was more impassive and dolorous than any Jarp's Quindy had ever seen.

"You said that you left *Coronet* . . . with a friend. Not . . . Kenowa, surely."

"You remember us all, don't you! Neg, it was not Kenowa. I can't imagine anything separating her from Jonuta, turning her against Jonuta. Even the fact that he obviously thought much of you and could not forget you."

Janja's face went ugly.

Cool it, dammit, Trafalgar thought. *You said the wrong thing that time, you proctological specimen of a Jarp! That, Janja does not want to hear!*

Under the table, he and Kalahari held naked stoppers. One was aimed at Sweetface, one at Janja. Each was set on One, only One. Each was ready to be squeezed—"fired."

"Kenowa owes him," Sweetface said, after a waver. "We all owe him or did owe him. I just couldn't stay with him anymore. Had I stayed I might have killed him. Or more likely tried, and been killed! The friend I mentioned was another Jarp. A . . . not quite complete one. In the company of Galactics, I called her Tweedle-dee. Kenowa called her Tweedle-dumb, I know. Jonuta's beloved Kenny. 'Her,' yes; Tweedle-dee is far more female than any of the people I have known. Was."

"Tweedle-dee. Tweedle-dumb," Janja said, and shrugged. The words meant nothing as words or as name. "What do you mean, not quite comple—oh. Mostly female—you mean she has no testicle?"

Sweetface shook its head and its increased sadness was obvious. "Neg. An incompleteness of the head. She was called something else before I met her, Janja."

The others stared at the Jarp in silence. Trafalgar glanced over as Shonya started to approach. He nodded but waved her away, hoping that she understood: *Pos, we want another round, just don't interrupt us*.

"I'm just not sure you want to know that Jarp's name, Janja."

"I've only known one other Jarp," Janja said slowly, quietly, staring. Remembering, thinking about the planet Resh, and the house of those true sadists, Sicuan and Chulucan. And the half-wit Jarp there . . . "And it was . . . a half-wit. You're talking about . . . no, you say the name."

"Whistle, she was called. On Resh."

Janja shook her head. "Incredible."

"Isn't it!" And after a moment, "I was . . . infatuated. That was part of the trouble between Jonuta and me."

"You took Whistle onto *Coronet*? As companion? And you fell out with Jonuta because of her?" Janja shook her head, muttering, *"Whistle!"*

"Partially."

"You chose that poor creature over Jonuta, then, and let yourself be dumped—on Front."

"Set off, not dumped. No lies, no exaggerations, Janja! I *asked* to be set off there. With Whistle."

Janja sat slumped, looking small, looking at nothing. Shonya set another drink before them all, and left one for Cinnabar. Trafalgar nodded and winked; Kalahari patted her thigh. Shonya departed in response to the signal of another patron of the Pig's Eye.

Very quietly, almost forlornly, Janja said, "I don't want to kill you, Sweetface."

A wave of relief rolled over the tables with an almost palpable aura of relaxation. Five people sagged a bit, and were happy to do it. Kalahari Cuw and Trafalgar Cuw exchanged a look, nodded, and made furtive movements under the tables.

"—in the damned *women*'s room, you damned Jarp!" a voice yelled, and it slurred a bit. "I'm not used to pissin' beside somebody with tits!"

With a considerable amount of noise five people pounced to their feet. Four rushed toward the rear of the Pig's Eye and the restrooms. One was at the bar in an instant.

"Nobody's going to get hurt, Haj," Trafalgar said, staring into the bartender's face. "Not much, anyhow. Let's say no one's going to get *killed*. Just keep your beamer down and stand by to serve a round to everyone here, on me. Except the drunken fobber who just yelled at our friend and crewmate Cinnabar. That drunken fobber will be leaving."

Haj stared, trying hard because he wanted to look toward the commotion in the rear. "Who the vug are you, anyhow?"

"A man with an awful lot of cred and even ready stells, Haj, who knows that no one's going to be killed or seriously hurt and that the best thing you can do is be cool and draw yourself a Starflare, on me."

Haj shook his head. "You sure you people don't have someplace else you'd really rather be?"

Trafalgar smiled. Oddly, so did Shonya.

Sweetface, meanwhile, had got there first. Cinnabar stood with its hands partially upraised, not in menace but in a fending motion. The snarly drunk was drawing back a large bony fist. Sweetface caught the cocked forearm. As the man started to turn, Janja made him grunt by punching him in the ribs. He looked down to see that the punching object was a stopper.

"There are six of us," Kalahari said from just beside her, "all together. You sure picked a bad night to try proving yourself! What you really want to do is go on home, don't you?"

The man blinked and went rather limp.

He went on home. As he exited, Haj called out the beautiful words, "Trouble's over without a punch! Drinks on the sty! Here's mud in yer eye, pigs?"

The laughter was out of all proportion to the words, but the cheer was happy and warranted.

"Can we celebrate now?" Cinnabar said, on a plaintive note.

"Oh, Cinnabar!" Janja hugged the Jarp again. "I'm sorry—and I'm so happy for you! Your voice is beautiful, too!"

They were all happy for their translator-implanted friend, and now they had the time to express it. Now too came realization of the deception, and its confirmation. Trafalgar and Kalahari had known that Cinnabar was here, of course, waiting to surprise Janja. No, they had not known about Sweetface.

Sweetface's presence here was perfectly logical, and either fortuitous or in-. One of those coincidences that everyone knew happened constantly, because everyone experienced them, but which would have been hard to accept in fiction.

"No death by accident," Sweetface said with a solemn face and a minute shrug, "ever took place that didn't involve coincidence."

"Tao's balls," Kalahari said Hellfirishly, "that's true, isn't it! I never thought of that!"

Still recovering from stress and now from the draining effect of relief, they babbled about that. Eventually they wound down. Janja established eye contact with the Jarp across the table, then spoke very seriously.

"Sweetface: I'm armed. Are you?"

"Positively."

"I don't see it."

"Do you want to?"

"No no, Sweetface," Trafalgar said with ebullience, "don't you dare take out that big hard thing in public!"

For the first time, Sweetface of Jarpi joined in their joviality.

"Do you think we should be armed?" Janja pressed on. "Are you worried about it?"

The others hushed again while the Jarp looked at her. "Janja . . . I'm not. Should I be?"

With a small sigh, she looked down as if in resignation. "No. You should not be, not now. Should I be worried that you're armed, Sweetface?" Again she looked into those dark, huge Jarp eyes.

"Positively not."

"I won't then," she said, and she reached out with her right hand.

Solemnly, the Jarp took it. Four long fingers and double thumbs, all of a shocking true orange, a hairless orange, enwrapped the shorter, minimally tan fingers of the Aglayan. They stared at each other, and no one else said a word. (All about them the other patrons of the Pig's Eye had gone noisy in natural jovial response to a free round of drinks.)

It was Kalahari who broke the silence that existed only at those two joined tables. "Sweetface—my name is Kalahari Cuw. Are you . . . do you count yourself enemy of Jonuta, Sweetface?"

The Jarp looked at her. "Hello, Kalahari Cuw. Yes."

Janja nodded, her eyes seeking to search those of the Jarp. None here knew of her ability to cherm, though Cinnabar suspected, or knew something. The cherming ability was taken for granted by Aglayans. Such a talent was a matter of fiction and phantasy among Jarps and Galactics. Any paranormal mental ability was a wistful wish and phantasy of humankind. Humankind—Galactics— still believed that the jelly-blob inhabitants of quarantined Shirash were the only telepathic race in the galaxy humans considered theirs. (Without limbs or tentacles or even pseudopods, the Shirashi compensated very well indeed with a superb and frightening telehypnotic ability. Coupled with a pretty well-developed telekinesis, it made them formidable and dangerous. After a disastrous first contact, Shirash was quarantined. It was forbidden, shunned.)

The galaxy-conquerors Janja called Thingmakers did not know about the Aglayans simply because Aglaya was pre-steel age, and its culture was mostly agrarian/pastoral rather than hunter. Aglaya's presumed sole value to the Thingmakers was its magnificent flower called phrillia. So said the encyclopedic references Janja had consulted.

Those edutapes did not mention that Aglayans were valued, too—but only as exotic slaves. The Galactic race was dark. Pale of skin and eye and hair, Aglayans brought good prices on any Galactic-settled planet. Humans knew the planet was "barbarian," because humans said so. Humans considered Aglayans human, merely undeveloped. A bit less than human, then.

That was not quite right. The blonds of Aglaya were not less than human; they were a bit more.

Janja of Aglaya could not read minds or influence thoughts and actions or objects by mind alone. She did not possess telepathy then; she possessed the cherming ability. She could sense and interpret emotions as many animals (and Jarps) sensed pheromones. Powerful aroused emotions in the minds of others were easy for her to sense, and read, even at some distance. Rage and anger were the easiest; they constituted menace.

She sensed no menace here. Not from Sweetface, or anyone else. Kalahari, she thought, was sexually aroused.

(Cinnabar knew that for certain, and knew that Blue Shonya was, too. Pretty naughty, it thought, for a lesbian to be working here, displaying herself as she was, exciting the males and inciting them to greater spending!)

Quindy asked, "What is your ship now, Sweetface?"

Trafalgar glanced at her. Did they have to keep questioning the damned Jarp? At any moment a new cause for hatred might come forth from it. It and its ". . . unusual" memory.

At the query the Jarp looked away. Janja took the opportunity to study it in quest of the weapon it said it bore.

The orange hermaphrodite wore a kaftan that, while very lightweight, was not clingy. It was slimly cut, and the sleeves were sufficiently fitted so that if a weapon were concealed there, it had to be a mighty flat knife. Self-belted, a bit past ankle-length, with a hood that lay in almost flat folds on its back. Nothing concealed there. The garment was base white, with clusters of thin navy stripes running in vertical bands amid broader ones of a deep wine-red. A (non-functional) zipper ran all the way down the front.

A slim strap, also dark red, lay diagonally across the torso between the breasts, which it emphasized. It supported a plump little equhyde case on the Jarp's right hip. The case was not long enough to conceal a stopper. Janja had never heard of a collapsible one. A knife or a jangler, maybe—but the case's lid was visibly strapped down and *locked*.

Something valuable then, Janja mused, *but surely not a weapon*.

"I don't have a berth now," the Jarp said quietly, looking at no one.

When neither Quindy nor anyone else commented,

Sweetface added, "I'm out of work. Looking. This is a bad planet for that. I've found a couple of people who'd be delighted to have me as slave, though."

"Bad planet for Jarps, too," Cinnabar blurted. Then, "I'm sorry, Sweetface. I left Jarpi as a slave. You?"

Sweetface nodded. "Oddly, Jonuta saved me from that and freed me, as crewmember. I feel that I repaid him. I have next to nothing. Of course . . . for all I know, by now he may have nothing, too. It must have been TGO that set out to ruin him. He had no idea why. Now I have."

Janja was opening her mouth to speak; Trafalgar hurriedly said, "Oh?"

"A TGW ship—along with a Murph policer—were destroyed in a brief action out off Murph's moon, Dot. The mining satellite. The man who did that was positively identified as Jonuta. TGO obviously had to take action."

"You didn't say 'was,' " Cinnabar pointed out.

"True. It was not Jonuta. A mistake."

"No," Janja said. "No mistake. It was Corundum. He was very clever in leading a man on Dot to believe that he was Jonuta, while pretending to be trying to disguise that 'fact.' "

Sweetface gazed at her, big-eyed. "You know that?"

"Pos. I was with Corundum at the time."

"And you left him. Corundum is a space pirate and you left him. Jonuta is a slaver and I left him." After a moment it added, "Dare I ask whether you left him because of a conflict of philosophy, morality?"

Janja sighed. "You dare. It is a good point and I understand the message. No, not the way I meant when I asked you that, and not the way you mean." She sat back. She stared at her plass, toying with it. Turning it around and around. Without looking up she asked, "What happened to—where's, uh, Whistle? Tweedle-dee?"

"Gone. Enslaved again."

Janja or not, Cinnabar reached over and squeezed its fellow Jarp's arm. Sweetface glanced that way, nodded appreciation, drank.

"It happened on Front," Sweetface told its plass, empty again. "I only just escaped. I don't mean I ran. I killed one of them and they fled. With Tweedle-dee. I had an awful time clearing myself. A *Jarp* had slain a *Galactic!* Never mind that he was a slaver, and that his companions had stolen a free person off a free planet."

"Not person," Cinnabar said with an uncharacteristic bitterness. "Just a Jarp."

"Firm. Just a Jarp." Sweetface looked around.

"I already signed Shonya for another round," Kalahari said.

Janja said, "I'm sorry, Sweetface. Truly. I understand—believe me."

Sweetface wouldn't look at her. "I know. I believe you."

"And Jonuta's a slaver."

"Pos. It's . . . different now, seeing it from this side."

Kalahari said, "This is the heaviest celebration I ever attended!" Then, "Uh—Janja. I'd like to whisper about one sentence in your ear."

"I'll bet I've already thought of it," Janja told her. "Listen, I won't call my spacer *Tarkij*. I think I'll name it *Sunflower*."

The others saw the steady, ever-thoughtful eyes; the clamp of that firm little Aglayan jaw. Made her look so determined, Quindy mused. So . . . daunting, menacing. But so young! *She is, too. So young.*

Sweetface sighed. "I like that, Janja. But you can't. There's already a *Sunflower* on the spaceways."

"Always has been," Cinnabar amplified, "since that first spacer called *Sunflower* landed on Jarpi."

Janja nodded. She drained her metal-based plass. "Not

Tarkij, then, and not *Sunflower*. All right then, I know what I'll call my ship."

Kalahari looked at her. "I know too, Janjy."

"I just decided!"

Kalahari flipped her fingers. "Sure. But it's obvious, isn't it. You'll call your ship what I've heard you say again and again. The god of Aglaya you call on—or name so often, anyhow. Not Sun-*flower* . . . but Sun-*mother*."

"You're right," Janja said, gazing at her in surprise. Then at Quindy: "Cap'n Quindy, tomorrow you are master of spacer *Sunmother*."

"It's a good name, Janja. An odd one, but we're an odd crew. A weirdly black woman, a weirdly *almost*-white one with *almost*-white hair, a regular rainbow of an Outie, and a Jarp."

"Damn," Cinnabar said, and shook its unhelmeted head. "I always get last billing!"

Kalahari and Trafalgar chuckled, but Janja was answering Quindy—while looking at Sweetface.

"No, Ship's Master Quindy. Two Jarps."

7

If every kid had a funny tooth to bite down on whenever the world disappointed him, prussic acid could solve our population problems in one generation.

—G.C. Edmonson's Albert,
in *The Man Who Corrupted Earth*

"I need to talk with Sweetface," Janja had told the Satana Coalition. "We'll just take a walk and see you back at the hotel."

"Firm, Janjy, but why not just move to another table for that private talk I thought you'd be wanting . . . with someone who knows so much about Jonuta! This place's getting noisier by the min and no one's going to hear your conversation."

Janja stood; Sweetface did. "I'd rather take a walk," she said (noting that the Jarp still showed no evidence of a concealed weapon) and Sweetface nodded assent/agreement.

"Go ahead then," Cinnabar told them. Cinnabar was clearly delighted at Janja's very sensible decision to take Sweetface into her crew. Its attitude was definitely "There aren't all that many of us Jarps and we ought to be friends, sticking together and mutually propping-supporting, taking care of each other as fellow aliens among Galactics (aliens to us!)." That was Cinnabar's obvious attitude. It did not state it and did not need to.

Now Cinnabar waved a hand. "Do let me pay for you both."

"Oh," Sweetface said frowning, "I can't—"

"Never mind," Trafalgar said. "Cinnabar's wealthy and we haven't been rich long enough to become properly tight-fisted. We'll see you two at the hotel. If you get there first and are still in deep converse, just put a sign on the door."

"Careful, Cloud-top," Kalahari said.

Automatically Janja had said, "Firm, Cap'n Prass-top, and thanks."

Only as she and Sweetface departed had she remembered that Hellfire was no longer Hellfire, nor prass-topped, nor captain.

Then the double doors closed away all sound and sight of the Pig's Eye, and she and Sweetface were ambling along the dimly illumined street of Thebanis's capital. Way up ahead a couple was walking in the same direction. A girl in high-necked jerkin and short-shorts pedaled by on an orange-and-violet bike. Otherwise, all stores and offices were closed and traffic was almost nonexistent.

In their wake Kalahari Cuw was saying, "You don't think Janja's being unwise, do you?"

"Of course not," Cinnabar said, going all defensive.

"Oh stop, Cinn. Your knee keeps jerking because of your bias. Traf?"

"I hope not," Trafalgar Cuw said. "I can't believe she wanted to get away from us and alone with Sweetface just to renew their quarrel. I think that's over. That kind of trickery doesn't sound like Janja, anyhow."

"My opinion is that Sweetface won't try anything argumentative either," Quindy said, "much less violent. I think that's a very sincere individual. And a pretty beaten-down one, too."

"Besides, Sweetface just got a berth!" Cinnabar said, knowing that was logic and not knee-jerk bias.

"Well," Kalahari said, "let's have another drink."

"Order for me," Trafalgar said, getting up. "I'm going back to the rest room to deposit the first three drinks—and pop a red while I'm at it, too."

"An antintoxicant's a good idea for us all," Quindy said. "Let's have a red all around."

"And lose this buzz?" Cinnabar protested. "Not me! I'm celebrating!"

"I'll pass on an antintoxicant too, Mother Quindy," Kalahari said, and she grinned.

Still wearing that smile, she glanced over at Shonya, all blue and not *quite* all naked. Shonya returned the smile, and winked.

Janja glanced up. "It hadn't occurred to me that they would dim the lights on the underside of the Municipal Complex, at night. It's a nice touch."

"Thoughtful," Sweetface said. "Who wants to walk out of a bar late at night into broad daylight—especially Thebanis's!—simulated or otherwise?"

"Good point. I like it. Those odd lights make everything sort of misty. Sweetface—I'd hate to be wrong or gone fobby, but I'm convinced that I do want you on my ship."

"I hope you're right—and that I am, in readily agreeing," the Jarp said, and neither of them mentioned that it was just about down and out, and just about fresh out of alternative choices. "Uh—your ship, you said. You are . . . Captain Janjaglaya?"

"No—ugh, look at the junk in this window! Those Bleakers don't care what they export, do they! No, I failed the test today. Not enough experience, obviously. So— Quindy will be registered as captain. She is marvelous at con, and with SIPACUM. I own the ship."

"You . . . *own* a . . . spacer," Sweetface said, standing beside her to stare through the store window at the display of overpriced imported . . . junk.

"I do. My life did end that day on Aglaya, and I'll try not to mention it any more. My new life has been rough. Now it's begun to look promising. 'Out of adversity, character,' the saying goes, and I can add 'and profit'! For one thing, all the people you've just been sitting with are rich. The first time I escaped from slavery I carried the balls of my former masters and was too stupidly naive to take anything else. The second time, I carried away wealth. So did the others—all four back in the Pig's Eye."

"You were all . . . enslaved? Together?"

"Pos. It was awful, but at least we made it pay. Now none of us *has* to do a dam' thing."

Sweetface politely—and with incredible control—did not ask for particulars. The last time it had seen Janja, she was Aglaya-pale, with very short almost-white hair. Jonuta was taking her offship onto Resh to sell her to a dealer. That had been just over a year ago. Now she was free, had friends, stells, and a great deal of confidence. And she owned a spaceship! That was any spacefarer's dream, realized by only one in hundreds. Now she had calmly, coolly said that she was rich. *Because* she had been enslaved again, and struggled free—again.

Sweetface merely asked, "Then why are you going into space?"

"Kalahari isn't, unless she hitches a ride to . . . wherever she might be going. She is retiring from the spaceways, to join the idle rich."

"She is wanted."

"No comment," Janja said serenely. "I can't be sure that Trafalgar Cuw will come along. I wish he would, that's all! He's a, ah, never mind. Mysterious, 's what Trafalgar Cuw is. Quindy and Cinnabar . . . well, Quindy is just wedded to space and the con, and the three of us have been through so much together! Danger, horror, attack by Corundum, slavery . . . you'll hear all that later.''

"One question—are you all wanted?''

"One way or another, one place or another, pos.''

"Me too. We never need to talk about any of that. I've taken my chances for years. I'll go on taking them. Oh—what should I call my ship's *owner*?''

"I am now Janjaglaya Wye. Call me Janjaglaya or Janja. Here, let's walk on—I just saw that sickening blue dildo. I am going into space solely in quest of Jonuta, Sweetface. In quest of his home planet, I suppose, to begin with.''

"To kill him.''

"Yes. That thought is what has kept me alive and striving all these months. Partially in revenge, of course; I certainly don't deny that. But also to *stop* him. To save all the people he'll otherwise steal and sell if he's allowed to live. All the Aglayans.'' After a moment she added, "And Jarps.''

Under the dimmed, mist-colored lights forming the underside of the AMC, they ambled on in silence. Alone. Another bicyclist had passed. That was the sole traffic along this street with its dun-colored sidewalks and an occasionally-sighted ramp leading up to the guv-bureaus above.

"That's my goal and my mission, Sweetface. To hunt for a man, and hunt him down, and kill him. A very dangerous man, as you know better than I do! Sure you want to sign on my ship?''

"*Pos*. Firm!''

"Very definite. Hmm. I'd say that what H—Kalahari wanted to whisper to me back there is that you could be dangerous, or a great deal of help just because of all you know about Jonuta.''

"She would be right, Janjaglaya. I *will* be of help. He is an extremely canny man, almost ridiculously careful with a thought to everything or nearly. A genius in a way, and I was in his company for years. You would not believe the number of policers, TGW included, and officious officials we made fools of. Or the ways we did it.''

''Won't I?''

''Merely a figure of speech. You will. You are asking whether I will tell you, show you. I will. I will also help you to find Jonuta.''

''And—''

''I . . . really don't desire to kill him, Janja. That's why I left his ship. I feared it would come to that.''

''But I do desire to kill him, Sweetface,'' Janja reminded.

''You are my captain, and I also have no desire to *save* him. I do not subscribe to the philosophy that vengeance is shallow or unworthy.''

''It provides a reason for living,'' Janja said, and the Jarp glanced sharply over and down at her. Janja's dull voice had returned, and so had the staring, burned-out eyes.

They were approaching an alley for service to adjacent offices and stores, with a nearby ramp leading up to AMC. For the first time, a car hummed past. A three-wheeler, yellow, electric, and incapable of speeding beyond fifteen kph. Any traffic was so unusual at this hour in this roofed ''town''-within-a-city that they glanced after it. It turned a corner and was gone.

''You are telling me that you will help but can't be expected to push the firing stud,'' Janja said.

''Exactly. That does not mean that if you are in trouble, I won't—''

''LOOK OUT!''

The two men didn't exactly step out of the alley directly into their path; they pounced. They had been in the Pig's Eye earlier that evening, and both had left precipitately though separately. Now they appeared to have formed an alliance, and waited in ambush. They looked emphatically mean.

"Hello there, *Jarp*!"

"Hello there, *Sunflower*."

"You shouldn't've messed with us, *Jarp*; Sunflower."

Their faces were ferally snarling and their voices were snarls. They were only two, but their faces were those of a mob. Their confidence came from their being together, and the fact that they had found weapons. The bearded man carried a mean-looking piece of pipe, blued. His chartreuse-pantsed ally held what appeared to be the handle of an ax, which he was thumping into his left palm.

Sweetface began, "She didn't do any—"

And Janja interrupted: "I had a stopper, remember?"

"I don't see no stopper, li'l gurl," chartreuse pants said—the one his companion had called Fon. "Maybe it's stuck in yer pretty shirt with your little warheads, hmm? Try reaching and you'll getcher arm busted."

"I don't see no stopper," the other man said, the one from the rest room. He started to close, swinging back and up his forty-sem piece of piping, which was about three sems in diameter. His glare was directed at Sweetface.

"Well, you see one now."

Before the two men and Janja could wonder how the slender tube of a stopper had materialized in the orange hand, it was there and had been squeezed and the pipe-wielder was dancing to the tune of a number Two setting.

"Goddam sisterslicin' *Jarp*," Fon snarled, and he thrust his long polished chunk of rock-hard polymer past Janja. Its slim end rammed into Sweetface's side, hard.

The Jarp's loud groan was followed closely by Fon's, as Janja grabbed the club in both hands and used its owner's grip as fulcrum to slam it back across his midsection. It clicked against his buckle, which did not absorb the impact. One arm was wrenched, too, and he let go with that one. Now the knuckles of his left hand were digging into his own side. Janja tried jerking a knee up between his thighs, but he swerved both knees to save his genitals.

Meanwhile Sweetface had staggered back, mouth sagging and eyes filled with pain. Attacker number one was relieved of the stopper beam. He stopped jiggling, sagged, caught himself. With Janja conveniently between him and the Jarp now, the fellow regained control of his jangled nerves and brain. Without even glancing at the pipe he had dropped, he slammed a fist into the side of her head and another into the fine target a man naturally chose: her breasts. (At that he groaned loudly and a tear spurted from his eye—his knuckles had just found the barrel of her bra-tucked stopper. Only the stopper hurt her, since the big bra was padded with more than the weapon.)

She fell sidewise and forward, which meant against the gasping, weak-kneed Fon, and his ax-handle. He was bowled off his feet and Janja was helpless not to fall on top of him. The club was between them. That way it hurt both their guts and cost them all breath. On the other hand, it didn't break Janja's wrist. It did his. He made a brief shrill noise and succumbed to pain by sagging into unconsciousness. His hand relaxed on the club; Janja still hung on. She was busy trying to drag in a breath.

"Rotten Sunflower whorebitch," the other idiot said, reaching for her hair with one hand and his pipe with the other and, since he was conveniently squatting, Sweetface kicked him in the side of the face.

The impact sent him caroming a full meter or so. The other side of his face made an ugly sound when it slammed into the pavement, rolling up skin in a long patch. He jerked violently. He didn't get up.

Sweetface looked both ways. Not a soul in sight. Just three people lying here at its feet and the way clear to run for all it was worth.

On the other hand, it heard the sound of voices, and footsteps. Above. A male and a female were coming down the ramp just on the other side of the alley—less than two meters away!

Sweetface never wavered. Years on the outlaw trail had taught it that no matter how much in the right it was, explanations were best avoided and flight was the very best course. It bent, yanked up its kaftan's hem to the waist, clamped it there with an elbow while it picked up Janja.

"Hang onto that club," it muttered, and lunged into the alleyway in which their assailants had lurked to await any of the six who had cost them so much machistic face.

Janja hung onto the club and the Jarp kept running, trying to be as quiet about it as possible. It danced over discarded rubbish, staggered, bounced a shoulder off a wall, grunted, clung to Janja, and kept running.

It passed a recessed doorway (hearing a scream from behind, the woman's cry as she and the man emerged from working late or playing soar-games, to discover the two fallen men, one bloody) and lurched to swing back and into the twenty-sem recess of the service doorway. Back against the well-secured door ("Get back up to the office and call the policers, Lu!"), it lowered the confused Janja's legs and pressed her back, too. The cover was minimal ("I'll see if I can do anything for these two") but neither Jarp nor Aglayan wore any spare meat. ("Maybe they're just drunk, Ticker! Maybe they got drunk and fought?")

"*Just . . . don't . . . move . . . a muscle,*" Sweetface murmured. "*This is not . . . unfortunately . . . a proper alley . . . It isn't dark!*"

Janja, who had had enough experience with an alley of the dark variety back on Resh nearly a year ago, now mentally cursed the nice overhead illumination that managed to light nearly every corner and crevice.

They stood crushed together and crushed back against the door, frozen, hearts pounding. Listening:

"I'm not going back up there in the dark and leave you here alone, Ticker! If one of these risers wakes up he might decide to take out his drunk and his hurt on you!"

"I've got his pipe. Let him try anything."

"Ticker—*please*. Let's just go! No one's around to see. . . ."

"Someone might! We're GOV-ERN-MENT-EM-PLOY-EES, Lu! How would it look?!"

"Maybe if you slammed that club back their way, real hard, they'd run, and we could—"

"All right then," Ticker's voice interrupted Sweetface's whisper, *"I'll* run back up and call the policers or get the watchman, and *you* stay here to keep an eye on them."

"Are you kidding?!"

Two sets of footsteps rushed back up the ramp. Neither Lu nor Ticker had so much as glanced into the alley. That would have required thought on their parts.

Janja and Sweetface kept holding their breaths until the footsteps receded. Then they popped out of the recess to head down the alley, at speed. The longer-legged Jarp was astonished at how rapidly the short Aglayan could move. It remembered her planet's high gravity, and the overdeveloped muscles of those calves now concealed by the flare of her scarlet pants.

"Hang onto the club," it muttered beside her. "It can be tested and you can be traced. Far more than fingerprints shows up to policer scanners!"

"Uh," she said, and that was her only answer. She was racing, taking three steps to its two.

As they approached a cross-street, Sweetface panted, "Go left. I'll wait a little and go right. Turn right at the first corner, right at the next. I'll meet you on that street, whatever it is."

"Uh-huh."

Sweetface stopped running. Janja slowed. By the time she emerged from the alley, she was walking. Nor was she winded. It didn't matter; there wasn't a sign of traffic, although across the street a store was lighted. She went left and walked rapidly, ready to slow on sight of another person. The club, almost diamond-hard yet hardly heavy, felt very good in her hand. She tried to carry it inconspicuously.

One block and two halves later, she looked for Sweetface. She saw others. Two bikers. Four people walking. One staggering. Four people in two vehicles. No Jarp.

Janja inhaled deeply, let the air out slowly.

So much for that, she thought, not without sadness. The Jarp had thought better of all this and had hurried away to remain in deep cover until she was safely off Thebanis. If only—

That was when she spotted it, peering out of the door-way of a lounge across the street. Eye contact made, it motioned and vanished inside. Its kaftan, Janja noted, was gone.

Wearing a little smile, she ambled up the street. A yellow tri-wheeler stood before a lighted shop. The big carrier-box mounted on the vehicle's rear accommodated the club easily. *And so much for that, too.*

Then she noticed that the still-open shop was a bou-tique. She sauntered in. *Just in case,* she thought, in a standard phrase-now-joke of the Satana Coalition. It was possible, at least, that she and Sweetface were being sought.

The clerk had eschewed calorie-consuming foods suffi-ciently to build a bit of extra weight, which looked good in a white-arabesqued black dasheek, full length. The owner of the three-wheeler was just leaving. Since she did not come back, Janja assumed that the ax-handle was being pedaled away to another area of Raunch.

"I'm burnin' up in this flainin' thing," she lied, trying to put on a Mott-chindese accent which the clerk would presumably never recognize. Just in case.

"It is handsome, but . . . perhaps something a bit more . . . revealing?"

"Let's skip pants," Janja said.

Soon the delighted clerk was delightedly handling the unusual: a cash purchase. Janja was happy in a loose blue blouse with huge short sleeves all in soft folds, an extremely short black skirt, and a nice imported-and-thus-overpriced shoulderbag. Having left her scarlet jumpsuit in the dressing cubicle, she returned for it while her stell certificates were being routinely scanner-checked.

In the cubicle she tucked her stopper into the new shoulderbag—"kerdragon," an electric blue lizard easily bred on one of the planets of the Tri-System Accord.

"You do have beautiful legs," the clerk enthused, when Janja approached carrying a crumpled wad of red cloth.

"You don't think they're, uh, too big?"

"Oh, *no*! Let me just wrap that hot old jumpsuit, dear. No, if I were you and your height, I'd emphasize those calves even more on a pair of really high heels. Say—strap sandals in white. They're really all the tune-in this year," she said, by which she meant they were the in-thing to wear.

She wrapped the one-piece while helpfully informing her very welcome late customer that the bag came from Andor, T.S.A. Then they went to look at shoes. The clerk—and owner, Janja surmised—made no argument when the short customer completed her new ensemble with a pair of lightweight, clingy boots that molded her legs to the knees, in blue. With eleven-sem heels, slim.

More cash; another quick scanner-check required by law, effusive thanks and hearty best wishes for a wonderful evening. An invitation to return, and a bonus: a tiny squeeze-tube of the paint-on "jewelry" so popular in Raunch. Blue-and-pink.

Janja strolled out, short-stepping now on the high thin heels, and crossed the street. *If I have to run I'll have to get out of these heeled boots first,* she mused, *or break my neck! Beautiful legs, hmm? Bet she'd have said that if they'd been the size of my wrists—all the way down!*

Janja, Janja—you're becoming as suspicious and cynically questioning as They!

She entered the lounge—the Green Jinni. It was a name she didn't like. It reminded her of Corundum. It was what he had called his ship's SIPACUM: "Jeannie." *Jinni,* one of the magical beings of myth which the undereducated called *djinn* or "genie."

She walked into eddying, swirl-shot green mist that she realized was illusion. Its apparent source, a fat, garishly-dressed and grinning jinni—chartreuse—sat crosslegged in mid-air, twice life-size.

A holocube, Janja mused. *There is more imagination in the bars of Thingmakers than in their museums of art!*

"Hel-*lo,* darr-ling," someone called, over the tinny-tinkly music of a ravisynther and a tenor drum. "Buy you a gin 'n' quinette?"

"—she c'n wrap them calfy legs around my neck any time," another male commented, *sotto voce,* and Janja was only just able to hold back her smile of pleasure. No use being insulted when compliment was intended, however crude!

Sweetface sat at the bar. Its long lean legs were really displayed now, in plum-colored tights previously worn unobtrusively under the kaftan (which was nowhere in view) and dull black softboots. Otherwise it wore only a Thebanian strap-titser, a bra that was mostly straps and displayed plenty of shining orange breast-flesh. The Jarp's warheads were not large but hardly tiny. The openwork bandeau was the color of dried blood.

Before the Jarp stood a plass of beer, draught. On its left, a woman in green glo-bra—full—and SprayOn patch-pants in five colors. High-heeled sandals, white, were gaitered up her legs. On the Jarp's right, an empty stool. Janja took it and her eyes widened immediately at the unexpected coolth of the seat so high on the backs of her thighs.

The bartender was human and female, in silky-looking yellow teeshirt and loose straight pants, black. The tables were tended by servo-tubeways. The woman looked questioningly at her newest customer.

"Starflare," Janja said, naming Thebanis's truly superior beer.

"Dark?"

"Green Circle."

"Umm." The bartender moved away to her nozzled pipes.

"Grand Khan Hotel," Janja muttered quickly. "Seventeen-oh-nine."

"Seventeen oh-nine," Sweetface muttered. "Kaftan—rest room."

"Seventeen how many?" That came in a whisper from the man to Janja's right and she stared at the mirror across from her. Then she smiled.

"No no," she murmured, leaning his way. "Seventwo-nine."

"Got it."

She slid off the stool—forgetting how much showed, with the ultra-short skirt, and receiving two whistles and more comments—and moved through the swirl-smoky room to the rear. She found the women's sitter and went in. She searched. No kaftan.

Thoughtfully she emerged and stood leaning against the wall beside the door, across from the men's. A very young man or youth came out. His brows went up at sight of her.

"Someone played me a mean trick," she said. "Hid my kaftan in there."

His grin was sly. "Saw it. What'll you give me?"

"Greedy jacko! A fat kiss if you get it, fat lip if you don't."

Grin broadening, he started for her. She fended with both palms: "After."

Still grinning, he went back into the men's and soon emerged with the Jarp's kaftan. Still grinning. Janja took it—he didn't let go—and gave him a kiss with a lot of tongue. He jerked away!

"Daughter of evil!" he snapped, making some sort of ward-sign, and hurried back into the safety of the rest room.

His grin transferred itself to Janja's face—after her initial expression of shock. Poor baby! Sick cults never died out, and one never knew who was a religious sickofobber and who was a rapist! She got the cruelly wadded kaftan into her new electric blue lizardskin bag and returned to her place at the bar. Her plass of beer waited there. Standing close to Sweetface, she put down three stell-notes.

"Got the kaftan. Drink mine." And she left.

"Well I'll be sliced sideways," the bartender yelped. "Hey! You—legs!"

"She paid," Sweetface said. "Covered mine, too, not to mention the price of another. I'll drink hers."

"No you won't," the bartender said, snatching Janja's beer just as the orange fingers touched it. She stepped back smiling. She sipped, gazing at Sweetface, eyebrows up and eyes mocking; challenging.

Sweetface sipped its beer slowly, staring right back. Slowly it pretended to reach for the stell-notes she had forgotten or pretended to forget . . .

She spilled beer on herself in her haste to snatch the paper money before the Jarp could touch them. "See what you made me do!"

"Sorry. But after all—I gave you the beer."

In the next few minutes Sweetface turned down the woman who took the stool where Janja had been (and struck up a conversation by remarking that her strap-titser was just like Sweetface's); popped a hematite-red citromine to counteract the alcohol of its beer and the one she forced on it; drank half the Starflare (dark: Red Circle) a hopeful man sent over; turned off its translation helmet and called something to the bartender ("Turn on yer dam' translahelm, Jarp, damn it!"); stood and scratched its balls obviously as it paced to the door; and redshifted the Green Jinni twenty minutes after Janja's departure.

Just to be on the safe side, it took the public transport to the station right beside the Grand Khan, standing all the way. Inside the Grand Khan, it hurried to a public rest room to rid itself of the urgency of beer anxious to be on its way.

And it was propositioned just outside the hotel lift. This time the importuners were a man and a woman. Together. Both were unusually attractive and the pupils of both were huge. Their breath reeked of redjoy.

"It really isn't true what they say about Jarps," Sweetface said.

"Prove it," she said, blatantly extending a redjoy stick— an aphrodizzy smoke—as offering.

"I already have a date," Sweetface said, gesturing at the lift.

"Oh—a foursome!" she said, chuckling, and the tall well-built man giggled. He winked at Sweetface. His glance dropped to Sweetface's crotch.

"I have a disease," Sweetface said.

"Slice off, sisterslicer," the man said, and tugged his fascinated but horrified partner away.

Sweetface picked up the redjoy stick from where she had dropped it, and rode up sixteen floors, alone.

Janja was waiting in room 1709. She sat in a shadowy puddle of ultramarine light from a single neon lamp, a gold freeform.

" 'Lo. Do you think maybe we saved each other's lives tonight?"

Life had been so busy and interesting for Sweetface that it had nearly forgotten the scuffle. "I think. Thanks, Captain."

"Me too. Then thanks again for rushing me down that alley and otherwise thinking fast and directing our . . . escape."

"Uh. No use having to talk to policers. I think no one saw us there, or fleeing. Those two may try talking and they may not. If the one I kicked in the head can talk. He was reaching to grab you by the hair and pull you off his ally—and he was picking up his nice piece of pipe. Single-minded idiot thought I was out of it and forgot me altogether."

"Just a Jarp, remember?" Janja showed the Jarp a small smile. "I didn't know any of that, of course. Thanks a third time, Sweetface." She gestured. "There's your kaftan. You all right?"

"Not a scratch. You?" It glanced at the hanging kaftan, nodded.

"A scratch is all. Maybe a bruise."

"All because of Jarps."

"All because of stupidity. *Their* stupidity. You and I are aliens among *them*, Sweetface. I don't see Jarps. I see people. Then crewmates, and friends. Where'd that stopper come from and how'd it get into your hand so fast and where is it now?"

Sweetface smiled. It reached down to the little case slung at its hip—the little locked case—and its fingertips seemed to *change*, or disappear, or something definitely odd. Then the case vanished.

Where it had been, at the end of the shoulder-chest strap, hung a holstered stopper. Normal length.

"Lesson number one in the cleverness and trickery of Captain Cautious," Sweetface told her, and began talking about holoprojections. It progressed to telepresence coifs, aurasuits, and worse.

8

We know next to nothing about virtually everything. It is not necessary to know the origin of the universe; it is necessary to want to know. Civilization depends not on any particular knowledge, but on the disposition to crave knowledge.

—George F. Will

All the way out to the star called Galileo and its settled planet Qalara, Janja studied, and learned, and observed and listened to Sweetface and Quindy. And she asked questions.

Jonuta was not on Qalara. He had been. Jonuta's *Coronet* had departed for Luhra, two weeks ago. His crew now included two of the felinoprimates from newly "discovered" HRalix. Oh yes of course, Kenowa remained onboard *Coronet*. Along with two Terasaks and a newly employed Qalaran, and one passenger.

"Shit," Kalahari Cuw said (who also said that she was "along for the ride and the joy of not being boss and responsible" and who seldom left her cabin. She shared it with various members of *Sunmother*'s crew, including its captain. And she read a lot, or studied, or both. Or something.).

With Captain Quindy presumably oncon, Janja moved *Sunmother* away from Qalarastation. Then she watched,

111

while Captain Quindy hurled the ship away from Qalarà and Galileo and straight at the unbearable brilliance of the Corsi Cluster, parsecs away and still visible as more than a point of light.

The new ship's racks were packed with Quindy's course guidance cassettes off *Satana*, and labeled. Quindy worked at preparing new ones when she had opportunity. Janja put old ones onscreen, and studied. *Sunmother* sped.

This SIPACUM was newer in every component than *Satana*'s—or whatever *Satana*'s name was or would be. Quindy had requested an extra module and had got it. *Sunmother*'s SIPACUM was vocal. It had also been fed most of *Satana*'s stored data. (And a lot of information in *Satana*-SIPACUM's memory had been wiped.) New study guides had been fed in, for Janja. Also input were the texts of piles of books. General knowledge and pure entertainment; specific knowledge and pure frippery.

Janja was in a hurry, and had elected to wait to add or adapt to the vocal supercomputer she had fallen in love with on Jorinne.

Sunmother sped. The Corsi Cluster became a lot more than a marmoreally white point of light.

At a specific point Quindy thought she was sure of, she arrested the ship and sped her in, in toward galaxy center and the horror there called The Maelstrom—and then hurled her onto the Tachyon Trail, arrowing it for Luhra. Everyone onboard was sick except Trafalgar Cuw and Quindy. Sweetface was embarrassed. Two of the seven stigluls died. Trafalgar sadly consigned them to space and lovingly tended the others.

(Despite some talk about it, no company had been formed, no arrangements made for the introduction of stigluls to the galaxy.* They did reproduce happily onship, Trafalgar pointed out, and could make mighty fine trade-goods. He

*see SPACEWAYS # 4, *Satana Enslaved*.

became Chief Stiglulation Officer and named every one of them Stillwell, with a number. He loved tending them and professed to love them. Now he said that the "names" Stillwell-2 and Stillwell-7 would be retired forever, in honor of the first of their "noble race" to die in space. And out went numbers Two and Seven, the youngest. The others kept right on being living garbage and cess disposals, and kept right on providing sugar—left-handed sugar—and alcohol in exchange.

("The most efficient conversion systems along the spaceways," their doting supervisor enthused. "The greatest race in the galaxy! Have a drink?")

Quindy was not embarrassed; *Sunmother* reconverted from tachyons—"came out of subspace"—close enough to Luhra to spit on the planet. They had made it nearly a week faster than anyone else could have done. Thanks to Quindy, master of *Sunmother*.

Jonuta was not on Luhra or its station or in that sun system.

He had delivered his merchandise and his passenger and had redshifted with *Coronet* messily trailing exterior cargo: an assortment of huge bales and packing crates. Laboratory equipment, bound for Resh.

"Resh!"

Firm. Resh.

"Grat-shit!" Kalahari Cuw said. Resh was a long, long way. "Elusive devil! Then why'd Janjy go down onto Luhra?"

"Secret. Sweetface's doings. Working on some sort of disguises, I think. Jonuta's good at that, and Sweetface knows it all, or nearly."

"HRal-shit!" Kalahari threw up her hands and returned to her cabin. She was studying, she said. Furthering her education, she said. Sometimes she "inspected" the stiglul "farm" with Trafalgar and sometimes Trafalgar was in her cabin with her for hours. Certainly for no sexual purpose.

"Talking. Just talking. My sister you know." That was all he would tell anyone. Kalahari said the same words, in the same way, substituting only one word: "brother."

By the time Janja and Sweetface returned onboard, burdened, Quindy had her plan together and most of the necessary calculations. SIPACUM was still at work on them. She would get them from Luhra to Resh faster than possible. She and SIPACUM were sure it was possible.

"Faster than *possible*?"

"Pos," Quindy said, unsmiling.

(Her hair was back to the color of fresh jonquils. Both she and Trafalgar liked it that way. When they spent long hours together, the hours were not long for them and were not devoted to talk.)

She hurled them across the space-dusted parsecs while Janja studied and listened to Quindy and Sweetface and Trafalgar. And she asked questions and learned, learned. The secretively private hours she and Sweetface spent together in the smallish hold just off the stiglulation chamber did not, presumably, have anything to do with sex.

What Quindy enforced this time was hard on them all. They remained tachyons nearly all the way. Chrons would have to be reset and Stillwell-4 was ill. So was everyone onboard *Sunmother*.

They came out of it to, as Quindy said, "bounce off" Ghanji's sun, Cospar, and pop over to Resh on an arrow flight. Janja learned. She also threw up twice. She had company.

They also reached Resh in less time than anyone would have believed, because it simply was not possible.

"Captain Supermaster," Trafalgar called their marvelous Quindy. Besides, even Stillwell-4 was fine; it had just reproduced.

Jonuta had been there. The shipment had been delivered. He had left Resh with no cargo to speak of.

"Ha!" Sweetface snarled, hunched over computer-drawn

star maps with Quindy. Janja stood by, staring. Waiting. "He sneaked his *real* cargo onboard, then—he *must* have picked up 'walking cargo' on Resh! He's either zipped over to Ghanj or on to Franji. He and Kenowa both like Franji."

"Either/or, hmm?"

"Pos. Ghanj or Franji. Sorry. But you can't plot a dead-on course for Franji anyhow, Quindy. Not even you. Try it and we'll become part of The Maelstrom. No; fastest course is dead at Terasaki and bend off to round Cospar close, *in normal drive*. Expense doesn't matter?"

"No." Janja stood behind them. She wore the high-collared jumpsuit this day. She had three of the scarlet one-pieces now, each slightly different and yet all nearly the same. Janja's uniforms. The color of blood. Jonuta's blood. They had become her only daily attire. The almost military sameness signified her single-minded purpose and reminded her companions of their mutual goal. "Expense doesn't matter. Terasaki is not a possibility?"

"Firm. Jonuta can't go near Terasaki. They want him *bad*."

"Right. You're the expert, Sweetface. Forget expense."

"So, then. As we round Cospar, Quindy, you take ship on manual and get Ghanj's station oncomm, tight and fast."

Quindy nodded. Tachyon message riding laser beams. Fast and tight.

"We learn whether *Coronet* is there, and if not whether it has just been there."

Grown past her shoulders, Quindy's yellow hair flashed in the con-cabin's bright amber lights. "Very good," she nodded. "If yes, we swing on in. If no, I throw us at Chandrasekh hard as I can. Firm, I'll work it out, starting this instant. Janja!"

"Chandrasekh," the voice of the ship's owner said from behind them. School was in session: "A *hot* red-orange sun with five planets. The third is Franji. Settled over five centuries ago. Seventy-eight per cent ocean, point-seven-three gravity. Capital is Velynda. It is in trouble, because of socialization of industry and services.''

"That's enough. Very good, Janja. Sweetface, get lost. Boss, come in here close. We need to plot this very very tightly with minimal allowances for possibility of error. Everything based on speed—swiftness I mean—as the main criterion. Sweetface: Warn the others. Let's work it out together, Boss.''

"Yes, sir!''

Janja slid into the captain's chair beside Quindy, who would not sit in that one, ever. Sweetface left smiling . . . and was aroused from a nap three hours later by its boss. She desired to ask a few questions. She did. Sweetface answered, to the furtherment of Janja's education.

Their course bent around the star called Cospar so tightly and close-in to that ravening furnace that SIPACUM issued warning when a solar flare licked out toward the ship: *No closer!* Good thing the ship wasn't a grat, Trafalgar said, else its whiskers might have been singed off.

No one laughed. Aircon was on Highest and every viewscreen and several scanner-heads were shielded. How *could* the man make such jokes when they were flirting with eternity, likely to be vaporized and part of that vicious sun at any moment?

At the precise moment when sun-generated static cleared between *Sunmother* and the star's habited planet, their message blazoned to King's Station. And they waited. Whether they could feel the spacer rocking with solar winds or not, they thought they could. Quindy's fingers were poised over her console. Inship commsender was arced to hang directly above her forehead. In the adjacent chair sat Janja again. Beside her was the rack of course guidance cassettes. She held one ready.

Having seen to the stigluls, Trafalgar stood ready to

strap in. He licked at the sweat on his upper lip without thinking about it.

New numbers flicked on the chron, and Quindy darted looks its way. Her tongue darted out to lick wet salt from her upper lip. Ten seconds remained before major and time-consuming corrections must be made. Solar static was increasing steadily. Ghanj's station in space was just about to go out of sight behind the sun, and deafening static.

Seven seconds remained when the reply came. Jonuta was not on Ghanj. Computer log showed no visit from *Coronet* within a half-year-ess at least. King's Station assumed that spacer *Sunmo*—

Cospar's radiant thunder ate the rest of the message. The station could have allowed for that, of course, but why bother? Straightline comm required little thought and no work.

"Inslot cassette forty-one repeat four-one," Quindy snapped, and lifted her head toward the commsender.

Without looking, she noted that Janja gave the number a last check before she snapped in the cassette. It snicked in. SIPACUM acknowledged with a flash of lights in three colors and two shapes. (All necessary information was recorded on a wafer smaller in every way than a fingernail, and could have been put on the point of a pin. But trying to grasp anything so small and poke it into computer scan-slot was hardly feasible. The guidance wafers were imbedded in 3x3x1-sem cassettes for human convenience— for those clumsy grapplers humans called hands.)

SIPACUM said BEEP. A red light began flashing rhythmically.

"Stand by for tachyon conversion in seventeen seconds re-peat six-teen secs I do say fifteen secs," Quindy told the all-stations commlink. She knew her news was met with groans and was happy not to be able to hear them. Janja did not groan. "We will now arrowflight straight into the Chandrasekhar system, kiddies. Maintain opaque screens and twy not to fwow up. Three seconds and that's all—Boss?''

Despite Janja's pleas that it was embarrassing, Quindy insisted on calling her that. Not so long as Janja called Quindy Captain, which she did.

''Excute,'' Janja dutifully said. ''*Uh*!''

Her stomach and every other stomach on *Sunmother* lurched and viewscreens gave it up along with chronometers as ship and crew became subatomic particles that hared past rays of light as if they were laggard tortoises.

This time even Sweetface and Trafalgar were ill. Not Quindy. Lips clenched and face beaded with sweat, she stared at instruments she hoped had not been jolted into lying to her. Sweat tickled its way down her right side.

She brought them out so deep into the Chandrasekhar system that they were chastised by a Franjese patroller. Quindy did not tell them how long ago they had left the vicinity of Cospar and Ghanj. She would not have been believed, which would have led to more than chastisement for ''endangering lives in busy planetary space.''

They settled in toward Franjistation, were assigned a berth and directed, and eased in. They were docked and advised when their airlock was surrounded by the sealed inspace mouth of the umbilical tunnel into Franjistation.

For once, Quindy left the ship. The simple reason was that she had never been on Franjistation and was not known to Kislar Jonuta. She did not wear the *Sunmother* ''uniform'' and was back in eleven minutes. *Sunmother* was magnetically docked at berth E-2; *Coronet* was in J-2. Furthermore, its captain was in the station's lounge, in earnest conversation with a man, presumably Franjese.

Quindy described both men and their location to a tensely staring Janja and Sweetface. The Jarp nodded.

''Dickering with a local for the walking cargo on *Coro-*

net," it said. "We could get him in a lot of trouble merely by calling an anonymous tip to station security, Captain."

Quindy made no reply. She was "Quindy" to Sweetface, who always called Janja "Captain."

"No," Janja said, tingly and trembly all over.

"Very well, Captain. We have chased him down. What do you want to do, Captain?"

What do I want to do? Collapse, Janja thought, and silently bade her heart ease off its rapid banging. Some excitement just was not manageable, even with Aglayan mind-body control. *This* excitement, as a matter of fact, was well-founded and welcome. She did not want to control it. She was very bright of eye as she spoke:

"It's what we've waited for," she said, and her voice did not quaver. "This is what Quindy has bested every record for and what we've chased across all these parsecs for. Now . . . now we out-Jonuta Jonuta! Sweetface: aurasuit. TP. Princess Perisiti,* I think. And . . . Humperlong?"

"Good choice," the Jarp said, nodding, and moved to the cabinet.

It took out the materials to help the short woman prepare her Jonuta-style disguise. The bundle of dark silky fabric rustled as the Jarp shook it out. It held the suit's pants legs, which looked too small for the Aglayan, who had stripped. That fast, in her excitement and her eagerness.

It was nicely silky and clingy, with a nice little close-fitting hood anciently called a *coif*. The coverall's odd bulkiness was provided by its extensive interior network of filamentous wires.

As the clingy suit stretched to encase her body, Janja was made indecently sexy. Every curved salient and hollow was molded and outlined, including her navel and the crease of her vulva. No costumed superhero of old had

*"Perry-See-Tee."

been sexier, though all had been more colorful. The aurasuit was a dull charcoal gray, from coif to attached, self-covered boots.

Sweetface aided her into a short skirt of slate blue. Its purpose was to make sure that the suit was not so bemazingly and even licentiously attractive, with the projector off. Meanwhile its length and side-slit allowed maximum movement. Planned, all planned.

Janja meanwhile got the coif up onto her head and drew it down over her face. All the way down, past the chin. Her face was totally obscured as though she wore one of those kinky old bondage helmets. Yet unlike the captive— or masochistic, or both—wearer of such a head-encompassing "helmet"-hood, Janja could see perfectly.

The coif was equipped with a TP—a telepresence, long available to the non-implantable blind. About the size of her thumb, her tailored-to-measure aurasuit's TP camera moved with her head. She saw what it saw, instantly, with a two-way feedback. The coif could have contained a viewscreen, but Janja was fortunate as well as stoic: A self-illuminated miniscreen was unnecessary because she was hardly troubled by the DRA—direct retinal attachment.

"DRA-TP functioning?" Sweetface asked, having closed the miniskirt along one side by engaging its field.

"Functioning. I see you perfectly and in color." Her voice sounded natural enough, or would to anyone who didn't know different.

"TP setting?"

"Two to one," Janja said, meaning that she could turn her head a quarter way around and see a full half-turn— behind her. "My vision's perfect," she said, turning her head this way and that.

"Suit comfortable?"

"Not quite. I don't have all that much in the warheads department, but it's so tight it's trying to mash them right into my chest. And it's mighty tight in the crotch. Next time I'll wear heavy underpants. Otherwise—pos. Comfortable. The snugness is . . . reassuring, you know?''

"My captain will pardon me if I say she looks absolutely marvelous, warheads included.''

"I will," she said, and reached to the bauble that appeared to dangle between the tautly-molded warheads. Provided with a chain, the copper-and-enamel piece was made to resemble a partially-eclipsed blue sun, and to seem a pendant. It was not; it was securely attached to the coverall. That was absolutely necessary. The seeming decoration was far more. It was really the aura-projector. It was provided with four settings: OFF, ONE, OFF, TWO. The projections they called "Princess Perisiti" and "Humperlong" were already installed as minicartridges within that little "decoration." It was not merely that the pendant projected a holographic image; it surrounded the suit with one. The holoprojection's arms and legs moved when the suit's did.

Janja's hand went to the bauble, dropped away. "Well?''

Behind her, Quindy gasped. Sweetface smiled. "Princess Perisiti," it said, in a low voice.

Janja was gone. The strangely faceless charcoal gray creature was gone.

The aurasuit was functioning. Its built-in projector surrounded it and its wearer with a holographic aura: the full-bodied image of the exotically beautiful woman they had chosen. She had been a Ghanji noble, hardly a princess, and she had been dead over fifty years.

A broad jaw and considerable makeup under her high, pronounced cheekbones gave her a strikingly attractive hollow-cheeked aspect. Every feature was large. Almond-shaped eyes the color of walnut; slightly aquiline nose with a tiny ring in one nostril; mouth frosted pale orange, wide and full of lip. Her color was a deep tan. The pale orange shirt plunged low to reveal half of her taut, well-separated breasts that could not be expected to move much when she did. ''Princess Perisiti's'' warm brown gloves disappeared up under her three-quarter length sleeves.

Narrow of waist and rather broad of hip, she wore the pants the computer on Luhra had provided. Attractively snug without being blatantly tight, they were of burgundy velvon. Flat-heeled, beaded ankleboots matched their color.

Since Janja's aurasuit propped her on its built-in tensem* heels, she would appear *naturally* taller, on her apparent flats.

''Princess Perisiti'' wore no weapon and carried nothing. (They had carefully not learned her real name and had made up this one only as a whimsical sort of identification of the little holoproj wafer.) A gold serpentine circled her slender neck. A Chardik opal decorated her blouse just above the right breast.

Her hair was glossily black, coiled with neon beads resembling unfaceted rubies with an impossible glow. She wore matching ear-studs—four—and was just short of breathtakingly beautiful. ''Striking'' was the word, or ''arresting.''

''Turn,'' Sweetface said.

She did. Again the staring Quindy gasped. Head to one side, this stranger in the captain's cabin spoke in Janja's voice.

''I see you perfectly, Sweetface.''

''Good,'' the Jarp said, directly behind her. ''You look perfect. Perfectly beautiful! I'd forgotten what a nicely long-sloping oval ass Princess P. has—sorry, Cap'n!''

She turned back. ''Don't worry about it,'' that lovely vision said, in the voice of Janjaglaya. She lifted a hand to her cleavage then and she was Janja. The transition-transformation was instantaneous, the holo-aura dying to leave charcoal-suited reality.

''Ready?''

''Pos.''

---

*Ten centimeters; about four inches, Old Style.

Her hand went to her "jewelry" and they inspected her second disguise.

The coveralled laborer was so dolorous looking, so resigned and beaten down—or on drugs—that they had visualized the way it must have walked, slumped and shuffling. That birthed the ID-only name "Humperlong."

The image was perfect, again. Again the gesture to the loosely coveralled chest, and again Janja deactivated the projector and was Janja.

"Janja," Quindy said from behind her, in a subdued voice. Quindy had heard what they were doing, of course, but this was her first sight of the "secret" of Sweetface and Janja.

Janja turned. The other woman handed her a holstered stopper trailing a system of straps. The faceless creature in miniskirt over skintight charcoal took it. Sweetface had to help her into the harness, which poised the stopper's grip just beside her left breast, emerging from the holster in her armpit.

"We're assuming that she won't have to make a fast snatch for it," Sweetface told Quindy. "But even in the Princess P. image, a familiar movement toward the hip might be worse than suspect—especially with Captain Cautious."

Quindy nodded, watching Janja draw the tubular weapon, gaze at it, and sigh. It was one of the outer planets models, with the Two setting adjusted to induce swift unconsciousness rather than Dance. Everyone on *Sunmother* had one of these, now. "Trafalgar's treat," as Janja had arranged and paid for the scarlet jumpsuits. The stoppers had come in from Barbro Transfer Station, illegally. They were unregistered.

"I've never worn one set on Three," Janja said, in a resigned voice that was rather wistful. She thumbed the weapon over to its third setting: Fry. That activated the second of the two barrels nestled inside the larger one. It emitted the disintegrator beam no one called a disintegrator beam or ray because the phrase was as ghastly as the effect—and because the phrase was too, too corny.

Neither of the others spoke. It was what she was here for. If she did not use the Three setting, all this chasing would have been for nothing. And she might well wind up dead.

All three knew that she might anyhow; or incarcerated or, worse, a captive of the master slaver Jonuta.

Janja relieved herself of another big sigh.

Sweetface nodded. It produced a tiny box and opened it to display a pill. "Trafalgar suggested this."

"What is it?"

The Jarp shrugged. "A compound. Contains an upper, concentrated testosterone for aggressiveness, and—"

"I don't like pills. I won't need it."

Sweetface shrugged and tossed the box onto the bed. Then it reached up to cut off its translahelm. It "said" something in its own whistle-trill language and made a sign with one six-digited hand.

Janja nodded. She knew she had just been wished the more fervent version of "Good luck," Jarpi style, doubled by the gesture. Her whistle was not perfect, but it astonished Sweetface; Janja replied *thanks* in the language of Jarpi. The two aliens among so many billions of Galactics exchanged a long and solemn look.

A familiar phrase ran through Sweetface's mind: *"Dammit, Sweetface, turn on your dam' translahelm!"* How many times had Jonuta said that?

It was the tall orange hermaphrodite's turn to sigh.

Janja turned back to Quindy. Throughout all the preparations, the legal captain of *Sunmother* had said only one word; Janja's name, when she proffered the stopper. The executioner's weapon. Now she stood, looking dumpy in dull boots, dust-colored leggings rather than tights, and purely utilitarian brown smock. A simple and harmless analectrical field held the full smock well out from her. The dull black rinse applied to her long hair enhanced that aspect, and the slouchy cap of green added nothing. Now her face was set, and very serious.

"I admit my nervousness. I've never done this bit, Janja."

"Neither have I, Quindy."

They gazed at each other in silence, Quindy nodding slowly, knowing what Janja's eyes looked like without being able to see them.

"I've never committed murder before either, Quindy. Not coldly, premeditatedly, I mean." Again she was silent, her face deeply pensive within the coif that concealed it. Then, "We'd better be about our business, before he finishes his dickering and either shuttles down or goes back onto *Coronet*."

Quindy nodded. Janja slipped on the tiny bracelet that was a one-channel minicommunicator. Quindy wore its twin. Sweetface made sure that the sleeve of the aurasuit was down over the comm, and warned its wearer. Janja nodded in silence.

In silence, the two left *Sunmother*.

They were an unattractive pair when they emerged from the umbilical; two bulky figures, one in a brown smock and boots with dun tights between and a throwaway cap on top; the other in greens, a laborer of some sort. Who would or could know that the dolorous face of this "laborer" was that of a person who had suicided on Luhra, seventy-three years ago?

9

My Mission is that I want Jonuta. That is my purpose and my life. Since he destroyed my life on Aglaya, he provides its purpose.

—Janjaheriohir of Aglaya

Death is Nature's way of saying, That's It, Slaver!

—Trafalgar Cuw

Like most spacecraft docking stations high above their planets, Franji's was an enormous wheel. The hub housed rest rooms, offices, Medical and Security and Customs; a couple of overpriced shops, a bar-lounge and fastfoodery, two electronic involvement-game areas, and a pair of tiny detention cells. There were also two huge warehouses and employee lounges.

A concourse surrounded the hub. Radiating from it were the wheel's spokes. These were numbered tunnels leading out to the perimeter concourse. Every seventh tunnel was extra large, to accommodate huge loader-haulers capable of handling tons of cargo. Docked spacecraft were outside, in space, electromagnetically grappled to the wheel's outer rim. Once the mouth of each berth's umbilical tunnel—a giant hollow worm of flexible construction that formed an enclosed ramp—was sealed in a position surrounding a spacer's airlock, the airlock could be opened safely. Immediately the ship on the outside was connected with the station's interior.

Quindy had seen Jonuta in the lounge between the hub-ends of Spokes Ten and Eleven. She had established that *Coronet* was in berth J-2. Now, one more colorless worker, she hurried in to the hub and around that much smaller section of arc to the Starlight Lounge—one of scores by that name, all along the spaceways.

Janja had no time to lurk or worry or consider all the things that might go wrong. Despite all her planning and the preparations with Sweetface, she was acting precipitately and knew it. A space station was hardly the place for the ultimate vengeance-taking of assassination. Had she been provided time to ponder, consider consequences, and grow nervous, "Princess Perisiti/Humperlong" might have reconsidered.

This was not after all a city in which she could lose herself until she got offplanet, more at her leisure than the station would allow. Nor was this after all just any mark, any target. This was the ever-watchful man rightly called Captain Cautious.

But Janja had no time to lurk or worry or reconsider.

Moving among spacefarers and stevedores she tried not to touch, past a securitywoman who did not so much as glance at her, "Humperlong" reached her chosen position. She began moving around the cottage-sized loader parked between the rim mouths of Spokes Ten and Eleven. Pretending to examine it.

Almost immediately her wrist tingled. Humperlong raised her hand casually to scratch her head. Quindy's voice came soft and clear:

"He's just left the lounge. Taking Spoke Eleven toward you."

Humperlong glanced about, turned, and sprinted. She did not slow as she entered Spoke Eleven. Far ahead a trio of spacefarers was headed her way. She saw no one else in the tunnel. She hoped they were too distant to notice what happened; on the run, Humperlong adjusted her projector, twice. That took her from Humperlong through faceless Off to the lovely young Ghanji noble.

Princess Perisiti sprinted up Spoke Eleven.

"Kenowa is with him," Quindy's voice told her. *"She's showing a lot of skin and no armament. He's wearing a stopper."*

Within the coif that was invisible behind the lovely face of her disguise, Janja frowned. She did not, however, slow. *"Run* all the way to the ship, Quindy. Give me an hour. If I'm not there by then or you know there's big trouble—redshift, fast! Out—no further comm."

And Janja ran. She had eliminated any chance of Quindy's arguing, reasoning or trying to. She ran easily, an athletic young woman from a high-grav planet sprinting with little effort in Franjistation's .7G. The heels built into her suit slowed her to perhaps a normal speed rather than her own norm, which was competitively fast. Her steps were loud, echoic in the broad, high tunnel. Her breathing was not.

She approached the trio, who stared. She met and passed them at the run. They stared, but since his two companions were female, the man did not call out to the racing beauty. It must have hurt him not to turn and watch her from behind.

She was two thirds of the way to the hub when she saw the approaching couple.

Jonuta and Kenowa were ambling as if they were in no hurry at all. She assumed they were talking casually.

Suspecting nothing, she thought, and kept running.

Even from this distance Janja's TP showed her that Kenowa was indeed showing a lot of skin. Janja kept running. She wanted to be as close to the hub and its throng as she could possibly get herself—her selves.

She wasn't too happy that the two stevedores were

coming along behind the slaver and his "aide," also in no hurry.

On the other hand, they might be of value. The two workers might provide a screen of sorts. *If* they didn't think too fast, and/or try some stupid heroics . . .

The familiar couple off *Coronet* were only ten or so meters from her when Princess Perisiti staggered, slowed, clutched at her chest. She moved toward them at a walk now, pretending to be gasping for breath. She hoped her image was looking past them, so that they would not notice the staring eyes.

She paced toward them, they toward her. Looking at her, she presumed. As she, by means of the telepresence cam, was staring at them. Breathing only a little hard. Astonishingly unexcited, thinking even to apply her mind-body control to still her heart and dissipate adrenaline.

Kenowa was blatant in a silver halter with long gloves to match, a metallic-thread azure skirt as short as Princess Perisiti's, white kneeboots. A blue Terasaki coil rose high atop the busty woman's head. There was no way she could be armed . . . *unless the wig is hollow,* Janja reminded herself and was surprised at how cool she was.

Jonuta wore unrelieved black. That was unusual, but there was no doubt that this was Jonuta. Medium tall, well-built and rather rangy, too good-looking, glossy black hair cut so as to cover his ears to the lobes. And wearing a stopper, of course, without swagger. Approaching her, the man who had caused Tarkij's death, who had enslaved her and countless others, who eluded all policers . . .

"Jonuta!" she called, and now her heart leaped into a rapid pace. "Captain Jonuta!" She broke into a trot, Princess Perisiti apparently holding a hand to her chest above the heart.

She was four meters from them, speeding up as she grasped the cylindrical butt of the stopper and drew it.

"Remember Janja of Aglaya, Jonuta?" she called, leveling the stopper, and she squeezed. The stopper trembled, hummed.

Kenowa clapped a hand to her deep dark cleavage as the approaching beauty's stopper hummed its faint song of evil and the nearly invisible beam leaped out. Almost instantly Janja was thumbing the weapon's setting down to Two.

Jonuta shimmered in the bathing ray—and vanished. Fried. Disintegrated. Removed from the spaceways.

Already Janja was directing her stopper at the woman beside him. Kenowa jerked as if struck physically, trembled in a brief sort of rictus, and sagged. Jonuta was gone and Kenowa was collapsing, unconscious, as Janja raced on past. Directly toward the two stevedores. Now she cried out.

"Out of the way! Hurry—see to that woman. The shot came from behind you—stay low and see to the woman!"

She ran toward them, waving her arms. One glanced behind him. Behind her, Janja assumed, dust-motes drifted. Atoms that had been Kislar Jonuta of Qalara. Captain Not-cautious enough.

Why hadn't Kenowa screamed?

The stevedores didn't part, but stayed close together, staring at the beauty racing toward them. She had been on the far side of the vanished man and the fallen woman and they could not have seen the stopper in her hand. Then one broke into a trot—past Janja! Running to "see to" Kenowa as she had bade them! The other naturally followed, starting to run. . . .

Just in case, Janja swerved once they were past, to keep them between her and Kenowa, or possible armed pursuit. And she ran. She assumed that Kenowa was down and out for a while, but Janja's experience with this second stopper setting was nil. It certainly made sense, she thought, too keyed up to think only triumphantly.

She knew more excitement and apprehension than elation. The elation would come later, when there was time.

Elation, and celebration, and . . . deflation. Let-down. Her Mission was accomplished. That which had sustained and driven her for over a year had just been accomplished. Soon enough she would have to deal with purposelessness, and seek some new purpose. What, after all, was she fit for, among Them?

That was for later. Just now she had to keep running, to escape, elude, be cool. And get back to her ship.

Just as she reached the hub a hurrying man stepped into the tunnel's mouth. Beyond him were many others, and colored lights and hubbub, and people noise. She ran directly into the man in the collarless green shirt and baggy white pants.

"Here now, you needn't be in such a—"

She wrenched free of his clutching hands and swerved away from his stupid smile. She chermed no menace. Lust, perhaps. She hurried on, sure that he was looking after her and hoping that he would not try to follow, in hopes of making the acquaintance of a lovely young woman dead over half a century.

Trying not to touch people who might possibly feel other than what they saw—and notice—she followed the sign to the Women's Room. The hub was the usual place of excitement, full of Galactics and a few Jarps, nearly all of them spacefarers just off their ships or returning from planetside, wearing clothing of every description and most colors, even uniforms. What if . . .

What if . . .

She reached the door to the Women's Lounge and went directly in. She did not so much as glance at the split-skirted, pink-legged woman who stood before the mirror, checking her lipstick and looking at the reflection of Princess Perisiti. Oh yes, the holoprojection reflected as solid.

The first stall was locked. The second was ajar and not occupied. Janja locked it behind her.

She had made it. She stood still, staring at the back wall

of the cubicle/staring at nothing. She sucked in a long quiet breath and eased it out. Another, putting her mind to work to quiet her self. No one had said a word. No one had noticed her other than as an unusually good-looking woman moving purposefully through Franjistation's hub. Too purposefully for eye contact or even an attempt at staying her, at converse.

That didn't mean it was over. That didn't mean she was safe.

She turned to avail herself of the stall's one-way peephole. It was a sensible addition to such stalls, and this time Janja was unequivocally appreciative of it. She watched the woman turn from the mirror and leave. She had not glanced at Janja's stall. Janja waited.

Another woman emerged from the first stall—wearing blue hair and a Franjese sari—and went her way without so much as washing her hands.

Only then did Janja raise her hand to her suit's "ornament" and change her image. Then she made a few appropriate noises and left the stall. Just as she did the flusher/water-recycler actuated itself, in every other stall, and Janja jumped as if struck.

Settle down, she told herself. *It's over. No one suspects you—look at you!*

She did, and was shaken anew to see her reflection: a dumpy, dull-eyed woman in a nearly shapeless coverall of medium olive. No makeup. Hair like a black mop grieving for its missing handle. Humperlong. Without one feature, one hint of Janjaheriohir of Aglaya; Janjaglaya of *Sunmother*. (Or *Firedancer*, lost somewhere along the Forty Percent Trail; or *Satana*, renamed and left to gain a new master and a new and better use.)

Oh, the magic of it! This was how Jonuta had fooled so many! And now she had learned so many, many of his secrets from Sweetface—and turned this one against Jonuta himself!

In no way did the unassuming and unattractive creature in the mirror resemble the arrestingly attractive Princess Perisiti, or the exotic Janjaglaya. The poor woman who stared dull-eyed back at Janja looked . . . lost. *Suicidal,* Janja thought, and knew pity and an anguish that was ridiculous across the three quarters of a century that had passed since Humperlong had ended her misery by ending her life. No, her *existence,* Janja thought, and shuddered.

Hello Humperlong Janja. It's done. What do you have to live for, now?

She grasped her mind and yanked it from that dark trail. *They really are terribly clever with Their science, and Jonuta really is a genius at using Their . . .*

Was.

That thought left her feeling weak in knees and belly. *Was.* Captain Cautious had become past tense.

She forced herself to stop staring at this piteous reflection that was hers but was not Janja at all, not at all, and she left the rest room.

Not one person said so much as one word to her amid that bustling space station throng. No one even tried to make eye contact with this nothing in the green coverall; as a matter of fact those who noticed her assiduously avoided seeing her.

She walked among their noisiness and flashing ID and advert-lights, and into a tunnel, and along its seemingly endless length, forcing herself to pace slowly—shuffle-humping along—and out of the spoke, pausing a moment to gain her bearings, and along the station's outer concourse, and into the yawning worm's mouth of an umbilical, and up the ramp. To the airlock of spacer *Sunmother.* The inner hatch was closed. That was ever sensible; this time it was also ship-owner's orders.

"Light of Aglii," she said in Aglayan, and the inner hatch made a *snick* sound as it unlocked for its master. She entered *Sunmother* without glancing at the man who waited there, Trafalgar, and paced to the con-cabin.

Quindy, Sweetface, and Cinnabar were gathered there. Awaiting her, or bad news from some voice of authority via the comm's station channel. They looked relieved at sight of her, but only Cinnabar smiled and nodded. *I knew it,* that nod said, *all the time!* They said nothing.

Janja had considered making a dramatic utterance: *Captain Cautious is past tense*. She had decided against it. That was not her way, and would only bring loud noises of relief, happiness, congratulations. She wanted none of those. She had done a job.

"It is done," she said very quietly, and used the suit's ornament to become Janja again—that is, a faceless charcoal-ensheathed creature that was recognizable only as a short, female primate with hard thighs of good size and a dancer's big calves. An assassin; a *ninja*. And she was shaking.

"Captain Quindy, let's get away from here."

"Right," Quindy said, and turned to the console to request clearance for redshift as if this were the most routine of days and the most routine of departures.

"Sweetface, come give me a hand with this confounded suit," Janja said, and then her trembling legs gave way and she collapsed.

10

"All that is demanded of us . . . is to realize our own nature."

—Henry Miller

"No magic had ever been found that would let a man see himself."

—Vardis Fisher

Janja awoke lying on her back. She was in her cabin, in her bed. She had been stripped and lay under a light coverlet. She stared dully at the ceiling, then moved her head. Her eyes focused to find Cinnabar sitting by her side.

Months and months ago, it had seen her potential and called her "Captain Janjaglaya." It was an unwelcome title then, and Janja had remonstrated with her orange friend. Cinnabar's loyalty—and devotion?—had never wavered. It did not see her as a goddess, but as superior, to be listened to and followed, and as eminently desirable. Janja knew that it loved her. She supposed that she loved Cinn, too. Whether it was in love she could not be sure; that alien mind remained not quite penetrable to her cherming ability.

She was glad to awake and discover Cinnabar keeping vigil.

" 'Lo."

"Hullo." She returned its smile.

"Your body went on overdrive, or something . . . imitated an earthquake, maybe. Then it was over and you had done it but didn't let go until you got back to us. That's when the aftershock hit. You've slept nine hours. Mostly peacefully. We put you in shipdoc for two hours, for an IV of glucase and . . . drainage," it said, referring to the cybernetic daktari's fixtures for drawing off urine and excrement. "We felt you'd need the energy from glucase. Feeling energetic?"

"Negatory, but not feeling bad, either. Feeling weak . . . no I don't! Fine. I feel fine! Thanks, Cinn!" She reached for the Jarp's hand, having discovered that she was not at all weak. She squeezed to prove it.

"Ow."

"It *is* . . . over? I did it?"

"Franjistation channel advised all ships that there'd been a murder. Since we wanted to leave and had already applied, security came onboard and checked us. Naturally they didn't find the unknown beauty they were looking for! They gave us a release. We redshifted. By now they've probably decided that the hit was so professional and untraceable, it must have been good old TGO."

Janja sighed and lay back, clinging to the orange hand whose slim fingers were over a full joint's length longer than hers. She stared at the cabin's ceiling, elated and yet still muzzy, confused.

"Franjistation Control wouldn't have held up shipping if they hadn't had proof of a killing, would it," Cinnabar said. It was not a question, and the Jarp had substituted the less loaded word "killing" for the more accusatory legal phrase "murder."

"Um," Janja acknowledged, staring upward. Clinging to that hand.

"Since we had looked a little suspicious, Quindy made

a suggestion and we agreed. We took on cargo. We're respectable merchanters, hauling.''

"Cargo?! For—for where?"

"Terasaki. Easy run from Franji. Even a good price." Cinnabar chuckled. " 'Course, we won't get the bonus for speedy delivery."

Just keep talking about normal things, Janja thought. "Why? Where are we?"

"A long way from Franji. Not too far from Terasaki, though. Quindy put us into orbit around a dead planet of a burned-out sun. Scans show the only life to be lichen. We're just orbiting. Around and around, on momentum."

Dead, Janja's mind whispered along its dim-lit corridors. *Dead. Dead star, dead planet, dead Jonuta . . .*

"Oh, shipdoc did its usual job of trying to fix everything it found wrong or even quotes wrong! Your color is your own, notice? And your hair's back to normal, too. Looks beautiful, Cloud-top." Two hands exchanged a pressure.

Janja said, "The others? Quindy, Traf—"

"When last heard from, Sweetface and Trafalgar had the con and were talking, mostly, I think. Quindy's with Kalahari in her cabin. The stigluls are making happy noises—sickening! Hungry? The soft guitar music all right? That's three Terasak brothers. Call themselves Stopgap. Want a drink? Stillwell's becoming a regular zoo!"

Dead, dead, dead . . . "No. No, I don't want anything . . . music sounds nice, thanks . . . O Sunmother's Light! I really did it then! Jonuta's career is *ended!*" *Dead, dead . . .*

Cinnabar squeezed the hand that grasped it too tightly. It felt hot. *Because she's been asleep, that's all,* the Jarp reminded itself. Not to worry.

"Pository. Ended. Gone. Jan? Want to talk about it?"

She shook her head forcibly. "No. Later. Plenty of time later. I feel . . . I feel . . . I just . . ."

"Feel like you need to take another nap? I'll stay."

Nervous, Cinnabar was being too solicitous. Janja's headshake was impatient. "I—oh! It's *done!* Really done then, Cinn—I really did do it!"

"You really did do it, Captain Janjaglaya. There really should be a reward. After all, the most competent and infamous slaver along the spaceways! Billions will praise you without your ever knowing—billions will thank you. and never mind that you can't hear them."

Maybe Cinnabar was her best friend, despite all the time she had spent with Sweetface. That was business, although the teacher and the learner had grown close. Still, she liked Cinnabar better as a person, and they had been through so much, and Cinnabar loved her . . .

My best friends. Jarps; two Jarps. And that was Cinnabar's third or fourth attempt to make her feel heroic, a hero, rather than a triumphant murderer.

Dead. Dead!

Janja retrieved her hand and brought the other out from under the coverlet. Pink hands, overlaid with a bit of tan. She clapped them, then pressed both clasped hands under her chin. She sighed and stared at the ceiling. Her eyes caught the light. Cinnabar saw the flash, the glitter.

"I . . . hm! Strange! Um! Cinn . . . you know what— what I'm feeling? What I want?"

"I'll bet I do!"

The Jarp bent suddenly to kiss the pale breast Janja's movement had freed of the cover. It was bare and uprounded muscularly. Its crest had firmed in response to the cooler air. It was beautiful. Cinnabar kissed it and felt its supine friend shudder, almost violently. The Jarp smiled. It probably wasn't occurring to Janja just now that Jarps *knew;* they could smell sexual arousal, even sexual willingness. To those of Jarpi, pheromonal scents were strong and unmistakable.

Janja did think about elementary biopsychology: "Oh,

oh Cinnabar . . . it's natural, isn't it! So—standard. After violence, fear of death, then triumph . . . it's standard: sexual need! Are you . . . is that insulting? I mean it seems so—so mechanical, my wanting you just now."

"Don't be silly," it murmured, nuzzling. The pretty pink peak grew some more, under its lips. "I always want you, Janja. I could add 'And if it's a "natural and standard" need right now, what else are friends for,' but that's too tame. I said I want you."

"Then come to bed. Please."

Cinnabar squeezed the pale hardness of that bared breast, and rose with a laugh. "Please, she says! You couldn't stop me now, luv! See me try for a galaxy-wide undressing record!"

Janja saw. She watched the revelation of that long rangy body. Red-tipped breasts definitely female. Hips too narrow for most females and yet no more angular than Kalahari's. Buttocks womanly longish and yet quite round, like a man's. Legs tauter, more definite of musculature than those of most women, and yet little more so than Janja's. Certainly the penis and testicle were not womanly! On the other hand, the thin-lipped slit was there, too, and it was all female. A functioning, congenital hermaphrodite, ready to be man and woman, woman or man to its friend; to "Captain Janjaglaya" in need.

Janja sat up, coverlet slipping down, and held out her arms. Cinnabar smiled and held up a staying finger.

"One second," it said throatily, and hurried to the light control. That was unnecessary; on *Sunmother,* lighting in this cabin responded to vocal commands. Cinnabar programmed "R" for "red" and "Twi" for twilight level. In that sexily ruddy glow, it returned to the bed, and Janja.

"One second," Janja said, holding up a finger to stop the naked Jarp just at the side of the bed.

She leaned that way, sliding a hand around to cup one tight orange buttock. Tugging, holding Cinnabar that way, she bent to kiss the smallish penis, to lick and nuzzle, to slide her mouth over it. She moved mouth and tongue and head until the Jarp organ thickened and grew inside her face.

She was more devoted, more orally fixated and attentively loving than she had been in months. Months. Cinnabar's hands felt good, warmly good, gliding over her hair, long firm fingers combing through the blond strands. She felt its body quiver against her forehead and under her hand, and she was pleased to be the cause.

"Would . . . uh, ummm . . . oh, would you . . . like my mouth, too?"

Janja sucked hard, shaking her head. She made the negative a definite one. That side-to-side movement made Cinnabar groan in pleasure. Her own idle left hand rose to her breast.

The standing Jarp watched her fingers caress her own warhead, pluck at its nipple, cup—and then crush the whole unusually tight mass against her chest as if determined to squash it, to force it somehow to retract into her own chest. The Jarp saw the blond's arm quiver with strain.

"Uh," Cinnabar gasped. And, "I want to do that! You want your breasts fondled and crushed, and I want to do it."

"Ummm," Janja said, answering with her mouth full. She nodded against the Jarp's lower belly.

Abruptly its hands were pushing her head away, forcing. It joined her in the bed, hurriedly. They curled swiftly to arrange themselves allowing for the centimeters' difference in their heights. Lengths, now.

Janja continued her loving tonguing and mouthing along with her rearward fondling, while a hand enveloped one of her breasts and an unusually round mouth the other. An unusually long, slim tongue moved rapidly over it. Pointed birdlike tip slithering and whipping over a nipple that erected rapidly.

Long minutes passed in that sensuously red glow, and the only sounds in the cabin were of two delighted people in the grasp of rising sexuality, of pleasure given and simultaneously received. An unusual urgency ruled Janja, and never mind its violent catalyst. She had become a doting, ardent lover to a being who always was.

Their hands grasped, tightened hard. Dark fingers clamped like thin cables into glowing pink breast, and kneaded. Their teeth teased and nipped. They guided each other with wordless sounds and little movements. Neither could be still, as both rapture and need intensified.

Janja's whole head was moving now, with a force that rocked her body, so that she took in every bit of that alien slicer again and again. The sounds of that were salacious, positively obscene. Waves of sensate pleasure strobed through her every nerve and cell.

"You . . . are going to . . . end me," Cinnabar gasped, clamping its hand hard. "And . . . I will love it . . . but don't you—don't you want me in . . . I want *in* you, darling!"

Janja took reluctant leave of the beloved morsel she had forced to grow so much. The bed bounced with her movement, which also dragged her breast out long, before it tugged free of the six-fingered grasp. Turning on the bed, gasping, eyes alight and aglow in the ruddy twilight.

Cinnabar gazed at the tautness of upturned buttocks, the kneeling, parted legs that displayed the sliced purse of their juncture. It hurried to kneel upright behind that demanding vista. When it started to use a hand to guide itself into her, another hand came back under the kneeling woman. It seized on that mouth-wet Jarp slicer, and tugged.

"Uh!"

The gasp of union was almost in unison, and then the long orange body was straining hard against the upturned rearward cheeks of the shorter woman, striving to imbed even more of itself in her. And that was impossible.

"If you don't want it hard," the Jarp muttered in a voice that quaked, "you'd better jump up and run, now!"

Janja's reply was to brace herself and jam back with strength.

"Uh!" And the Jarp grasped her hips to return the pressure.

Janja braced and moved; Cinnabar moved long and slowly, then faster and with increasing force that filled the air with slapping sounds.

The delighted, gasping Jarp knew that women took their men in this position, on Aglaya. It loved the position and the way she ground back.

It did not know that in just this way, animalistically and deep-reaching, another Jarp had taken Janja long ago, on the spaceship of the man who had fed her an animal breeder's aphrodisiac before commanding that his crew, each and all save only the big-wigged woman, rape the little blond "barbarian." Then he had sold her. Jonuta.

"You are absolutely sure you're all right? Please—if you aren't, *please* tell me!"

"Can I get you anything?"

The two women hovered anxiously over the man propped up on the bed. With a restrained smile, he shook his head. His voice rumbled up from his chest, which was only partially covered by a short robe of midnight velvet that in another era would have been reserved for a sultan enthroned.

"I am absolutely sure I am all right, Kenny. Yes, HReenee, you can get me less wurra-wurra wringing of hands, and some more bioflav juice."

The HRalix-born felinoprimate named HReenee nodded and moved back bonelessly. Seemingly she *flowed* to the door of the spaceship cabin to fetch more of the vitamin

C-rich drink. She knew to add just a little Qalara Passion dry gin.

"Kenny: quick, while she's gone—I love you."

"Oh, *Jone!*"

The big woman fell upon the prostrate man, holding him and kissing him, leaking tears on his neck and chest. His hand pressured her back, moved on it.

"I think I love her too, but we both know what a fickle mercurial bastard I am, and how many times I've fallen into infatuation. Not love, Kenny. Infatuation."

"I know, I know," she said, holding him fiercely, kissing and kissing while the tears flowed.

He held her loosely, half-sitting and half-sprawled in his bed. Patting and rubbing her broad back while he stared at the cabin's ceiling.

"*Listen.* I want you to hear it . . . *I* want to hear it, Kenny.

"I was suspicious of Kenyaras, even after we made our bargain for walking cargo. I made sure he left the lounge first. Then I went into the rest room with my briefcase. I did it all, alone. Put on the aurasuit and activated the image of you in the silver halter—the Thrilling Wonder Damsel. I became you, wearing that outfit. Then I tried the new projector. It worked *fine!* It made it appear that I was walking by your side. Except that *I* was strictly an empty holoproj, while the 'you' anyone could see was really me, in the aurasuit surrounded by your holo-image. Confusing?"

"Oh Jone, oh Jone. Don't talk about it!" She was leaking a lot more tears, now.

"I want to." He patted her back, with some force. What he did not say was that he didn't just want to talk about it; he needed to.

"I walked up the spoke—'*we*' walked along that tunnel, Kenny! I saw her way up the tunnel, running toward us. Ghanji, surely, and absolutely beautiful. About twenty-five. Suddenly she seemed to stumble. Clapped a hand to her chest and slowed. Oh, that was clever! Diverted my attention and eased my nervousness about her, all at once. I could see her gasping for breath. I never saw the stopper. Never.''

She made a gulpy sobbing sound and held him tight enough to hurt. *He was nearly killed, nearly Killed!*

"She called me by name, Kenny. Twice. The voice sounded familiar, I think. Vaguely familiar. Then she was running toward us again. Close, now. 'Remember Janja?' she called, and I *heard* the stopper. I swear, just for an instant, and saw the beam because I know what to look for—Booda knows I've seen enough stopper beams! She was firing at my image, not at me—I was you or appeared to be, and that tricked her. In an instant I realized that I'd been tricked too, and how—with another aurasuit and holoprojection! My own methods, used against me!''

And it was Janja, Kenowa thought, clinging tight. Hate rose in her. *It had to be. We checked every ship docked at Franjistation . . . and who else could it be—spacer* Sunmother, *owned by Janjaglaya Wye of Outreach! Outreach my butt—it was Janja! And that ship was the first to redshift—immediately!*

"And I slapped my hand to the projector that created my image . . . to let it vanish as she shot—as she Poofed it! *Fried* me—in cold blood! Anyone behind us was either mighty lucky or Poofed, because there's nothing about a holoprojection even to slow a stopper bolt.

"See—I hit the cut-off to let her think she had Poofed me, and I thought she would run on past. Keep running, to escape. But as I was reaching for my stopper, she hit me with an Outworlds-type Two beam. It had to be one of those. And that was that. I was unconscious. Naturally the aurasuit kept showing me as you. I came to being carried to station medical, by two cargo-handlers. Too dumb to know they were carrying an unconscious man and not you, I suppose. Mustn't have tried to grab a feel, or they'd have known. I made a fuss, started kicking and squalling, and they let go. Without a word for those nice boys I ran, back to the hub, and kept running until I was in the women's lounge. Anyone who was looking saw *you* run in there, of course.''

Kenowa tried to giggle while she was busy sobbing and nuzzling. The sound was uninspiring.

''Any enterprising male who hung around waiting to see you again when you came out—well, he's still wondering what happened to you. The woman who was just about to enter when I left was shocked, of course. I just kept moving. I came straight here to the ship. With the shakes, and a real headache.''

She was burrowing, streaking him with tears, going for his crotch with her kiss-dispersing mouth because she was Kenowa and he was her man and he had almost been killed and she wanted to do this, had to.

That was how HReenee found them when she returned to his cabin with a big plass of carbonated juice of bioflavonoids.

She stopped still, gazing at them, staring, loving him, hating Kenowa right at this minute, wanting to kill. On each hand the single remaining claw of her ancestry slid out, retracted, slid out. . . . The punctured plass began to dribble pinkish yellow juice.

He put a hand on the wigged head bobbing over his loins. His dark fingers gripped loosely, holding her there, silently bidding her continue.

''Thanks, HReenee. I need that. Pour it into something else quick, will you—seems to be leaking. You can go if you want, but I really do wish you'd stay.''

And in his cabin on *Coronet*, Captain Cautious smiled at her.

11

Descartes: Since I think, I exist. Obviously it follows that no person can logically doubt its own existence. Therefore . . .

Arauca Pragma: Each person must strive to be ruled by logic and concerned with self. This is true practicality, and is surely the highest purpose of humankind.

B. Theriole: I weep for the Critique of Pure Reason in this day of Pure Practicality.

Morffillon Jasjit: The only purpose of the cockroach is to fill its "belly" and to reproduce itself (as often as possible). This High Purpose it holds in common with humankind.

Yul Brynner, as Pharaoh: His god . . . is God.*

The flight to Terasaki was short and yet seemed long. Janja had succeeded and so her shipmates felt that they had all succeeded. They had triumphed. Jonuta was dead. All of that was reason for joviality and the celebration they had earned.

There was no celebration and little joviality.

Janja Quester proved far preferable to Janja Triumphant. She was about as bright and celebratory as an aged Basset hound. The others could not bring themselves to celebrate

*see chapter 12

146

when she behaved so and looked the way she did. Even smiling made a person feel guilty, on *Sunmother*.

Almost the only blessing now was that at least they didn't see much of her and her long face and flat eyes.

"She isn't like the rest of us," Trafalgar Cuw said quietly, while Janja as usual was doing them the favor of relieving them of her company. She was in her cabin, moping. Very alone. She did not want company. That she had made consummately clear.

A few ship-days after their departure from the Chandra-sekhar system, captain and crew of *Sunmother* were gathered in the spacer's lounge (which had been intended as an overlarge and ornate master's cabin. Janja had decided otherwise, a few minutes after first setting foot on the ship). While the ship's owner was not present, *eau de Stiglul* was, in various plass containers. SIPACUM and *Sunmother* ran *Sunmother;* Quindy monitored from the lounge.

"She grew up on Aglaya," the Outie went on. "Ever punch up 'Aglaya'?* She's mentioned that entry, with both scorn and bitterness. To Aglayans on Aglaya, it's the universe. They aren't barbarians—they just haven't had the disadvantages of technocivilization as we have. That was all she knew, and she was in love. About to marry, for life. Jonuta ended all that. Very soon, her 'barbarian' idyllic illusions were shattered into a million pieces, all painful. The Universal Edutapes entry added an exclamation point. It says openly that Aglaya has no value except for that big blue flower, whatsitsname."

Sweetface looked down, and grim. It knew all this. It had been a prime participant in Janja's capture and the smashing of her illusions. It was neither proud nor happy

---

*AGLAYA (N175-2Gs 13 a, u, p). PROTECTED/UNDVLPD. XANTHOCHROID (CAUCASOID?) INHABS: LT. IRON AGE. TOP. 2/3 LAND SPARSELY POP: HVY RAIN FORESTS. UNIRELIGIOUS: SUN + PLANET-RY. APONYM. THOT TO BE FORM OF GYNECOCRACY. ONLY KNOWN VALUE: *phrillia* (q.v.)
—*Universography Edutapes*

about it. The trouble was, now it was also not at all happy or proud about having betrayed Jonuta.

Sweetface wished it were with Janja now. They could mope together—and maybe bring each other out of it. But Captain Janjaglaya did not desire company.

(She didn't want to be called Captain Janjaglaya, either. "I failed that test!" she had snapped, cutting them off further as she cut herself off inside.)

"She has told us all, more than once, that she has stayed alive and striving—enduring and coping—only by thinking of her goal. Her *Mission*. For a year, she has dreamed of it. The quest for Qalara and the destruction of Jonuta. Corundum promised her that and she joined him. Hellf—excuse me, Kalahari; let me put that another way. Janja felt that Kalahari promised to help her get Jonuta, and so she joined *her*. On Resh she was not only a slave, but in the hands of certified textbook sadists. She stayed alive by thinking of escape. She escaped! *She* got herself free, and she killed those three bastards into the bargain. *She* got herself off Resh, with a little help she won't talk about. And in a shockingly short time she had learned enough to be a student advisor—and had killed Srih, and had become Corundum's . . . had joined Corundum.''

"Would you kindly stop repeating that goddamned furbaggin' whoremongerin' sisterslicer's name?" Kalahari snarled. "I'm going for another drink." And she stood.

Trafalgar hardly glanced at her. "Already she had changed. Janja on Aglaya was no killer! She soon had enough of Co—that murderous flainer, and joined you of *Satana*. You know what that led to. The riot on Mottchindi. Corundum's inspace revenge. The forced-planetfall on Knor and slavery to those—''

"Sawed-off stump-legged furbaggin' sadistic sons of frogs," Cinnabar supplied, without smiling.

Trafalgar glanced at Quindy. She wore flop-top and shorts. At the outside of each upper thigh a decoration gleamed; four fifths of a thin ring of large diameter, each of gleaming crystal quartz even brighter against the jet of her skin. The other fifth of each ring was imbedded in her flesh. Souvenirs of the Knorese captivity.

"Exactly," Trafalgar said. "We all escaped—and Janja killed again, for all of us. Next—Jorinne. She tried to rescue Hellfire all alone, and was captured by the same kidnappers. More sadistic swine! She endured, she survived— *she* attacked the captors and rescued herself and Hellfire! And all the while it was her goal that kept her going through monstrous adversity—the goal she saw as a Holy Mission. Jonuta. And then she had the means! This ship, and us. Mostly you, Quindy and Sweetface. Then came the excitement of the chase. Does any of you think she ever gave thought to what she'd do *after* she got Jonuta?"

He gazed at them in silence. They looked back silently, and looked down.

"The chase! Lord lord and Theba's navel, from Jorinne to Thebanis to Qalara to Luhra to Ghanj to Franjistation! And brilliantly—with your brilliant help, Sweetface—she got him. She used Jonuta's own ingenious methods to end Jonuta's career, at last."

"And good riddance," Quindy muttered, staring at nothing at all. "And I suppose we all see your point, Traf." She sighed. These days she looked as dolorous as Janja, or nearly.

"Well, I'm not sure *I* do," Kalahari said, reentering the lounge bearing a new drink. "What's your point, Truhfalgrrr?"

He glanced at her, one eyebrow up. He made no sweeping gesture. "Sister mine, if you retired from the spaceways only to booz, you're better off returning to the owl-hoot trail."

"Nag, nag—the what?"

"Just an old cliché. Sorry. My point is simply this, and it is all our problem: Janja grew up elsewhere and elsewise from us, and never thought about what it was she wanted to do. Now she has accomplished her Holy Mission that was her reason for living and continuing to try. So what's she going to live for *now?*"

Janja's friends gazed at him.

In Janja's cabin, Akima Mars displayed an extraordinary litheness and, for a definite masochistic secret agent, an astonishing penchant for cruelty. Once she had got herself extricated from the awful tri-penile Ape of Balto, she swung to her captor and kicked that villainous Lazareth Lang directly in the face. Blood sprayed. Holographic genius had made viewers of this Akima Mars mellerdrammer dodge and squeak, all over the galaxy.

Janja didn't dodge or even blink.

She was staring at the microtaped holomeller, but she was not seeing it. Or if she saw, she was not registering any of Setsuyo Puma's ("The Biggest Pair In The Universe") travails or heroics or, currently, cruelties designed to appeal to the so-called darker side of her viewing fans' natures.

What do I do now, Janja of Aglaya was thinking for the hundredth or perhaps thousandth time. *I've killed my reason for living . . . what do I live for now?*

Her thoughts wandered along murky trails again—for the hundredth or thousandth time in the past few days—and she did what she had never done. She availed herself of what Trafalgar called "Stiglal'kohl" for the fourth time in the past hour and a half. She poured a strong one. She also added the lemon flavoring she liked and skipped the antintoxicant.

Staring unseeingly at the screen, she prowled the cabin. Thinking of Jonuta. Remembering Aglaya, and Tarkij, and an Aglayan spacefarer known variously as Whitey or Flash— an Uncle Tom, in ancient phrasing. Thinking of slaves and masters and corpses. Masters she had slain. Chulucan and

Sicuan and their major-domo Izhan, on Resh. Boskar and . . . well, another, she'd forgot the name—the Knormen. And Jonuta. Jonuta, master slaver.

Oh. Oh yes, she thought, reversing polarity on the closure of her "uniform" so that it gaped open to the crotch. *I almost forgot Srih!*

Oh you're one of Them now, Janjaheriohir! Gray, gray, but splashed red with the blood of men you've killed. Slavers, all slavers and slavemasters. Evil men, oh yes. Killed with these gentle little hands off "barbarian" Aglaya!

She glanced at the screen. The makers of the Akima Mars series starring Setsuyo Puma, "The Biggest Pair In The Universe" at 134E-64-100, purported to be making holodramas of pure black and white, pure good and evil. Akima Mars versus all the bad guys. The baddest. Always she suffered and always she prevailed, after torture and sometimes worse. Good prevailed, and everyone assumed that the spaceways were better for it, for Akima Mars's presence along its parsec abyss. The whole galaxy was better for it. The universe!

"The whole dam' universe is better because 'Kima Mars beats the shit out of all its nemeses—all bad guys!"

She hoisted her plass in toast to the hyper-busty hyperstar in the holoval screen, just now good guyishly blowing away an entire spaceship full of presumably totally evil followers of the totally evil nemesis of *this* film.

So what do I do with my life now? Akima Mars is fiction. Just fiction, and purest fantasy at that.

And Janja staggered. Angrily she drank, put down her drink to haul off her scarlet jumpsuit (stumbling back to sit down suddenly and unintentionally on the bed, snarling at a universe safe for the good guys that nevertheless made her clumsy).

Oh, he was a cool and handsome dog, badguy Jonuta was. I'm glad I met cool and handsome goodguy Tr'falger Cuw, or I'd think Jonuta was the coolest and handsomest man I've ever met. The only one who taught me something like respect, because he was cooler than I was, and cleverer too—except once.

(Why didn't Kenowa scream? I'd have screamed.)

He treated me worse and better than anyone! I showed the swine, I actually backed him down . . . and damn him, he showed me he wasn't a swine. He turned and left. No no, he would not rape me. Oh no—he just proved his power and my position by drugging me so that I was a willing victim when he had Srih rape me, and Arel, and Sw . . . Sweetface.

She wrestled the pants off her legs and flopped back on the bed.

"Maybe I should go kill Swee'face too," she told the ceiling. "Make it seven. Kill 'em all, Janja. Kill 'em all. You an' 'Kima can make the whole slicin' universe safe f'r Aglayans!"

Why didn't Kenowa scream?

I can't go back to Aglaya and I can't be another damned badguy pirate. I even have a spaceship, but I can't pass as its captain. What am I going to do with my life now? (I'd have screamed, seeing him get killed, if I were Kenowa.)

"All I know is piracy and killing," she called out to no one, and she began to cry.

She awoke with a foul brown taste in her mouth and a headache and she was alone. Quindy hadn't come to bed.

Oh. I locked the door. Sorry, Quindy. Bet you had to spend the 'night' with Trafalgar, you poor thing!

Why hasn't that oh-so cool handsome hyper-competent walking enigma ever tried to bed me?

Why didn't Jonuta force me? He could have. Jonuta was stronger!

She dragged herself up and, holding her head carefully erect and still against its pounding, went over to unlock the door.

On her way to the closet she remembered that she could have unlocked the door by voice command, without getting up. That brought anger at herself, which led irrationally to tears, and she whirled to fling herself at the bed and weep.

Sometime or another Cinnabar came in, dear solicitous Cinnabar, and she ate Cinnabar like there was no tomorrow. After she had done using the Jarp, it made silly er-uh excuses and fled.

There's no tomorrow, Janja thought. *What can I do now—what am I qualified to do, among Them? Be a fobbin' dull merchant after I've gotten used to so much excitement and rushing about? Retire with my ill-gotten fortune? How do I retire? From what? (From my job: killing Jonuta!) How? There is no tomorrow. I've ended all my tomorrows.*

And she wallowed in self-doubt and self-pity some more, and wept some more.

"Hi," Kalahari said brightly, pushing a smile. She was wearing a low-slung, side-hiked miniskirt in green silkeen, with a gold stripe and a slanted row of little tassels, and a weird sort of criss-crossing, one-shoulder bandeau or "bra" that made even her look sexy. "I came to see how you were doin', Cloud-top. Thought maybe you'd taken root in here!"

Her voice and tone were too bright, just as her smile looked forced. She was trying. Too hard. "Hey Janjy— bet you'll pardon me if I mention that you look like hell."

"Go to hell with your solicitous shit, you goddam lesbian!" Janja yelled.

Kalahari twitched, stared, blinking, and left without a word. After a while Janja wept some more.

• • •

She shaped up—to a degree—when they were docked at Terasaki's Ukiyo Station. Decented up and even vanitized to presentability, Janja approached Quindy. Quindy and all the others had donned their red "uniforms," seeking to please her.

They had judged wrongly; Janja wore a white bare-midriff blouse and loose, hip-slung pants the color of lime sherbet. She also carried a spacefarer's go-bag.

"Can you handle the cargo dealing, Quindy? I want to visit the station shop and get some clothes. Whatever they're wearing in Yamato this year."

Quindy was taken by surprise but recovered with admirable swiftness. "Of course, Boss," she said with aplomb. "Good idea."

She watched Janja go, with mixed emotions. Ship's owner should be with her in this matter of dealing for the offloading and transfer of cargo. Janja needed the experience, and besides *Sunmother* was her ship. On the other hand, she had obviously spent some time in her cabin researching; at least she knew the name of Terasaki's planetside spaceport. And her avowed purpose for leaving the ship so quickly sounded promising.

It sounds as if she cares again, Quindy mused. *Maybe she'll rejoin the living now, rather than continuing to imitate the living dead.*

She had no way of seeing Janja walk directly past the station shops and to the shuttle depot. She took the first available shuttle down, took some note of what the apparent natives were wearing, and found a shop. Inside, she found what she wanted: a helpful clerk and currently fashionable clothing.

She chose a loose tunic in turquoise, with a wedge-shaped front and center insert of imitation chainmail—in gold. Self-sashed, the short-sleeved tunic was worn rather sloppily outside, over very long and very loose black pants. She even went along with the wig that made her hair the color so popular in Yamato of Terasaki this year, red. Neither she nor the clerk mentioned doing anything about her skin or her eyes, which showed absolutely no hint of epicanthic fold. To try to copy that would have been silly, though some did.

The clerk and shop's manager both paid plenty of attention to the second Aglayan they had ever seen. What pale skin! Those round, pale eyes and incredibly pale hair— almost a shame to hide it under the ukigumo wig!

Both Terasaks stared, uncomprehending but politely silent, while the exotic customer calmly fed the trash converter the contents of her go-bag. One, two, three handsome crimson jumpsuits. She did stuff into the bag the clothing she had worn into the store—on top of the jewelry the clerk spotted there.

Her cred was very, very good. She bought soft shoes and a black kimono with a meteor shower hand-painted on its back. They went into the go-bag, and she left the shop without ever having smiled.

Her very, very good cred swiftly obtained her a room in a small hotel the Satana Coalition was not likely to consider. In that nice old-style room, she spent the next three hours staring at the holocube. She registered none of what it showed and remembered nothing of it. Her mind was busy, though it didn't accomplish much.

About the time she began to take note of her hunger, the knock came at the door. Plain old-fashioned knuckles on lacquer-look pressed plass.

She ignored it.

Three times she ignored that knocking.

Whoever it was did not give up and go away, and at last she sighed and flounced off her body-accommodating cushion to unlatch and yank open the door. Her mouth was poised to chew out the members of the Satana coalition— her crew now, technically—who must have spied on her and tracked her here.

The man who stood there was not Trafalgar Cuw or anyone else she had ever seen. Nor was he a member of the old Homeworld "race" that had anciently settled Terasaki. He was alone. Not particularly tall, neither ugly nor handsome, and he was staring at her without expression.

Those cold flat eyes were like chunks of frozen black jade.

He flashed some sort of credentials at her and asked to see her papers.

"Papers?" Janja was nonplussed and felt stupid. What sort of world was this, anyhow?

"Proving who you are," he said, moving forward, a wirily slender man with a forehead full of hair and down-curved mustache that looked as if it could never participate in a smile.

Janja did not give away as she should have done under such pressure, as he obviously expected her to do. Consequently they remained rather close-pressed in the doorway of her hotel room.

"Where you're from, inoculations, and all that," he said. "It's simply a routine check."

"Oh, I—" she said, and started to turn back into the room.

He gained another step. "Have no papers," he finished for her. "Don't bother showing me that you're-from-Outreach junk!"

And Janja was caught so well, taken so completely by surprise and now so completely aback, that he succeeded in entering. The "lacquer" door wheeped shut behind him, framing him in black.

"Bet I can get a stopper into my hand faster than you can, Janja," he said, and now he and that mustache and those frozen eyes did indeed smile.

12

Pragmatism is the rule along the spaceways and, according to Arauca, is the highest cause and only true philosophy of humankind: Pure Practicality.
I say bullshit. I'm a pragmatist who doesn't believe Arauca, isn't sure about Descartes, and thinks Morffillon Jasjit is probably the greatest genius in the galaxy.

— Trafalgar Cuw

Janja and the stranger stood just inside her hotel room, immobile and staring as though they were playing a game of frozen tag.

"You have no papers. None that are real, anyhow. You have never had any papers. You are Janja, not Janjaglaya. You are *from* Aglaya. You were stolen by slavers and sold on Resh to a dealer and sold again to Chulucan, retired priest of Gri. You murdered him and his son. You bought passage to Franji by selling yourself to a Spacefarer First, serving on *Rambler*. He too is Aglayan and he is called Whitey—and Flash. You were also helped by a hust-house keeper on Resh, a woman named Kitsko. You used the name of one of her girls, Linshin. You signed on as ship's girl on the IP spacer *Lion of Islam*, which was due in seven days to depart in three—for Qalara. You were very, very intent on getting

157

to Qalara. Willing to whore yourself to the crew of *Lion of Islam*.

"Instead, you blew away a man in a bar a few days later—his name must have been Srih, hmmm?—and left Franji in the company of the pirate Corundum. He seems to have vanished from the spaceways, but we admit we're not sure what part you had in that. Now you have your own spacer and a faked Outie ID. We *know* this, Janja; please don't bother trying to lie. One question I would appreciate an answer to, Janja. Are you still anxious to get to Qalara?"

Hurricane, volcano, earthquake, holocaust.

The universe came apart with a great red crash about Janja as the man with the curly black bangs stood there and recited her history. It was all over. Ended. She would be arrested, executed (publicly, to help stave off war or for whatever other reason They invented). She had been destroyed by Jonuta, and she had killed him. Now she would be tried briefly and executed for that "murder."

Well, at least he won't continue murdering and stealing people until he dies of old age, wealthy and fat. I did get him. This is the best time to be caught by Authority.

Who? What authority?

Wait a min— She found no menace in this man's attitude, in his mind. Only a . . . blandness. Interest? Perhaps some in her as a woman. Some in her as a woman off a "barbarian" and "Protected" planet who had nevertheless accomplished what she had accomplished. But she chermed no menace.

"Could I see your identification again?" she asked, trying to be as quiet and calm-cool as he.

"No. Oh, I forgot; on Franji you also tapped a young ass named Banerjee and a woman named Caramyl. Slavers. And you *acquired* a few stells, and proceeded to spend every day and most of the nights in the public library. Studying. Your hair is naturally white or nearly—

here's a phrase you didn't know: 'ash-blond'—and your skin naturally much lighter than anyone's and I'll bet there's a stopper under the white miniblouse and pale green pants. Please don't make a try for it, all right?''

"Do, uh, do you have a name?"

"Not yet."

He slid his hand into the front of his jacket—he was dressed so as to be overlookable and thus "invisible," she noticed. Everything he wore was brown. Yet so as not to be conspicuous by his very drabness, the brown was in three shades and she had a glimpse of a pale yellow shirt. Only the collar showed.

His hand came out of the jacket with a little black package. It was labeled "Bluejoy," and the cover featured a picture of an ecstatic-faced female, young and attractive. He nodded to persuade Janja to follow his gaze with hers. She did.

He held out the package and carbonized one of her boots, standing over beside the low bed where she'd left them both.

"I do not intend or care to use this on you," he told her, "but I wanted you to understand that I am armed and not with just a flainin' stopper, either. I am fully cognizant of your dangerousness, Janja. You see, I hope to persuade you not to make an attempt on me because I would kill you if necessary but beat the blood out of you in preference. Please go over there and sit in that blue chair. I'll take the orange one with the dragon, so I needn't have to look at it.''

Doing anything else was not to be considered. When she had seated herself, he did. The chairs were a couple of meters apart. The little package with its deadlier-than-drugs contents lay on his knee. Noticing her gaze, he showed her how fast he could snatch and level it.

Janja nodded understanding.

"Now, Janja, are you still so desperately intent on reaching Qalara?"

"Who are you?"

He sighed. "You want a name. Call me Cougar."

That was something, she mused. Labels helped. At least she had something to call him, improbable or no. And he did continually use her name, without prefacing it with the civilizedly-respectful "seety" or even appending the "-sahn" used on Terasaki and a few other planets.

"I meant, who are you with, Cougar? I did not have the opportunity to study your credentials. And you did work hard at taking me by surprise and overwhelming me."

"Oh." He fished out the card-packet and tossed it to her. "So you are even clever enough to understand what I was doing, hummm?"

The ID said he was a representative of the Reshi Inner Police. The picture matched his face. The name was Sinchung Sin. She looked up.

"Nothing here about 'Cougar,' " she said.

He shrugged easily. "I like the sound of it. Why have you been so intent on reaching Qalara—and are you still?"

Janja regarded him in silence, turning the little ID cards over and over between her fingers. Considering the distance to him, the distance to her go-bag. Forget that; her stopper was poked down in the chair she'd been sitting in. The orange one emblazoned with the yellow-and-red dragon. The one Sinchung Sin/Cougar now occupied.

"No," she said at last. "I have no interest in Qalara."

"You mean 'no *further* interest,' since of course I do know why you've been on this quest. Did you know there was an attempt on his life on Franji's space station—while you were there? Won't you give it up? Is it only him, or all slavers?"

Attempt? She shook her head. "I have lived for no other reason but him. Other slavers I have not thought about. What do you mean—an 'attempt' on his life? *Attempt?*"

So he doesn't know everything then! Either he doesn't know I'm the one who made the "attempt" back at Franjistation, or he's playing with me . . . some more, she added mentally, knowing that he'd played with her quite a bit already. His use of the word 'attempt' to describe her slaying of Jonuta was probably just that. More toying, more of his amused playing with her.

Why didn't Kenowa scream?

"Tarkij was long ago. You were saving yourself for him, weren't you, Janja? But since then there have been many men—and women, and Jarps too, I'm sure. It isn't for Tarkij, your quest. It isn't a lover's quest or mission any more. It is pure personal vindictiveness. Vendetta—there's another new phrase for you; see how much I know? You've been intent on murder, all this time."

She shrugged. She was trying to keep her eyes as flat as his, and her expression.

"You won't even deny that, Janja?"

"Months ago, I had trouble calling up Tarkij's face in my mind," she admitted. "But Jonuta had to be stopped. You are right, Cougar or Sin. It was a personal thing. Vindictiveness, vengeance. It will also save the Aglayans that he would otherwise have killed—or mind-kill, as he has me."

"Nonsense. There are other Jonutas."

"Then I have ended one of them," she said immediately. Neither of them had raised its voice a microdecibel.

"You are using an odd verb tense—the past. Have you given it up, then?"

She stared. Then she made herself appear impassive: "I have succeeded."

She saw his start, and his own swift control of his expression, his reaction. "Oh. So it was you, on Franjistation. You are guilty of multiple murder on Resh and theft on a couple of other worlds. You are guilty of theft in space—piracy! Doesn't any of that disturb you?"

Pain lashed into her with that, and she shuttered her eyes while she worked anew to calm her self. She nodded slowly, but when she opened her eyes and answered, her gaze and voice were steady and as cool as his.

"Of course. It all disturbs me—though if you know so much, you must know what sort of slimy swine those creatures were, on Resh; ex-priest and his son or not. Reshi Inner Police certainly weren't interfering with their cruelties, their murders! Jonuta is guilty of far more, though. As to the man you called Whitey . . . I practically forced him to get me off Resh. He is an honorable man, and totally innocent. And Captain Tachi didn't have any idea who I was. Still doesn't, I assume."

He smiled. It was not, she noticed, a mocking smile. This man seemed fully in control of himself.

"Kitsko, Linshin, Whitey—all these are guilty of harboring, aiding and abetting a criminal. A murderer. Also of aiding a slave to escape. That of course is a separate charge. One must always search for as many charges as possible in an attempt to be certain that some idiot does not acquit the accused—the guilty. And Whitey? Honorable? Have you heard the phrase 'Uncle Tom'?"

She nodded in silence.

He raised his black, black eyebrows a little. "I am impressed. You remember its meaning, its ancient application, back on Homeworld? You have studied that deeply?"

"On Homeworld there was one race. Galactics. A pale sub-race subjugated the darker sub-races. In one tribe the pale people released the dark from slavery, but continued to dominate them. I think it must have been because it was cheaper to force them out on their own, so that the paler people would not have to house and feed them. The chains of slavery have two ends, after all. By pretending to free their slaves they freed themselves of responsibility for them."

He smiled without apparent amusement. "A new theo-

ry. You do not possess all the facts, Janja. There was a
war and murders and a lot more. But do go on. It is
refreshing to hear a new interpretation. Especially from a
former slave, hmm?''

''Why are we sitting here talking this way? You came
for me and found me.''

His eyebrows went high. ''This is better than executing
you or cuffing you to take you away to Resh, isn't it?
Humor me.''

''I think that you are enjoying this, Cougar. A cougar is
a cat, and cats play with the prey they have caught, don't
they. Are all you of Resh sadistic lovers of toying with
others?''

''Not all anybodys or anythings are anything, Janja.
You know that. If you don't, you deal in generalities, and
that defines 'bigot.' All Aglayans are barbarians and all
Reshi are sadists? Hmm?''

She elected to answer his earlier invitation, to go on
explicating what she had learned and inferred. ''The mili-
tant former slaves called those of their own kind who
consorted with or sucked up to their former masters and
served them meekly . . . 'Uncle Toms.' The edutapes
referred me to the phrase 'boot-licker,' and also to an
ancient book, which the library did not have.''

''You have it very well,'' he told her, steadying the
deadly little weapon he carried while he crossed one leg
over the other. (They appeared to be good legs, although
his brown trousers were not snug.) ''Whitey is an Uncle
Tom. Whitey told us about you.''

''No! That is false!'' Her eyes suddenly blazed at him in
the most defined display of emotion he had seen from her.
''He would not have—he could not! An Aglayan . . .''

''Whitey is not an Aglayan,'' he told her equably. ''He
is an Uncle Tom. Would you wear a wig if you were not a
fugitive?''

''I had forgotten that I am a fugitive,'' Janja sighed. ''I

do not think of me as a fugitive. I bought the wig for another reason.''

Since there was no reason to continue wearing the red wig, she jerked it from her head and tossed it in his direction. (The ''Bluejoy'' package seemed to leap into his hand and point itself at her. She tried not to smile mockingly.) He studied her hair with a little frown.

''Do not all women on Aglaya wear their hair short?''

''Pos. Until marriage,'' she said, using the term of *his* people; Them. ''I am not on Aglaya and we both know I am far beyond virgin. But Whitey—''

''—is not worth discussing, Janja. He wishes to serve, to be accepted. He will never be accepted. You don't give a millistell whether you're accepted or not. Thus you might have been—are, to a degree. Among some. But no, we have taken no action against Whitey. Or Kitsko, or Linshin. We wanted to find you first, Janja. Someone else might.''

''Someone else might find me first, or might do something to those good and kind people you mentioned?''

''Yes,'' he said, frozen of eye.

She sighed. ''Cougar: in my go-bag are only clothes. My stopper is stuck into the chair you're in. On the right.'' She waited until he had found it—never taking his gaze off her—and brought it forth. He held it high to see it, nodded, checked its setting. He boosted it from One to Two.

''That stopper is of the outworlds type,'' she told him. ''You wouldn't want me unconscious, would you?''

''Oh, I recognize its make. No, I wouldn't. But you aren't going to try anything, are you. That's why you just gave me your weapon.''

She shook her head. ''Right. I am not. I do not believe that Whitey told you of me, Cougar. He is an Aglayan. You do not understand Aglayans, no matter how much you know.'' She leaned a little forward and fixed him with a steady stare. "What must I do to insure the safety of him, and Kitsko, and Linshin?"

This time he showed his shock. This time she had forced him off balance. Janja was glad, for now he had displayed more emotion-reaction than she, and thus had told her more than she had told him. In other words she was right; Cougar or Sinchung Sin wanted something.

"What makes you think—"

She cut him off with a triumphant trace of scorn in her voice. "You came here to catch me by surprise and tell me all this. You wanted me to know that you know everything about me. But you do not, and you want something from me or you'd have arrested me. What is it you want? My body?"

"What makes you think—"

She tried to flip her fingers, but could not. With a sigh and a grim face she said, "Everyone wants my body."

"I'd not turn it down," he said, appraising her with bold eyes. "But if everybody wants your body, Janja, I continue to be the odd one. I want your brain too."

She studied him a moment with her head on one side. "My brain is not for sale," she said, wondering if he knew its value. Could he know the secret of Aglayan cherming? Could Whitey have—*no!* "Those men who have had my body, Cougar . . . none of them has had any part of my mind, or conquered it in the least measure."

"The penalty for theft on Resh," he said quietly, gazing into her eyes, "*by a slave,* is amputation of the right hand. Without regens, Janja. Unless the thief happens to be left-handed . . . The penalty for murder on Resh—*by a slave,* Janja—is death. Resh is a slaveworld. Do you know what death in the psychoid chamber is?"

Janja shrugged and stared with hooded eyes. "Something civilized, and therefore barbarously unpleasant. Slave or otherwise, Cougar, I slew two men who were monsters, on Resh. The father was worse, because he hid all his life beneath the yellow mantle of priesthood. I would gladly slay the present High Priest, too. He also is a murderer, who lurks behind the name of Gri, of religion. My arrangement with Whitey was our business. My action in getting off Franji . . . Jonuta of Qalara had whored me, and the only way to get to Qalara and him seemed to be as a whore. I am not a whore, and have no wish to play the part, any more than I have desired rape—any of the times your *civilized* galactic race has raped me. I am going to stand up, now; be ready with your killer ray and my stopper!''

"Y—" He broke off, for she stood, not rapidly, and moved about the room. He kept her stopper in his hand, without bothering to aim it at her.

"I knew no other way than to play the whore, Cougar. So whence came kindness and rescue? From a pirate! Corundum. An outlaw! You must know or know of the employmaster at the spaceport on Franji. That slug offered to house and feed me until *Lion of Islam* arrived, in exchange for the obvious. *The usual!* I refused. I passed up an opportunity too to be trysted by two spacefarers. With Corundum I went most willingly. He treated me as what he was—a gentleman. He was also a murdering trickster, and when opportunity came to leave him, I did. True friendship has come to me from Jarps, Cougar, not your kind!''

Standing behind her chair, she stared at him. "I will be a hust only when I must, Cougar. When I stole, it was enough to keep me alive until I reached another . . . plateau. A major error was in taking nothing from those swine on Resh!''

It was a long speech for her. She stopped to take a deep breath and stood straight behind her chair. Veiling her eyes, realizing that she had said much. Perhaps more than she had said at one time to anyone, ever. And to this stranger!

"Agreed," he said, leaning a little forward and fixing her with his nearly black eyes, which he narrowed. *(He should not have raised the mustache, she reflected. His eyes are too good to be distracted from by that mustache.* It was definitely not an attractive or flattering one, that down-turning growth above his mouth.)

"You could have stolen enough to pay your passage to Qalara."

"I did not consider it. It would not have been right."

He sighed, looked strangely at her, leaned back. "Janja, Janja. Not right, you tell me! Not right!"

"I have always been prepared to pay a price to get myself to Qalara," she told him. "Whatever the price was—whatever was necessary to catch up to Jonuta. If it had to be paid with this body, very well then. As I told you, those who have had the body have never had the mind. Only Tarkij could have had that. And Whitey, perhaps. But—"

He waved a hand, nodding. "You are a moralist. You are a fanatic, Janja! You have formed your own religion, Janja of Aglaya. And like the founders of many religions, you feel that you have a great and noble purpose. That you are right, in the Right. Therefore you give yourself license to do anything you want to achieve that purpose. No no now—don't remind me that you have scruples. Petty alley thievery and grand larceny are little different before the law, I'm afraid."

Janja was frowning. She saw the truth in what he said. When truth was present, she could not overlook it, no matter how it troubled or discommoded her; the attribute of a good disciplined mind. It disturbed her now. She knew that she had deceived herself, in some areas. But . . . *"Moralist?"*

"Absolutely." He bobbed his head with vigor, and she watched the flash-flash of light off the frozen chips of jet that served him as eyes. "Oh yes, you are a moralist.

Slavery is bad. Jonuta is bad. Jonuta did Janja wrong.
Therefore Janja must do him wrong. A worse wrong; she
must take his life, mental and physical. Janja's masters on
Resh were bad men, therefore it is forgivable for Janja to
slay them. She must reach Qalara—you thought, though
you'd not have found Jonuta there, of course—and so it
was acceptable to use Whitey, to use herself. Selling her
body for gain because of noble purpose. She needed money
and others had more than they needed and no such noble
purpose.''

He nodded, smiling. "Oh yes, Janja. A moralist. Most
of you moralists are careful rationalizers, you see. Whole
societies have been disrupted and nations ruined by your
kind.''

After a long while she came around her chair and sat.
"No nations improved, or birthed?''

"None worth talking about. At any rate, now what?
You killed Jonuta, is that correct?''

"You know that.''

"I do now. What about your purpose for living then,
Janja? What is going to drive you now?''

When the seconds dragged on and she did not answer
but only stared—looking sad, hard hit—he spoke again.

"You aren't of us Galactics, and even fancy that you're
better. Jonuta's death was your reason for living, wasn't
it?''

She nodded, looking down. A glaze came over her eyes;
it shimmered.

"Then you must seek new purpose, or languish or plain
die. You asked me what I wanted of you. Perhaps to give
you new purpose. Jonuta is far from the only bad man
along the spaceways! Others are far, far worse. A moral-
less demagogue can do more harm on one planet than
Jonuta ever could, selling a few people here and there.''

Janja raised her head to stare. "Who . . . are you?''

"Surely I will tell you sometime, Janja.''

"How nice. You want me to do something for you. What? How?"

He looked at her shrewdly. "Do you want to, Janja?"

Janja blinked. She put her head on one side. After a while she asked, "Do I have a choice? You are going to offer me some sort of bargain, involving whether or not I will be arrested and tried. And killed."

"The word is 'executed,' oh my," he said, with a satirical smile. "How delightfully quick and intelligent you are! Almost Captain Janja, and in such a short time!"

She was still, staring, waiting.

"Yes, of course I do. You could not only have purpose but be valuable, Janja. Why, you could actually accomplish something! I could have said that thirty mins ago. First I wanted to hear the depths of this self-set mission in your eyes, to hear it. To learn about you—moralist! I didn't want you to accept a proposition from me just to save yourself from punishment. Most would—and I really believe you would be silly enough to reject that!"

She sat still, chin high, staring and listening. Waiting.

He looked around. "Someone else might possibly be as sharp on a trail as I am. Suppose we get out of here. Suppose we get off Terasaki together. It's obvious that you are very, very interested."

"Of course I am. I also own a spaceship, and have friends. I can't—"

"Yes you can. You will." He stood, putting away the spurious stick-pak that housed the awful weapon and hanging onto her stopper as if negligently. "You have to. I want Janja. Captain Janjaglaya of *Sunmother* won't do."

"But I—"

"Janja! Listen! You failed. You failed, Janja! Jonuta is alive—alive! You tricked him—he tricked you! Jonuta is *not* dead. You need not give me that 'You're a liar' stare—any news broadcast can tell you of the *attempt* on Jonuta, on Franjistation. *He is not dead,* Janji. He is not even harmed. I will admit that he is most likely a bit peeved!''

He gazed serenely at her while she stared, her face working, her eyes bright.

''You see? Now you have all sorts of reasons to live again! Come along—get that go-bag and let's go.''

She came slowly to her feet again, supple as a wild creature. ''How do I know . . . how can I trust you?''

''You don't,'' he said, with a tiny smile, eyebrows up. He gestured. ''Going to bring your satchel?''

''Look here, Cougar, damn it—I have to tell my friends *something!*''

''Wrong,'' he said coolly. ''You do not.''

She lifted the go-bag—and threw it. Powerful legs propelled her after it, pouncing at him.

He sidestepped the satchel and beamed her with the stopper while she was in mid-leap. At that he was fast enough to drop the slim cylinder and catch the unconscious blond before she banged limply to the floor.

13

The wrong use of a thing is far worse than the non-use.
—Socrates, *Euthydemos*

"You rotten fobbin' bastard—you kidnapped me!"

"True. You've been kidnapped by the bad guys, Janja. Now you've been snatched by a good guy. That's called poetic justice, or something like that."

"Justice? I remember your mentioning that there's no real difference between grand and petit larceny!"

"You're judging by your own concept of morality, Janja. That's a learned attitude, from early experiences and formal teaching. It also depends on adequate emotional development. You're an emotional child, Janja. All scarred up in the head, too."

"Noted. Who are you, Cougar? You are *not* with Reshi Inner Police, no matter what your ID says. Bigger, I think. More scope and more power—that's made you more arrogant than most policers, even. Who are you? Who is 'we'?"

"You've played that tape. I told you I'd tell you later."

"Where are we going? What've you done that has my body paralyzed and my mouth and mind free?"

"Leaving the mouth free was a mistake. We're going to where I want you to be. I used a drug. Call it frabgipator."

"Fra—is that what it's called, really?"

171

"Why not?"

"You are just *wedded* to lying, aren't you? You'd rather lie than not!"

"Maybe I had my training in a hospital. Trust me."

"Can I trust you?"

"I can't think of any reason you should. I offer you no promises, Janja. Just purpose. I mean purpose *after* Jonuta, Janja!"

14

In time interstellar man will come to outnumber all the stay-at-homes who have remained on Earth or in its immediate vicinity. He's the future of our race.
—Chris Morgan, *Future Man* (1980)

It hurt, some of it.

There were gleaming steel surfaces, some sharp and some not, and blinding lights and a machine that taught her while she was semi-conscious, feeding information into her between the blinks of her eyes. Remification. Too, they went into her skull with something long and sharp and shiny and incredibly thin, and they did something there, and they did something else with a needle-thin beam of light too. Light with mass. When she was in position to wonder, she wondered if her brain was taking on mass along with all this information.

She received implants and transplants. All this from men and women all of whom were in gray or in white, in this shining gray-metal place on a gray world to which they had come in a gray ship without markings or name.

"Very good, Janja—nine bullseyes! But that tenth shot was off, and you're dead. Again. Turn, holster. Spin and draw and trigger at the count of five. One—two—oh, squat as you fire this time—three—"

and

"Ah, Janja, Janja. One very good hour on the simulator—but in the past two minutes you have taken us right in to the Demonhole. I wish I could just forget modern psychology and beat your ass when you screw up this way. Oops—missed! Naughty, naughty. Try for me again and I'll crotch-kick you—*understand?* Firm, then—let's go study Jonuta some more."

and

"Don't you ever get *tired*, Cougar?"

"Nahh—you Aglayans short on endurance or guts or what?"

and

"Yesterday her *adjusted* system threw off a direct injection of *Pasteurella pestis* in less than nine minutes."

"Sure, sure. That's only Bubonic Plague. What about something really nasty, like Shanki fever?"

"Nothing's like Shanki fever, Sin. You really are a baby-eater, aren't you? Anyhow, we'll try that in a few days."

"Great. If she survives she might make it at that. What's she doing now?"

"Treadmill. Two gravities, ten k.p.h."

"Shit. Why not give her something hard to do? With those fat-calved legs of hers she can run *twenty* kloms an hour, in *three* gravs!"

"You trying to kill her, Sin?"

"Nah, just raising her like a daughter I want to be strong and mean as a kalpy with mange and rabies."

and

"It took her exactly three mins thirteen secs to over-power Bull and Suko—she didn't know it was a test and broke two of Suko's fingers. Took her one min and fifty-nine secs to tie them with their own clothing. After ten mins they still hadn't got free."

"Good! Why the big frown, then?"

"She seemed to . . . go amok, Sin. If Suko weren't experienced it'd be a broken arm stead of two fingers."

"Berserker Janja! So set the fingers then, and tell Suko she should be ashamed. She's the one turned up her nose at training a 'simple barbarian girl from some skungeball planet,' wasn't it?"

and

"No no no, girl, you walk like some barbarian girl off some barbarian planet who's used to walking barefoot and never heard of polite society. Now try to get this through your AOWW!"

"Try teaching me without the snot, Suko, or I'll break the other four on that hand."

"What *are* you, Janja—some kind of sadist?"

"Don't say that to me, Suko! I've been in the hands of that kind of swine—have you? You don't talk to me that way. Ever!"

"All . . . right, Janja. Now do you want to try walking again, and this time think all the while that you're a lady of Ghanj?"

"Firm. And if I don't get it right this time I want to go wrestle the android again."

and

"What happened to Suko?"

"I'm your new trainer, Janja. Shut up with the questions and let's see you *sip* that saufee, instead of guzzling. You make noises like a pig."

"Listen you, you may be uglier and bigger than Suko, but you can't—*uh!*"

and

"Narzha broke one of Janja's fingers, Sin. 'sthat what you wanted?"

"Sure. That pissant Suko let her think she's tough. Finger all right?"

"Of course."

"Tell Narzha to try kicking her legs out from under her

if she gets out of line again—and stomp a little. Janja can take it. Now get *out* of here, damn it—I'm ears deep in reports. Can you believe some asshole out on Corsi's planetformed moon is actually doing research in nuclear weapons?''

and

''. . . capital, Norcross. Gravity point eight-two-ess. Exports as follows: mercury, enarpan, holomovies, the small, superb, prestige-priced groundcars called Hummingbirds, polykel bearings, Tabulata ceramic-ware—''

''All right, Janja. Now Panish.''

''Panish. Fourth planet of the star Kopernikos. Capital, Harmony. Gravit—''

''How many space stations?''

''Three.''

''All right. What color is Kenowa's hair?''

''What is this, Cougar, kiddy-time? She doesn't have any.''

''Try not to be such a snot, Janja. What's the gravity on Shankar?''

and

''Mulkraj refuses to have anything further to do with her. He was trying to teach her to walk like a hust—''

''*What?*''

''—on high heels and aware of her sensuality, and he made some remark about her background. She kicked him in the testicles.''

''The what?''

''Balls, balls.''

''How'd she do?''

''Good point, Ratran. She used the flying kick Narzha taught her, and the monitor got it all. Perfect technique. Absolutely beautiful.''

''Put Mulkraj on cleanup detail and let's see the monitor run of Janja's flying-kick tecnhique. Call me that again and *you* can try training her!''

and

". . . and when the light becomes blue in this quadrant, you then push lever three. All the way in, until it locks. That's in a standard Raushma cabin, Janja. If you happen to be in a Yuan control-cabin you push lever *two* down to *two*, key in B, and depress key three until it clicks. That sets the entire autoplanetfall mechanism into motion. Best thing then is make sure you're zipped and let computer do the rest. *However! If* the computer is not in full online status and/or you have reason to suspect malfunction—"

and

"Another report from KT, Ratran. The research on that moon of Corsi."

"Keep Janja occupied while I study it. Looks like a mission coming up. Nuclear weapons! The stupid son of a bitch!"

and

"—and machines machines MACHINES!"

"Stop being a silly barbarian. You are a machine, Janja. A machine fueled and driven by the internal combustion of hydrocarbons. Machines have made you next to immune to diseases—and accidents. Try not to be such a bigot—you are one of the 'Thingmakers,' now. *Things* bring health, ease, speed, practically instant healing and long life, and ability to acquire all the knowledge machines have made available. Using things and then babbling against them is just bigotry, Janja . . . terminal stupidity!"

and

"Ratran Yao! But—then why did you tell me your name is Sinchung Sin?"

"I didn't. I gave you some ID and you believed it. Think I'm Reshi?"

"You exasperating, lying—you *did* tell me your name is Cougar!"

"True. Cougar's just a nickname . . . Cloud-top."

Cougar/Sinchung Sin/Ratran Yao shrugged broad shoulders well padded with muscle. He was a deceptively slender man, packed with muscle. She had learned that he possessed far more strength than he "should," for his size. She also knew that was partly because he was preposterously fast, and just terribly expert. Still, when she wore the tall-heeled boots that she hated but which were "necessary," she was as tall as he. Whoever he was.

The pain of it was her inability to deny logic and evidence: She had to respect this man. Whatever his name was.

"Still a lie." She stared across his desk at him, still stripped after having worked out with some strong, fast, expert goon who had come in from . . . somewhere. Because, Janja suspected, she had become better than any trainer here—and maybe anyone here. Except, probably, Cougar. That is, Ratran . . . well, whatever his name was. "You always twist truth and avoid it as if it might burn you."

"I'm your chief trainer, Janja. Merely trying to set an example for you." He showed her his exasperating smile.

"You had me cold, on Terasaki. Why not tell me then that your name was Ratran Yao? What difference could it possibly have made?"

"A lot. You have used several names, remember? Ever notice that in the holomellers the villain usually says too damned much and that turns out to be a mistake? Something might have gone wrong. You might have escaped or passed a message. In that case you would have been able to pass my real name . . . 'Linshin.' Janjaglaya *Wye*." Now his smile had gone mocking.

The man who had entered her Terasak hotel room two months ago and "recruited" her seldom smiled or even laughed in genuine mirth. Instead he *used* smiles. Satirical, or cynical, or mocking. Of course there were those who said that cynicism never existed until his organization was born.

"You know how to use false names and places to confuse and cloud, Janja, and you're just a beginner. I'm an expert. On Resh I was Sin Yanshin. At the spaceport on Franji I was Humayun and some numbers. At my hotel there I was Tabash and some numbers. And to you, Sinchung Sin. And Cougar." He flipped his fingers. "One name's as good as another, don't you think. And some are better, at times!"

"How can I even be sure your name is Ratran Yao?"

Finger-flip: "You can't. Everyone here assumes it is though, and I answer to it. Use it." He shrugged. "I like Cougar, too."

So she ignored "Cougar," but began to use the new name. But she shortened it.

"Still another ship has been hijacked just outside the Tri-System Accord area."

Ratran stared at the messenger. "Damn! That's . . . what? Five in the past two months?"

"Right. And four in the previous four months. Six in the twelve months preceding."

"And even that's a lot! So it's stepping up. No wonder— T-SA hasn't been able to do a thing. So . . . ?"

"So T-SA has asked TAI for help."

"TAI!" Ratran Yao's exclamation wasn't in incredulity; it was an unmasked sneer at Terra Alta Imperata, which was hardly TGO.

The other man nodded. "Right. No contact to us. Our gal in the T-SA council persuaded someone else to suggest us. The prez—our old friend, you will remember—said he preferred not to ask us for *anything*, and he got council agreement."

Ratran slapped a hand over his heart. "Ah, how the galaxy doth love us, Yash! So all right, just keep compiling information and looking for some coordination—or a likely culprit! Obviously someone somewhere is getting mighty bold, and that usually means someone's getting mighty big ideas! Meanwhile . . . let T-SA suffer then, while TAI shows how wonderful it is. Oh—Yash. Anything from Blazer?"

"Nothing for two days. That was 'We're there. Working on the problem. Looks promising.' "

"That dam' Outie's sure tight with words, isn't he! All right then—let me get back to work, Yash."

He watched the man leave. Damn. Blazantagar Ehm was one of the best Level Two agents there was. He could take care of himself. But this T-SA thing . . .

Hmm. I'm going to contact the Iceworld Connection, no matter what names he/she/it four-dimensionally calls me for "disrupting research!"

She had been at her social studies for three hours and was taking a break before her dancing lesson: "Rat, this man Mockiavely. He said that the wise plotter either has no assistants, or destroys them after the plot is carried out."

He nodded, gazing at her with his large black-brown eyes, disarmingly dishonestly, disgustingly soft and languid when he wanted them to be. Charcoal brown eyes.

"Is that what I am to expect? Once we've completed whatever it is that you're preparing me for . . . will I be in danger?"

"Always. But not from us, Janja. Not unless you betray us or go the other way. Remember that we have something Mockiavely did not, and could not even conceive of. A *large* organization, all dedicated to the same purpose. Not even his ideal, Chezary Borzhya, could command such unity of purpose, such loyalty—such *competence*."

"Loyalty," she said, cocking her head. "How will you insure that?"

"To begin with, you *are* loyal. It's part of you. You even chased off singlehanded after two kidnappers who grabbed a friend. Considering your lack of knowledge and expertise, that was stupid."

She flipped her fingers. "No use stating the obvious, you've told me. I know it was stupid."

His smile looked as if it might be considering trying to be genuine, and he winked. Pleased with his student. Then his face and eyes went icy.

"Beyond that, though—leave here. Try to tell someone who you are, what you are, what we are."

"I don't even know!"

"Of course you do! You aren't stupid. You know where you are. What you're a part of, I mean—and you know that you *are* a part of that 'we'."

She gazed at him, studying his face with its tiny mocking smile. She had only respect for his intelligence, his genius, his utter competence. *And I'd still love to smear his smarty smile for him!* It was maddening, that smile.

She said, "Do I?"

"Of course you do, Janja. Say it."

"The Gray Organization."

He bowed his head, smile widening. It was the satiric one. "Ah, what drama! TGO, Tee-Gee-Oh doesn't stand for 'The Gray Organization,' Janja. That's just a popular phrase, invented by some grat's-ass politician on a minor planet. TGO is TransGalactic Order, keepers of. We aren't gray, Janja."

"Oh? What is TGO's purpose?"

"You know." (A section of his desktop went blueswirlish and was pulsing. He glanced at it, made a face, returned his calm, wide-eyed gaze to her.) "To maintain order along the spaceways. To work toward more law and order and to preserve what exists. To maintain a balance in the Galaxy, Janja."

"Balance. With slavery, enslavement, kidnap, piracy, illegal drugs . . ."

Somehow his finger-flip seemed borderline obscene, rather than the mere digital shrug it signified. "Some offenses are almost impossible to prevent. Those that affect a few are not worth trying to prevent. Really trying to stop drug-dealing, for instance. What a way for governments and policers to waste millions of stells and people-hours! How silly! Firm: There are piracy and slavery and drug-dealing and gracious-me pornography, too. TGO drew a line and those things are below the line. I'll tell you what's above the line TGO drew, Janja. War. *There are no wars in the Galaxy*."

She looked at him, thinking about that. *True*, she mused, idly scratching one bare breast. The blue patch on his desk was pulsing more brightly, as if in urgency. Damn. He seemed more aware of it than of her bare jigglies.

"The job is to maintain a balance along the spaceways," he told her, keeping his eyes directed at her face. "We stop wars before they start. That prevents wars and the deaths of millions—or billions. We don't protect individuals, Janja—we protect societies! Make that *society*." He held her gaze for a long moment, making sure of the effect. Then he said, "To be continued. That flashing light means incoming message. Important. Try coming back in twenty mins—and put something on. I've seen naked warheads before."

She rose and tried not to flounce as she departed his office.

Sounded a little dry in the throat to me, she told herself. *Not made of steel at all, hmm?*

That was why she returned wearing a skimpy white halter and skintights that began below her navel and whose crotch was decorated with a blatant black zipper (over the nevelcro closure). The trouble was that he wasn't there, and he wasn't there next day either, or the next.

15

Gray and white color do not belong to the same thing at the same time; therefore their components are opposed. . . . It is impossible that contrary attributes should belong at the same time to the same object.
—Aristotle

Technician Cleya came into the darkened lab while he was setting the bomb. She was quite pretty, with her round face and back-bound hair and dimpled chin, and she cared, he could see, about her appearance. The Tech's smock was an off-green, rather than tan, since anyone sensible knew that tan tended to make the wearer look larger. And her tights were in a medium blue, showing off her nice legs. It seemed odd, for a physicist who had chosen to stick herself out here on this damned little moon orbiting Corsi. And to work on this project with the idiot Vilarik!

"What are you—who are you? What are you doing here?"

He rose, blinking a little, since she had turned on the overhead lights. He had been working by the light of the spot-torch headbanded to his forehead.

"Uh . . . which should I answer first, Technician Cleya?"

"You are not authorized to be in here and you are being impertinent! How do you know my name?"

"You're wearing a badge, dummy," he said, and gave her a jolt with the stopper. The outworlds Two-beam made her jiggle, made her eyes cross amusingly, and dropped her like a discarded bag of vegetables.

He put away the stopper and moved quickly to her. Grasping her by one armpit and one breast, he dragged her over to where he was working. There he let her slump and returned his attention to the firebomb.

"Definitely the wrong day to come poking into the lab an hour and a half early, Cleya," he muttered conversationally.

She made no reply and he finished what he was doing. He straightened and backed away, a bulky man in a tan lab-smock and brown pants, not quite tight, and buckled sandals. He studied the scene.

Cleya lay crumpled before the open-swung door to a lower-level cabinet set in below a drawer which was below a stained ceramic plate atop a preswood work-area. The cabinet was 50 x 50 sems, and 40 sems front-to-back. Clamped to its "ceiling" back in the rightward corner was his bomb. It did not show and it did not tick or even hum. It would go off in less than an hour. Since he couldn't have stopped it or dismantled it now if he wanted to—which he did not—he assumed that no one could.

"Wrong day to be so eager, Cleya," he muttered, and got her out of the way so that he could apply his electronic unlocker to the cabinet to the right of the open one.

In a few seconds it too was open. He removed lots of papers and pushed them sloppily into the first cabinet. Grunting, he got Cleya bundled together and stuffed her into the second cabinet. It wouldn't be comfortable once she regained consciousness, and she wouldn't be able to move much. That was of no concern to him and soon would not be to Technician Cleya.

Closing both cabinet doors, he applied his electronic unlocker to each—just long enough to scramble their locks. Now no one knew how to open them.

He paced to the door, removed the headband with torch, shut off the lights, and stepped out into the hall. He closed the door, tried it, glanced around, and scrambled its lock, too. Then he moved along the corridor with its ridiculous mock-terazzo floor. Though he did not seem in much of a hurry, his rather tigerish gait moved him along swiftly. He entered the restroom.

The watchman was still in the stall and didn't appear to have moved.

"Still unconscious," muttered the man who had made him that way, and sighed. "But not for long enough. Just in case . . ."

He gave the watchman another Two-jolt. Storing away the stopper, he produced a plastic bag. With swift expertise he drew it down over the unconscious man's head and pressed it in all around his neck. The multi-purpose pen from his breast pocket generated enough heat to seal the bag.

Too bad. It's just that we protect society, not individuals.

He left the watchman where he sat. Having applied a minilock to the restroom's door and spun it at random, he departed the building the same way he had entered: the main door. He scrambled the main lock and hurried to the tiny electric rambler he assumed was Cleya's. She hadn't locked her little red car, but it would not respond to simple commands or, surprisingly, to either of the two overrides he tried.

"Cautious sort, this Vilarik," he muttered, and used the pen.

He drove Technician Cleya's car over to her boss's house and parked right in front. He walked up to the door of the house he considered an ugly monstrosity, one of those inflatable minipagodas. Looked ridiculous. So did the even more anachronistic doorbell, which he rang.

A few seconds later the door was opened by that idiot Vilarik himself. (The trouble was that though the phys-engineer was an idiot, he was also a bit of a genius. He had been in the *Observe!* file for years.) Vilarik gazed coldly at his visitor, a broad-shouldered, wiry man in gray and maroon. He wore a wide-eyed look and a droopy mustache. He was carrying some sort of package, nicely wrapped with a gloswirl ribbon.

"Oh—for my daughter?" Vilarik's face went pleasant.

"Uh—for the wife of the esteemed Vilarik-san, from someone on far Meccah," the visitor said, wielding the package he had taken from beside the seat of Cleya's car. He did not put it into Vilarik's outstretched hand. "It has come a long, long way and she is to sign for it, esteemed sir."

"I am aware of the distance to the planet Meccah," Vilarik said with austerity. "However my wife is not here. That must be a birthday gift from my wife's parents to our daughter. She is down on Corsi with her mother, since tomorrow is her birthday and we allowed her to choose her own present."

"How nice! And she chose a day in Newhope!"

"Ummm. I'm sure it will be quite all right for me to sign for the package. I say—that lectricar looks just like my assistant's!"

"Really!" the messenger said, handing the other man an ID-pak. "I am glad you are alone in the house, Vilarik-san. I am Humayun RE4435d, with TAI as the ID shows, and we need to have some conversation."

Vilarik looked up from the ID with a jerk, and he did not look pleasant. "Damn! However did you people find me?!"

"The genius Vilarik was worth watching. Might we step inside?"

"Do I have a choice?"

The man called Humayun RE4435d said nothing. After a longish moment, the physicist sighed and turned to walk back into his home. He threw words back over his shoulder: "Close the door, won't you." (Humayun did, and made sure it was locked.)

Vilarik did not see fit to suggest that his visitor be seated when they stood in another anachronism: a black and white and cream living room in the style called Kwampaku. Humayun didn't bother with small talk but made his attack at once:

"Vilarik, the nuclear weaponry system you are so busily and secretly at work on is both illegal and not compatible with the future. Any future. That is why they were sensibly made illegal, long ago. It isn't just all that easy mass killing—we have lots of ways to do that. It's just that the damned things are messy, filthy, and keep on being so for years. Centuries, even."

Vilarik absorbed the surprise attack, swallowed, and nodded. "That is nonsense. Nuclear weapons can be made perfectly safe. I am proving it."

The other man didn't bother to snort or sneer. "You don't feel that the words 'nuclear weapons' and 'perfectly safe' are mutually exclusive?"

"Of course, in a way. That is, no weapon is 'perfectly safe.' That is not their purpose. A slingshot and a pulsar and a stopper, however, are not dangerous when they are not used and not dangerous after they are used. My work will soon prove that nuclear weaponry can be just the same."

"I'm afraid that wise heads long ago decided that the trouble with what you are working on is that once it is set into motion, there is no call-back option. Long ago—"

"You are telling me that you know exactly what I am working on?" This time Vilarik's face showed his dismay, and his voice rose.

"I am. Long ago a whole planet was divided into two mutually-hating factions. The nuclear researchers and creators on both sides labored long and hard. The result was the creation of an entire planetary attitude with a foundation that was quite irrational." Humayun sighed. "The trouble with you, Vilarik, as with those smugly righteous monsters, is that you have never been in war. Anciently, such people were excused from what their societies called 'military service' so that they could educate themselves further, in valuable science. The science of war. Others fought them, and died in them."

Showing anger rather than pain, Vilarik swung away and stalked the length of the large and coldly furnished room. He stopped to stare—or pretend to stare—at a half-wall holo of a tall purplish mountain all snow-capped as if sprayed with cream topping. With his hands clasped behind him—strangely, in a rather military posture—he spoke without turning.

"I shall not debate such . . . points with a . . . *policer*," he said, making his scorn implicit. "All this is too ridiculous. Outlawing any form of research is evil, stupid. A seeker after knowledge cannot be bound by such antiscientific strictures!"

"Oh, only idiots are against science and research and the progress it brings," Humayun said. He imitated the physengineer's stance, addressing the man's back. "Yet nuclear weapons have a habit of getting out of control, people being what they are, and all wise persons are opposed to *plague*. You, Vilarik-san, are a plague-carrier. Worse, you are a willing one."

Vilarik seemed to tighten, then spun to stare, quivering, with eyes showing both rage and outrage.

"You . . . pompous idiot of an undereducated *policer*! What the bloody vug then do your masters at TAI intend—or demand?"

"Nothing at all. TAI probably doesn't even know about the clandestine work you came here to hide. You have just become one of the few to look into the face of TGO and know it, Vilarik, you little swine. And what TGO wants is absolutely no possibility of nuclear weaponry on Corsi or its fifth moon or any other damned place." He smiled. "Promise?"

"You—*ass!* As if I—*Glaph!*" The last word he called out loudly.

Both Humayun RE4435D's hands came out from behind his back then, and the right one held a stopper. "Better that you were tortured slowly to death, but . . ." A moment later Vilarik seemed to shimmer. Then Humayun squinted against the expected little flash. After that Vilarik vanished into component atoms that drifted like dust.

Immediately Humayun pounced to place his back against the front wall, so that he could face anyone who entered by way of the front door or the doorway leading back into the house. He put on a natural, open face, and again stood as Vilarik had, with both hands behind his back.

The large man came rushing into the room from within the house. He wore only trousers and a stopper, which he wore in one dauntingly large fist.

"Are you Glaph?" Humayun asked in an equable tone. "The esteemed Vilarik-san's bodyguard, I presume?"

"Pos," the big man said, and Humayun noted that his larynx had been adjusted to give him a dauntingly raspy bass. Glaph's stopper was leveled at the stranger in his employer's living room. "I heard him—where is he?"

Eyebrows up in a pleasant expression, Humayun nodded. "Behind the sofa," he said, and when Glaph glanced that way Humayun's hand moved with incredible speed and Glaph joined his late employer.

By the time Humayun reached his tiny spacer he had thoughtfully destroyed Cleya's birthday gift for her boss's daughter, on the grounds that it would only be a painful reminder. By that time Humayun was someone else altogether. By that time, too, the bomb had let go. All evidence of Vilarik's work, along with his assistant, was simultaneously lighting and smoking up the little moon's sky. The man called Humayun sped away into the smoke, into the sky and beyond it.

He strove not to think about the spoiled birthday celebration, but such knowledge was the burden of a TGO agent. Individuals suffered to make societies safer, and Aristotle was wrong. The universe was gray.

Kislar Jonuta came briskly out of Hakimit Medical Center on Qalara wearing a small smile and a loosely nondescript gray longcoat over white tights and white softboots. The wide-brimmed, flat-crowned hat shaded and shadowed his face—which was not his face at all. The miniprojector made it homely, skeletally bony, and provided it with an unfortunate chin. Since that near thing on Franjistation, Captain Cautious was a lot more cautious.

Again he wore—legally—a stopper, holo-disguised as an eyecorder in its beige case. Again he had visited with Fumiko Kita-daktari and that same assistant, to inspect himself and the monitors; and again he had made a memory deposit in a secret Hakimit store-against-need-for-recall holographic system.

That depositing had been a grimmer business this time, but he wanted every detail of the so-close murder attempt recorded. If there was a next attempt, it might come even closer. Like it or not, he would be visiting Qalara more often, in future.

He smiled, ambling along the walk as if he was in no hurry at all but was merely enjoying Galileo's afternoon brightness and warmth. At least more frequent visits would make Miko happier! Their screwing in her office had hardly been proprietous and not wholly comfortable, but it had been most enjoyable indeed.

He had decided: When he redshifted into space again in a few days, he would leave both Kenowa and HReenee behind, whether they liked that or not. Miko's assistant would go along on this trip, along with Sak and Shig and Yanger. A bit of business on Bleak, and then "down" to Jarpi and a sweeping trip "up" to Aglaya, to put him very much in business again.

Miko's assistant meanwhile would do his job, and if he didn't care for Captain Cautious's business, he could just look the other way.

"Glad to see you're back," Janja said. "It's been a long twenty minutes. Is there any use in my asking where you've been?"

Ratran Yao shrugged. "Oh, to Corsi or thereabouts. That's about the most obscenely blatant crotch-adornment I ever saw."

Knowing that he had returned last night, she had deliberately put on the skimpy white halter and skintights again. The ones whose nevelcro closure at the crotch was covered by a black zipper. She had decorated her navel to make it the center of an atomic symbol, the ellipses in blue and lavender.

Since she made no comment, he nodded congratulatory approval and spoke on. "We were discussing TGO, I well remember. It still functions. For society—societies—Janja, collections of individuals forming the whole that is the whole pattern of humankind, not mere individuals as individuals."

She sat and crossed her legs because, while she had chosen the pants that encased them just a little more snugly than skin, she could not help but be self-conscious.

"I hear you," she said. "You listed fine, soaring motives, I remember, and I have been thinking about that—"

"While making five perfect scores in three separate areas of study," he said. "Congratulations, Janja."

"How nice you are! Where've you been, out killing someone?"

He flipped his fingers, showing nothing. "Holy Musla—how nasty you are! And for a moment I had thought you had dressed so sexily in an attempt to arouse me!"

She tried to cover her reaction to that shot, which had gone home.

Damn! She said, "Human values. A force of purest Aristotelean good-white aligned against all the multitude of black-for-evil forces in the universe."

He kept his face wide open and pleasant. "That describes TransGalalactic Order, Janja, yes."

"And you kidnap," she said, "and murder, and steal, and lie and cheat, Rat, with or without legal authority. You—"

"Oops. Mistaken premise. You cannot arrive at a proper conclusion when your reasoning is based on a false premise. Remember Aristotle!"

"You told me he was just a dead ancient barbarian who knew nothing but a tiny sector of a small planet, and that he was dead wrong."

"Ouch. Make that 'wrong about most things, right about some,' then. We have full legal authority, Janja. The Empire was tried. It wasn't intended; it just grew until it was there, a space Empire, and then it proved that it was a contradiction in terms. Empire cannot exist on a galactic scale. Now every planet—every civilized planet, my sexy little barbar with your eye-grabbing navel—contributes to our upkeep. That makes us completely legal."

"Put that on hold," she said. "You don't like the way I'm dressed and painted? You don't approve, perhaps?"

"Oh my gwacious, I wuv it! You are a very sexy female, Janja, and you very well know it. So—" He gestured. "Flaunt it!'"

She returned to TGO. "But you've kidnapped people, you lied to me, you misrepresented yourself on both Resh and Franji and Terasaki—"

"—and other places!"

"—and you maintain what you call 'order' by illegal means."

"Neg. The means are legal because they're ours. We merely use 'sinful' means; methods that the judgmentally inclined judge 'immoral.' Do you think it's better to *serve* the Law and so let off a person who has murdered again and again because it makes a bargain with lazy enforcers and admits its crimes—and has to be let off? We do not agree with that. I do not."

She shook her head, wishing she didn't have to. "No. I do not either."

"That's only one reason you are part of the 'we' here, Janja! We *are* the law. The over-law. There is no way we can operate illegally. That is *not* mere semantics! We are a legally constituted authority, above all others, by their agreement. We do not *need* court orders. Yet unlike petty policers we don't swagger about intimidating people just because we can. We prefer not to be noticed! We haven't time to play legalese games with local authorities, and accepted, local-law rules for arresting and questioning, or judges or compujudges or twelve good persons and (sometimes) true. If we descended to that we would be trading away half our effectiveness, or more. TGO is *needed*, Janja—always!''

Ratran Yao gazed at her from behind his desk—warm gold-flecked plasteel—and his eyes were not frozen. He wore his usual brown, although the open collar of his jacket was black. Janja shook her head and the wisps of her delicate cloud-pale hair, uncut for three months now, flailed her cheeks.

''That *is* semantics, Rat. TGO is a shadow organization and everyone knows it. Most fear it. TGO does just what it wants, because no one has any control over it. TGO—''

''*False!* Wrong!'' Now he let her see emotion, or at least a deliberate show; he slapped his desk. ''*We* control it! This is the first super-police force in all history that does *not* abuse its authority and power! Does *not*, Janja!'' he snapped, and he looked ready to bite.

''To begin again then,'' she said relentlessly, ''TGO does just what it wants, controlled only by itself. TGO murders . . . *assassinate* is just a nice word, invented to cover a specific type of murder; the dead person was not just anybody but was important, so it was 'assassinated' rather than just 'murdered' like anyone else.''

It was his turn to give the finger-flip that reminded her of his lessons against stating the obvious. He said nothing. He merely listened. Meeting her eyes directly all the while.

''No matter what the goal, the accomplishment, that isn't Aristotle's white behavior—it's black-for-bad. Not good, but evil. Gray is white with black mixed into it— and black is stronger than white.''

He yawned elaborately. ''Ah, philosophy. An ignorant ancient who spoke for the teensy little part of the little world he lived on. Pure black and white just can't exist, Janja, in Aristotelean terms. Tell that to the Director!''

"How could I possibly tell that to the Director? I have no notion who he is—I wonder if you have.''

"Oh, you think it's a he?''

"Women would be even less direct,'' Janja said, almost smiling.

Ratran tipped back his head but did not laugh. He looked down his nose at her. It was a long and broad-nostriled nose, quite straight.

"I am the Director of TGO.''

Janja snorted. "Oh, of course you are! And you go about the planets, alone! Recruiting ex-slaves from undeveloped and 'Protected' worlds. In disguise. Director Hroon al-Rasheed.''

He shrugged. "We've already established that you can't trust me. All right then, the Director is Shieda of Balto—''

"That belly-heavy greasewad of a greaseheaded pirate? Nonsense!''

"Oh. All right then, we have reincarnated Mockiavely and enriched his education. Or I am the Director. Or I am not and furthermore do not know who she is, or he is a man named—'' He waved a hand in groping spirals. "Oh, Brahmin Allahme.''

Ratran leaned forward, shoulders bunching to threaten the brown jacket with severe strain or worse, his elbows on his desk. His eyes were drills, darkly piercing her. His hands were odd, large and hairy, like those of Jonuta. Jonuta, whom she barely remembered. Who, she had proven to herself, was not dead.

"You are one of the Director's people, Janja. You are a part of the organization. You are TGO, Janja—a gray woman, if you must!'' And he grinned. "You and TGO are naturally congruent organisms. I am merely the necessary . . . gardener, who spliced your shoot to the main trunk.''

Silence boded between them. She knew, staring into the

dark eyes that stared back, that he had a great deal of respect for her, and her ability and courage, her single-minded pursuit of purpose. No matter whether it was the main purpose—getting Jonuta and then the man Ratran had told her was behind him (but Ratran lied as a matter of course), or the secondary goals that were preparing her. Learning polite society dances as well as wilder, older ones. Backgrounding herself in the social studies, galacto-politics. Even learning the various ''proper ways'' to hold eating utensils and to drink on various planets, for Ratran Yao assured her that he could pass as native on many, and she had decided to believe that.

He wants me, too, she reflected, moving her back a little away from the chair and putting back her shoulders to jut the skimpily bra-''clad'' cones of her warheads. *He wants to tryst with me—no no, he wants to slice! If we ever do though, won't it be more an act of hate than of love? —Violence?*

In that case why shouldn't we—who has better reason?

Each of us hates, passionately, others and other things. And each of us hates itself a bit, I think. And each other too, for being part of something that we both know is very very gray, despite its noble purpose and great accomplishments. Perhaps he told the truth. Perhaps that greasy child-lover of a pirate Shieda is chief of TGO. What could be more . . . fitting! More gray! Poetic justice, Rat would call it.

Rat! I even think of him so. Each of us highly intelligent, competent—for I'm as sure I am as he is of himself, field-testing or not. I handled my own ''field-testing'' before I was brought here! (Wherever here is.) Each of us devoted and dedicated to what we think and know is good . . . and yet disliking ourselves for being part of such an organization. An any-means-is-justified-if-it-accomplishes-the-Good-goal organization! And . . .

And I suppose that both Rat and I think highly enough of one another so that each of us thinks the other should be doing something else!

That was a revelation, and it made Janja blink and show her surprise.

"You're staring," Ratran said.

"No," Janja said without looking away, "you're staring. I'm merely looking back."

His teeth flashed. "Very good! A silent stare is always disconcerting! Stare long enough and the other person will just have to say *some*thing, because few people can bear silence. After the kind of remark you just made he's even more disconcerted."

She flipped her fingers. "I've been well-trained."

"Of course," her beaming mentor said. "And of course you do understand that I am immune."

"Oh, do I? Listen, when you said 'Leave here and try to tell someone what you know,' or however that went—what did you mean, Rat?"

He showed her the trace of a frown, and she saw the faint movement of his arm that meant his fingers were doing something under the desk. They heard the *yatayata squeakyatata* noise, then her voice, followed by a little more playback noise and then his voice. Quiet and firm, in the middle tones:

"*Leave here. Try to tell someone who you are, what you are, what we are.*"

He brought his hand back into sight again.

"Rat? Why are you recording us?"

"I'm in love with your voice."

"Ha," she pronounced elaborately, "ha. My question?"

"One of the very first things we did was put into your brain the same little addition I have in mine. Everyone you've seen here has the same implant. You can't betray the organization. If you try you will feel both dizzy and *sick*. If you don't stop, or if you try again, you will lose the use of your larynx. If you try again, you will go to the nearest spaceport and come here."

She was on her feet, eyes flashing, her face twisted. "You . . . creature! You Monster! You tricked me into agreeing to join you—and now you leave me nothing else! What about after—after *him?*"

Ratran sighed and leaned back. "We will worry about that when that time comes, Janja."

"Will that time come?"

"Definitely. That is, unless you just fail. It will be up to you, and you will have the opportunity."

She spun, stiffly. On the ball of her foot because last time she had tried spinning on her heel she had nearly fallen. That was just for books. Stalking toward the door, she froze abruptly and looked back over her shoulder.

"Wait a min—what you said sounds a lot more like posthypnotic condition and command than an *implant*."

He waved a hand. "Well . . . whatever it is. You know how I lie."

"Yes I do," she said tightly, and went on to the door. It wheeped open; she turned back. "Wait a minute again. When you say 'here'—leave here. I have seen nothing but steel walls without windows, and people who are a part of the organization. Where is *here?*"

"Don't you know?"

"Of course I don't know."

He spread his hands. "Where else?"

"Rat?" She put her head on one side. "Not—Home-world? *Urth?*"

"Where else?"

Janja stalked out, stiff-backed. He watched the tight cranking of her buttocks with high interest. The door wheeped shut. He sat back and reached under his desk to play back their conversation, as well as to actuate the hidden wallscreen that showed him the world outside. He squinted a little against the light of both suns

16

. . . for what a man says, he does not necessarily believe. —Aristotle, *Metaphysics*

"You slime!" Janja shouted, her knuckles white-planted on his desk, her bare breasts heaving and leaping. (Pale blue, the left; and the aureole of each was a black that shone as if burnished. Left their own color, her nipples looked both dramatic and tiny.) "You just had to—you *slime,* Rat!"

Ratran Yao looked mildly up at her. He dropped his large innocently staring eyes to gaze at her tremulous breasts, looked again into her face.

"If you carried that blue coloring up a bit higher, those warheads might look a bit bigger," he said in a calm voice that was disgustingly sweet.

Her face went uglier and she raised a hand from his desk. He saw the fingers leap out of the fist, stiffening, and his hand shot out to close on her wrist like a gravitic clamp. He rose slowly, squeezing and ignoring her *"uh!"*, edging out from behind the desk. Her wide eyes fixed on his, she shot out her left hand. Thumb extended, it raced toward his head. His other arm seemed to rise absent-mindedly, care-lessly. It snapped at the last moment so that its edge rushed to strike her wrist. Her hand quivered and limpened, fingers dangling. Her arm dropped. He kept squeezing.

Slowly, her eyes glaring and her face working, her entire body trembling with effort, she was forced to her knees.

"Now that's provocative," he said, and kicked her.

Pain shrieked into her body and she doubled over. Twisting, eyes bulging. He let go her wrist and she clutched herself, slumping to the floor and curling. Trying to ball up to contain herself and shut out the pain.

"I don't give a pink-warted vug what you call me, Janja. But don't try to attack me. You'll never be trained that well, and besides I can't be sure I'll remember to hold back. I just managed to catch myself before I broke both your arms. Why are you bare-tiddied?"

"You . . . know," she gasped, without looking up. "I've had to wear nothing but paint for two days, calling attention to my sex. To make sure I don't suffer from the weakness of modesty."

"Oh. Hardly necessary, hmm? Now why all the screaming? Get up. Here."

She looked up. He was extending a hand. She considered, looking up the arm to his impassive face, the big dark eyes that held neither anger nor sympathy. How well the bastard masked! She *knew*, with the brain-power she had not revealed to them, that he felt compassion.

Solely in order to punish him then, she ignored his hand and got up.

"You *slime*, Ratran Yao!"

He nodded, circling back to settle into the molded chair behind his desk. "I got that part, yes. Why am I slimier today than yesterday?"

"I—I—you . . . that slinking crawling Santha . . ."

"Ah." He fitted his ten fingers together, wiggling the thumbs a little. Gazing at them, he said, "Your female pride told you that your irresistible charm prompted Santharama to tryst you. He just couldn't resist taut-bodied

Janjaglaya, hmm? So you condescended to allow him to gratify himself in you.''

He looked sharply at her. ''It had nothing to do with the fact that you're a passionate woman who needs sex, of course.'' He smiled his nastiest little satirical smile. ''Then you found it was one more part of your training, hmm? That you were monitored and holorecorded and Santha made a report. So,'' he said, raising his voice with a sigh in it, ''you had to blame someone. And so you decided to come and yell at ole Rat Yao. Because . . . what woman can accept that she isn't as irresistible as she thought. Firm?''

She stared at him. Slowly, naked (aside from the blue and hot-pink paint on her pubis and the red, yellow and blue on her stomach and the blue and black on her breasts—and the legs vertically wave-striped in blue and green), she sat. He saw not the hint of apprehensive gingerness about the temperature of the chair before his desk. Then she amazed both of them.

First the tears were an itch in her eyes, then a lake that blurred her vision, then glistening little streaks down her cheeks. And then a river. Janja's guts quaked as she raised her hands to meet her lowering head and put her knees together and bawled. Ratran Yao stared, dumfounded.

He said nothing when she rose and left, still weeping. He paid scant attention to the blue stripe that ran down the line of her backbone to vanish into her rearward cleavage. He was male, and he did note that those taut round cheeks did not jiggle in the slightest.

''Tacky,'' he said, activating his computer. ''Give me a vocal on the update on the activities of code-name *Cautious*.'' And he gazed at his desk's top, listening, thinking, doodling.

She was back two hours later and he said ''Shut up'' to his computer while pressing the WIPE key that cleared the electronic squiggles of his doodling from beneath the surface of his desk. Busy or not, he remained constantly available to her, save for the week he had been missing on what TGO called diplomatic mission. (In TGO "diplomish" was defined as a jaunt to recon, a recruiting trip, a surreptitious meeting with some planetary official, a brief trek out into the darkness with stopper or cardiac gun or monofil wire and/or bomb to effect the end of another dangerous individual, usually a demagogue and only once a brilliant nuclear scientist.)

She was just as naked when she returned. (This one was a superb trainee who would not break her training for any reason she could postulate.) It was just that now she had employed symbolism: She had wiped and coated herself with gray, all over except for her hands, which were black. She had left her hair, which looked even whiter against the open-pore paint.

Again she sat ungingerly, and this time she crossed her legs.

He took his cue from her composed face. "Afternoon, Janjy."

"Don't call me that. I have a *friend* who calls me that."

"She is well and happy, too. All of them are. I swear." She looked scornful. "Did you look at it?"

"Did I look at what, Jannn-jah?"

"The film of Santha and me."

He shook his head.

"Swear?"

"Why should I swear, Janja? You can't trust me anyhow."

"Please swear, or admit that you did."

"I didn't. I swear by Aglii and TGO and Musla and your preeety right teety that I did not watch the tape of you and Santharama . . . trysting."

She nodded, showing him a relieved and gratified look. Then, "Why?"

"Why?"

"Why didn't you watch it, Rat?"

He shrugged. "I've seen plenty of tapes of people slic-ing. Just nekkid bodies wallowing and scrabbling around. This one isn't my province. Santha and Rukminy are in charge of that aspect of your training. They viewed it."

"Rukminy says I need more training."

He shrugged. "What'd you think, that you were the best in the Galaxy?"

"He says I—make love like a child, and change into a tigress at the last min."

"Hmm! One does wonder just how Rukminy knows about the mating habits of an Urthly cat extinct except on Luhra and Ghanj! Well . . . as I said, that's their prov-ince. Mine is just to take your abuse. If they say you're a lousy lay . . ." He trailed off, waving a hand with a one-sided shrug.

Janja showed no anger. She leaned forward, swinging her left leg off the right. "Rat—don't make me. Not with Santha. You . . . you do it."

They gazed at each other. He forgot to mask his face. She began to rise; he began to rise.

They attained their feet, leaning toward each other, stares locked. They met somewhere between his desk and her chair. His hands covered her back over half its length, low, while her arms went around him to hold their bodies tightly together. His tongue seemed intent on exploring her tonsils and she sucked strongly at it, striving to pierce his jacket with her naked gray breasts. Her nails dug into the cloth, in back.

"Why?" he said, perhaps two minutes later, with his hand on the tightest pair of buttocks he could remember having felt.

"You know." She was exploring his neck with her lips.

"No. Tell me."

"I—can't."

"It can't be love!"

"No."

"We'll leave here tonight. I have a diplomish. You'll come along."

"All right."

"It can't be love, Janja. I think maybe we even hate each other."

"I know I hate you," she said, kissing the juncture of the powerful ligaments of his neck. "How could I not? You're a foul trickster and liar."

"True. You're a burned-out hust of a putative female with eyes like ashes, who lives only for hate and revenge. Everyone's a bleeder, Janja. Scratch your finger and it bleeds and scabs. We can make it heal without a scar. But your mind . . . you've got a nasty scar in there, Janja."

"Words, words. Must I gag you with breast?"

"Oh, do."

"How many times have you lied to me?" she whispered, twisting on the semisoft floor of the three-person pinnace skimming through space on auto. She moved her head and blond hair rose, hesitated, then settled lazily down in .5G.

"Several," he said, turning so that her lips were at one of the little eruptions of his chest. His own mouth was as full of scarlet-haloed breast as he could stuff it.

"Where's Jonuta?"

"In space. Heading for Bleak, maybe. Probably."

"What rotten taste! What about Whitey?" She trailed her lips down over his stomach, tongue out.

"What about him?" His fingers plucked at the blue petals of her lower lips, opened then, entered on a gentle diplomatic mission.

"*Umm!* What you told me about him—did he turn me in?"

"Firm," he said, while her body arced against his hand to impale herself on two fingers, deeply. He opened them inside her, closed them and opened them, as if he were a physician and his hand a speculum. "Just lick, will you?"

"I don't believe you!" And she bit.

He cuffed her with one hand and yanked the other out of her so rapidly that she almost convulsed. She licked lovingly. He stroked her head and her clitoris.

"You never believe me, with good cause. I'm a professional liar."

"I hate you, hate you, Rat, you filthy rat! Hate you—get it in me!"

He did and instantly she clamped so that he groaned. Nearly collapsing, he hated to begin the movements that might cause her to relax the *gebbadzeh* muscles she had been trained and conditioned and taught to control so superlatively. Then he did, in the act of their hate, and he moved hard. He slammed and shuttled savagely on her, in her until she screamed out obscenities and writhed beneath him and grasped his buttocks and would not let go even after he had yelled and groaned and jerked and quivered, and it was over.

"We've got here so fast," she said, kneeling before the hotel bed and clutching the counterpane as he stood trembling behind her, grasping her upturned buttocks and slamming them together to form a hot tight tunnel around his slicer. "Is . . . is—is—ummmuhmmmm . . ."

And later, when she could talk: "Is TGO really on Homeworld?"

"Of course it is, naïve barbar child! Of course not. Pos. Neg. It's on Aglaya I mean Jarpi."

She knelt up over him, her hair swinging in a cloudy cape over her shoulders to caress the tops of her breasts. She pounded his belly with both fists, and found it nearly as hard as his chest.

"You liar! You slimy sisterslicer grat-slicer! Oh Aglii, O god how I hate you hate you all you do is lie lie *lie* to me use me train me make me a *thing* and a liar too—"

He slapped her, several times, and then lurched up off the bed, spilling her so that they fell onto the floor and tore at each other in another act of hatelove, fingers gouging and scratching while her legs clamped his back and urged him deeper and deeper and deeper.

"Where have you been?" she asked when he returned, and "Diplomatic Mission," he told her, going past her and into the shower.

She followed, hurling away her robe and working to make her breasts bob; with paints from an artsupply store she had decorated them that afternoon, blue and pink and yellow like the colored living balls children played with on Franji.

"You haven't had time to go far or really confer with anyone," she said. "What was your mission. Rat? I know you took Tephur."

Tephur. Te + ph + ur. Testosterone and phosphoribosyl uricase, in carefully formulated combination. Both the male hormone and the uric acid served to stimulate aggressive behavior. That was ancient knowledge, and Janja had seen him take the caps, and she had seen what they were.

"Never ask." He was already in the shower. His shirt flew out.

A compulsive symbolic cleansing? she wondered, and said, "But—"

"Nag, nag," he said, and a hand shot out of the shower stall to grasp a polychromatic breast.

It hurt, but she grinned and went along as he "dragged" her into the sonishower with him. Once again he showed her his strength, slicing away up her while he stood supporting her entire weight, her legs dangling while he hoisted her up and down on him. She was exteriorly cleansed and interiorly inundated.

Forty minutes later when he pushed her back on the bed, she made an exaggerated face. The voice she used was just as silly:

"Oh my poor overused stash—*again*, you virile brute?"

"Must be the testosterone," he snarled, and turned her laugh into a squeal when he plunged into her.

An hour later he said, "I took out a man who within ten or so months local, ninety-one prob-fac, would have owned enough of this planet to have taken it over and got a lien against the spaceport."

"Ridiculous," she said, lighting a redhigh and passing the smoking, sweet-burning stick to him.

"Um. Unfortunately he was definitely no friend of the people. That kind of one-person monopoly is way too dangerous. Best not to let it happen."

She watched him suck deeply, then again, holding the smoke for a long min before he sagged back into the chair.

"How did you do it?"

"Local gun," he said, "loaded with the same virus they use for—among other things—cutting and shaping stone. There's absolutely no escape once the stuff is on you. It . . . eats. Then it consumes itself."

She shivered while he stretched out his legs and sucked again on the stick. It was more powerful than emjay, the most powerful nonchemical orbit-stick yet found. And redhigh increased, rather than depressed, sexual desire and activity, as both he and Janja knew.

She bent to kiss his hand. Her fingers drew it up to her bosom. "The hand of a murderer," she murmured. "A killer, a liar, a subverter. O Aglii, what a contemptible monster."

His fingers twisted to clamp, sinking into soft flesh under taut skin. Randomly swirled paint writhed into new patterns and she groaned.

"Stop calling the name of that barbar god," he growled. "This is a training mission, remember? You're failing."

"You're . . . hurting me . . . but . . . no, don't stop . . . who should I call on, then? And 'failing'? Huh!

Santharama and Rukminy wouldn't think so! What was he doing?—when you murdered him, I mean.''

He drew her down, arm tensing to pull with his hand twisted in the varicolored flesh, until she slipped to her knees beside his chair to relieve the strain. He caressed the swell of her hip with his bare foot.

"He was standing in the bathroom of a suite three floors up. Getting head from the hotel's assistant manager.''

"No!'' Her eyes widened. She gazed up at his impassive face, watching the strange pinkish smoke twist up out of his mouth. "And—and him?''

"It was a her. Women who attach themselves to bad men deserve the fates of their paramours.'' He shook his head and blew at an eddy of smoke before his eyes. "What draws a woman to a man like that, anyhow? He's ruined dozens and caused the deaths of hundreds. No exaggeration. A score of those were by suicide. Worse even than that General Filatravia.''

"Who?''

"Another of my good deeds, a few months back. So what draws a woman to a man like that, woman?'' His pupils were enormous.

Janja shook her head. "I don't know,'' she whispered.

Her shoulders were hunched. He seemed unaware of his fingers, like constricting serpents in dark tan. Squeezing, kneading, hurting. She sagged against his knee, her hand sliding along his thigh to his groin. *I don't know*, she thought, and said, "Let me have a taste.''

He passed her the narcostick. She sucked, coughed, sucked again. Pink smoke plumed from her nostrils. Her eyes widened a little. She squinted, because the room's light was brightening. His pupils filled the entirety of his eye-sockets.

"And . . . what of her?''

"Didn't see a thing. If she got her mouth off him in

time, she's fine. If she didn't, we're in a hotel without an assistant manager.''

She shivered. ''Monster! How can you sit there calmly smoking and tell me about something so awful?''

''How can you be so interested?'' he murmured, pushing her head down. Pain licked through her breast when he released it and the blood rushed back into the areas constricted by those cable-like fingers. They slid into her hair. ''Have a taste of that.''

She did.

She had tasted it before. She liked it, liked being between his wiry and powerful legs, liked it when he lost control and became savage or nearly, grasping her head and shoulder to make certain that she would not take away her mouth. And she always hoped, too. But no, this man's seed also had no effect on her mind. Someday she would find an Aglayan, and become more than she was, by sucking him. Meanwhile, she liked it.

Later, on the ship, he mentioned another man he had killed while he was with his mistress. A union boss on Franji.

''When you have finished what you want to do, Janja, we have a major mission for you.''

She didn't say anything. Did he mean murder?

Their little ship was flashing back to wherever they had come from (Ratran had set the controls). It was a tiny craft, a three-person ship that was crammed with high-tech devices and little for comfort. He had allowed her to experiment, to handle it a bit, to make sure that she understood its operation. To test her skills and reactions. So he said; obviously she knew it all and besides SIPACUM handled most of it. Janja and Ratran were mere passengers, unless SIPACUM—a CAGSVIC—called them. It had not done so for two days Galactic Standard Time and they had risen from the bunk only to relieve themselves and to wallow, once, on the deck—which hurt her back and buttocks and elbows and his knees.

Now they lay side by side, naked, staring at the light-show he had set to play on the ceiling. They had not showered or done anything to the bunk or the cabin for two days-ess, and the air was full of the odor of redhigh and sex and sweat and the pungent aroma of their own dried juices.

"It is a slaver, Janja."

"Good."

"A far bigger and more important slaver than Jonuta."

"Really? I thought he was the shah of slavers!"

"So do most people. The man who will be your assignment is much less visible, that's all. He wants it that way."

Janja's face showed more than interest. "Who is he?" She was rubbing his thigh, high up. "What's his name?"

He gave her a smile that was more satiric than satyrish. "Sorry. First things first."

She made a face, and clutched suddenly. He grunted at the minor pain. Then he rose on one elbow to bite. She grunted, twitched, and neither pulled away nor resisted.

"I hate you," she whispered, while her hand caressed the back of his head. Pressing his face to her.

He licked what he had bitten. "I hate you too," he murmured fondly. "I think you're nearly ready. To get this man, you'll have to take on another identity. Captain Janja will do it . . . a slaver."

She threw him off and sat up quickly. "A *slaver!*"

"Firm." Sinking back, he gazed coolly up at her. "To get to him, you see. He's inaccessible, otherwise. You'll go in as captive."

"Oh wonderful," she murmured, flopping back. "First a slaver, then a captive again. More bondage and rape, I've little doubt. Wonderful. Is *that* what TGO's about."

"Ummm. Been practicing for the past year without even knowing, haven't you."

She jerked up into a sitting position in an impressive use

of stomach muscles, and slapped him. Without hesitation he slapped her back, twice, and not in the face. She collapsed onto his chest and they held each other.

"So I'm nearly ready, hmm?" she murmured after a time, nuzzling his stubby little nipple. "Then when do I go after Captain First-Things-First?"

"How about . . . immediately?"

She pulled away and bouncily resumed her naked sitting position. Now her eyes shone. With the excitement of delight, he saw, not hatred. He wondered about that. Had she forgotten the *why* of it; her fixation of getting to Qalara, of getting Jonuta?

"Immedia—Rat? Really?"

"Nearly. All you need is a *little* more training." He was smiling.

She jiggled like an excited child. "In what, in what?"

"Fellatio," he told her, and chuckled chestily.

"Oh well," she said, moving down on him. Then she quoted from what seemed her interminable lessons: "The end justifies the means."

He laughed, but only until her mouth stopped that and made him groan in rising delight.

By the time they returned to base, a Panishi merchanter with an outstandingly valuable cargo had been knocked over just on the point of making its approach to Toktaga, in the Tri-System Accord. As usual, the hijackers got away with the whole bloody ship. Panish was madder than the owner of a stomped foot, TAI was "accumulating evidence and beefing up inspace surveillance," and the Iceworld Connection ignored Ratran Yao's attempts at communication.

Do Not Disturb, Ratran thought angrily; *Out To The Fourth Dimension!* And he slapped off the comm to that so-secret agent and resumed compiling his so-secret report to a superior he had never seen.

17

You can't have your cake and let your neighbor eat it too.
                                                    —Ayn Rand

Pleasure is a luxury; to enjoy it one should feel safe from his enemies.
                                                    —Stendahl

The light of both suns of the planet that was not Homeworld was bright, and the incredibly beautiful ship flashed bright in their combined light. It was as if poised, lean and sleek, fit for space and for in-gravity flying, equipped with the latest and the best. It seemed yearning, as Janja stared wide-eyed at it, toward the sky, toward space. It was the most beautiful spacer she had ever seen, and it had just struck her speechless.

Such a ship should be called Light of Aglii, she thought, and made no effort to interfere with the rapid beating of her heart.

"You understand that there's a price for all this," a voice said, and she turned to face Ratran Yao. He wore a white dasheek to mid-thighs and a pair of white shorts only a centimeter or so longer, sandals on bare feet, and dark glasses.

Janja's face did not try to suppress her delight with the ship and its crew as she turned an inquiring gaze on him.

"Oh no. You mean you've decided to come along after all?"

His teeth flashed in a grin. "Bitch! You know you wish I would! No, I said a price, not a blessing. It's called tit for tat. We are neither altruists nor socialists, Janja. The giving of sugar-tit without regard for some tat in exchange is the opposite of justice. It's also stupid. So—"

Janja blinked. "Why Rat darling . . . I thought that everything you've been telling me about the goodness of TGO was to prove that it *is* an altruistic organization!"

He stared at her through sunglasses that were dark only one way; she saw his eyes clearly. She was just short of resplendent in fitted but not tightly ensheathing black, picked out and edged with red. The stiffish stand-up collar added a military aspect that was carried out by the soft shoulder-straps, in red.

"Maybe you have a mistaken concept of what 'altruism' is," he said. "By its ancient definition, 'altruism' is unnatural and impossible. To do good without thought for self or hope for recompense is not just against human nature—it's against the good of humankind because it promotes the survival of the un-fittest." His satiric grin flashed briefly. "Unless one assumes that the race did further itself as a result of the stupid 'altruistically' giving their lives for those better qualified to survive and reproduce! Otherwise an 'altruist' is someone who helps or 'helps' others in order to appease and gratify its own inner needs. Usually it uses someone else's funds for this self-indulgence. That is the basis, for instance, of socialism in practice."

Janja sighed and glanced again at the sleek spacecraft awaiting her. Ratran Yao took advantage of the opportunity to let his gaze roam her. She was magnificent! And she had no idea that—just in case—her uniform was that of the personal bodyguard of a certain Ghanji duke. TGO? *Her*?!?

She turned back to him to find him studying the ship. "I'm sorry I brought it up. I'm too excited and delighted right now to concentrate on definitions and philosophical matters."

"Obey your teaching, then, Janja—cut through to the core."

She did: "Right. What is the 'price for all this'?"

"Your devotion and loyalty. Your cooperation. We are providing the best for you, and you realize that your goal is one that TGO does not share fully. We don't mind Jonuta's piddling activities all that much, Janja. The galactic population is so many billions of people I won't even state it—it sounds ridiculous! Jonuta affects only hundreds of lives. When he went too far and destroyed a TGW ship, though, we retaliated. Our way was to crush him financially."

"A slap on the hand. It hardly proved effective."

She added no more. If he did not know that it had not been Jonuta who destroyed that TGW spacer; that it was Corundum who had gleefully done it and set Jonuta up as the culprit—then Janja was not about to tell him. For her to say anything on behalf of Kislar Jonuta would be serving the slaver, not her. That would be altruism and that, in the terms of the long-accepted definition Ratran Yao had just quoted, would be stupid!

"We want you—I'll even say we need you for the mission I've so far only mentioned to you, Janja."

"You needn't fix me that way with those iceballs you call eyes, Rat, or try to sell me. The mission you've 'only mentioned' will benefit TGO, me, the galaxy at large—that 'society' you talk about—and more specifically: Aglaya."

"And more importantly?" He gave her a shrewd look that demanded answer.

Janja flipped her fingers. "What d'you want, Rat, altruistic noises from me about the society of the people who kidnapped me? Of course I have far more feeling for Aglaya than for Resh or Franji or Thebanis or all three combined.''

''Dangerously emotional,'' he said, ''but just irrational enough. Totally rational individuals don't make good TGO agents.''

Janja laughed. ''Certainly no one could accuse you or me of being totally rational! I'll be back, Ratran Yao. And I'll be ready for that mission.''

He shook his head. ''No—you'll be ready to begin training for it.''

And he thought, *Oh and I know you'll be back, Janja! The one little thing you don't know about your crewmember Mulkraj is that he's an ex-criminal who is ridiculously loyal to me and TGO. On the other hand he can't function as a diplomish agent because he still just loves to give pain. Any attempt to keep going with that finest-of-the-fine ship, Janja m'dear, and you'll be back anyhow, fast—and ready for medical treatment!*

''We take care of our own,'' he told her, and thought, *and we take care of ourselves . . . make that ''ourself.''*

As for your crewmember Suko—she can poison you merely with a kiss, and if you should be so stupid as to shoot her, the gas release is automatic and enough to knock you down for hours.

Mulkraj, of course, was immune to that gas. And Ratran had told Janja the truth when he said that Mulkraj was one of the very best SIPACUM interfacers and ship-handlers in TGO; and that Suko was indeed both a superb human calculator *and* gunner.

Just make use of those qualities, Janja, and don't even find out about the others. Come back to me, Janja.

And, since some said that cynicism had been invented by his employer, Ratran Yao added even to himself: *Come back to us, because TGO needs you to get Ramesh Jageshwar.*

Mulkraj came down out of the ship and toward them. A very tall man who had either had a bad accident or affected a bald head—Janja did not know which, yet—but whose chest was a mass of curling red hair. So were his legs, for he wore only trunks and boots. His beard was the color of rage and his thighs thick as Janja's waist. The rest of him was in proportion.

"Ship's ready and just shuddering to get off this piece of rock," he announced, in an anomalously high-pitched voice. He waved a hand the size of an outfielder's glove— of *course* baseball survived the centuries—and smiled his sweetest smile. On him, that was a feral grimace that displayed pale turquoise teeth against a face the color of old leather.

"And the message just came up," Mulkraj said, approaching with the gait of a man only three-quarters his size. " 'The crown goes to the barbarian.' "

Ratran nodded and half-smiled. (Code) "Crown" went to (code) "Barbar." Translation: Spaceship *Coronet* was on its way to Aglaya.

"That's it then," he said. "Time to go. See you later, Janja. Good hunting."

He turned and walked away. Janja stared as he approached the "huge chunk of granite" without a touch or another word. Slowly her mouth came open while Ratran Yao approached the obstacle. It masked the entry to the lift that would carry him back down to the shielded installation within this "unpeopled" planet. It was also supposedly poison.

Not too far wrong at that, Janja thought. *Rotten bastard!*

She turned to Mulkraj. "What are your instructions?"

"To obey you, Captain."

"Umm. Let's go, then."

Tingles of excitement ran through her as she and the hulking Mulkraj paced to the blue and indigo spacer without a name, and boarded.

• • •

"Sak," Jonuta said, "the con is yours. Shig will stand by DS and knows he's not to do a damned thing unless it's double-absolutely necessary." He turned to the smallish youngster from Hakimit Med Center. "We're always in danger here. Yanger and I are going down in the boat."

The biotechnician nodded, obviously wondering. He wore a sloppy shirt and shorts, one orange and one green. Jonuta was down to tights and a soft shirt of Panishi cotton with three-quarter sleeves. Now the man who habitually stood at the con sat in the little-used Master's chair to remove his tall boots.

Sakyo sat in the Mate's chair, half a meter away. "Captain . . . pardon, Captain, but since when do you go down onto Aglaya yourself? You're also about three times better at the con than I am. Sure, Yanger's the new boy here, and Shig's tops on the guns. But—"

Jonuta let his boot clump down hard. "But what?" he rumbled, staring. "But I should send you with a brand-new man? Or leave him onboard when you'll be busy? Suppose he is the very clever plant Shig suspects? No, Sak. With the things that have happened to me in the last half-year, I admit to being nervous. More cautious than ever. I want Yanger with me where I can keep an eye on him, and I couldn't do that here on the ship. I elect me to go down onplanet."

Sakyo still looked unhappy. So did Miko's assistant.

Jonuta smiled, dropped one stirrup-tightsed foot and lifted the other. "Sak, Sak. I'm not going to pull a blunt 'Cap'n's orders' on you now, and you know I could and that would be an end to it. My stopper has no power-pack. Once we're down, I will exchange it for Yanger's. If he's dangerous—he won't be then! I left Kenowa back on Qalara because I'm nervous and I love her. I left HReenee because I didn't have the guts to leave Kenowa and bring HReenee along! As for her brother . . . he's too flaining unstable to have along on this mission. Believe me, I am thinking, and being cautious!''

Spacefarer Sakyo nodded solemnly. He still looked doubtful.

"Now I think I'll be even more honest, since we all know I don't have to. Sak . . . *no* one has ever been hurt, going down onto Aglaya." He spread his hands. "So I leave you up here, ole Sak—where it might be dangerous if some policer happens to be lurking and eluded our scan. Too, I'll just pluck a phrillia or two, for my lady back on Qalara. Doubtless pinin' away . . . on a shopspree!"

Sakyo had to laugh at that, despite the fact that he still was not happy with the arrangement and wanted to show it. He nodded—extra far, Terasak fashion—and swung back to the con. He had no need for touching keys. Jonuta's "Mate," SIPACUM, was reporting constantly, all over the console and on three tilted screens.

"Minimum proximity maximum safe orbit in about two minutes, Captain. Under nine mins to target area."

Jonuta rose automatically to reach for the inship comm. "Spacefarer Yanger, suit up and meet me at launch bay in seven repeat seven minutes. Canned air and helmet are not necessary and we will use both anyhow." He paused.

"Firm, Captain."

"Spacefarer Shiganu?"

"On DS and just sittin' around, Captain. Standing by DS," Shiganu added, just in the event that Jonuta was not in the mood for the casual touch.

"Good. Captain out and suiting up."

Jonuta did that, hurriedly. He needn't worry much. Aglaya was certified safe. Atmosphere eminently breathable; a bit humid but the word *asthma* no longer existed. Gravity heavy but far from crippling—which was why he had increased G on *Coronet* several shipdays ago (to the dismay of the man from Hakimit Med Center). As for alien viruses and bacteria: well, Aglaya had been visited no one knew how many times, for almost two decades. Aglayans were on a score of planets and five or six ships in space. They throve. So did those they came into contact with. Naturally; the descendants of Homeworld had not conquered the galaxy or death or even their violence, but they had very nearly conquered disease, as they had long ago made obesity a matter of individual choice. Galactics were immune to just about everything, including bugs that hadn't yet been isolated or encountered. So were the inhabitants of Jarpi, now, and Aglayans were made so within minutes after being brought onboard *Coronet* and the few other ships that "visited" the cloud-shrouded but warm and jungled planet, for the same reason.

("In orbit, Captain. Target area eight and a half mins ahead. Scans clear.")

Nevertheless, Jonuta was Captain Cautious. Nineteen years along the spaceways, alive and unincarcerated, although he was a participant in one of its most dangerous businesses. All he had lost was a fortune, which was why he was making this run. Recouping.

He would secure his helmet, and he would breathe only the air refined by the systemry of his tailored green spacesuit. He'd take a pulsar beamer along, too, in addition to his stopper—which he would soon trade with the Yanger he was no longer quite sure of. Just in case.

The people of Aglaya were after all not mere rabbits! He well remembered Janja's feral attack—on him!—shortly after her capture, and here on his own ship!—and the fact that she had previously punctured Srih's suit after that ass had Poofed her companion, down on the idyllic sylvan planet.

I wish I had that to do again, Jonuta thought grimly. *I'd have taken them both and seen to it that they stayed together—and not on Resh, either! Master Janjaglaya of Sunmother, Franjistation Control told us! Booda's nose, how did she ever do it? Her own ship!*

His stopper—Yanger's, once Jonuta had it—would be

set on Two and would dam' well remain there. The pulsar beamer was strictly for big emergencies. Some of those big Aglayan animals, for instance. Otherwise, he would see to it that no potentially valuable walking cargo was destroyed without a lot of reason!

"Five minutes to target area, Captain."

Jonuta nodded. He made an autocheck of his air purifier-recycler. All go and better than the equipment of most planetary military and even more policers.

"Captain."

That was the voice of Saboura-not-quite-daktari, and Jonuta looked questioningly at the young man. Helmet on; visor open; suit secure.

"Won't you wish to leave your monitor onboard, Captain?"

"Breath of Booda, Saboura, you are thorough! No, this is just a jaunt down onto a pre-steel-age planet. There'll be no trouble. If I left the thing I'd be admitting that there's da—"

Jonuta broke off. *True*, he told himself. *But he's right. The thing's troublesome and we call it a "monitor" so that even Sak and Shig don't know I'm recording every memory. Saboura's here and I won't be and Hakimit's a long way away. Earn your nickname, Jonuta!*

He nodded, beckoned, tipped back the helmet, winced when the smaller man swiftly plucked away the mini-membank. Then Jonuta hurried out of the con-cabin without a word, fastening his helmet as he strode. Good for the legs, this beefed-up gravity.

He reached the bay of the in-gravity spaceboat a few steps behind Yanger, who had it open and was inside. Jonuta entered the bay and Yanger released the hold. The door closed and sealed. Both men entered the boat. It was small up front, just big enough for the two of them and the necessary equipment and controls. Behind, the hold was not exactly spacious, but it would hold as many as four adults, three comfortably. Relatively comfortably, anyhow.

"Good for you, Yanger. You're on time and I'm seconds late. That's a bonus for you. Situation?"

Jonuta rolled into the seat and lay back. So did Yanger, beside him.

"Ready. All checked out and ready, Captain."

Jonuta reached past him to actuate the com. "Sak?"

"Aye, Captain. Coming up on it in less than a minute, Captain."

"Unwind and make one unwinding pass, Sak. Take up geosynchronous orbit when you come around again, and we'll see you soon."

"Aye Captain. I read three humanoids in the target area, Captain. Pheromonal readings indicate two female, one male. Any time, Captain."

"Now, Sak."

"Now, Captain. Go with the Way. See you later."

"Later, S—"

Thump and *hiss,* and the boat was away. It rushed down, racing free into Aglaya's ridiculous cloud layer. Jonuta eased in the controls. Then he began piloting the shuttleboat down to Aglaya. *Coronet* was gone on, circling the planet, invisible above the clouds.

Gauges showed the two men velocity, altitude, distance from *Coronet,* and the small craft's worthiness. All systemry perfect. One screen showed them the immediate path ahead. Another gridded the planetary surface below. Radar fed into computer and computer simulated hills and forestation onscreen.

Jonuta had been here before, to this same area. It was a good place. An immense savannah of waving chartreuse grasses bordered on two sides by forest in turquoise, chartreuse, puce, and yellow. In the dark of that forest dwelt the kith of Janja and others he had taken here. They came fearlessly out onto the savannah; Jonuta had never visited

Aglaya without catching one or more natives, all pale and blond, out in the tall grass. Once he had taken a big cat here, too. Not alive.

Clouds blew by the boat, tearing.

"Easy breezy," Jonuta told Yanger. "We swoop over right above them, put 'er down fast, and pop out like collectors with nets. And back up we go, to rendezvous with *Coronet*. And then it's back to Qalara. Let me see your stopper, Yanger."

The comm crackled. Sakyo's voice, none too clear, but there and excited.

"Captain! *Ship*, Captain! All we scan is its heat, coming in fast and low, Captain—lower than we are headed for where we were—pos! Headed for you, Captain! Looks like deliberate intersect, Captain!"

"Swing 'er back, Sak, and stay off the air!" Jonuta slapped off the comm. "Heat only, hmm? Somebody's got a mighty fine ship. How could it just happen that there's such a fine ship here just now? Doesn't look like a just-happening, hmm, Yanger. No wonder we didn't 'see' it—we should have, even with everything focused on the ground."

Stupid, he told himself. *Not cautious enough, Captain Cautious*, he told himself, directing a radar sweep and swooping the boat into the steepest climb he dared. Warning lights flashed red, then orange.

"Captain!" Yanger jerked out, his voice too high. "What the vug!"

"Easy. Just take it—"

"*Hello, spaceboat*," the comm said, crackly, and Jonuta tuned it almost automatically. The light was so yellow it was almost white; the damned specter-ship was almost on top of them!

"*We monitored your conversation. Going down to dirty your hands yourself this time, hmm Captain Cautious?*

Remember Janja, Jonuta? She's here, Jonuta! I am worthy of Aglaya and *of the spaceways, Captain Slaver!"*

Already Jonuta was working at evasive action, letting her talk, trying to ignore Yanger who seemed looking for a convenient panic button. Almost negligently, in passing, Jonuta's racing hands touched DS keys so that the spaceboat sent its small-arms fire ripping out in two directions while he wove and climbed, swerved and twisted his guts, but it was all for nothing.

Janja had him locked in and she didn't just fire; she kept firing in a sweep that would doubtless give rise to new tales and legends among the "barbarians" down onplanet.

I am worthy of Aglaya, Jonuta, she had told him a year and more ago, *and you are not. I have only this thought for you, and this promise: I will kill you, slaver.* And this time she did.

Jonuta and Yanger knew no pain, only a violent lurch, the bare beginning of an eye-searing flash (which instantly blinded them both, but that didn't matter) and the merest beginning of violent nauseating disconcert. Then they knew nothing at all.

They and the spaceboat detonated together, in air, and became thousands, millions of tiny bits, thousands of tiny bright streaks rushing down to Aglaya.

As it happened, no Aglayan was hurt. A leapfoot took a piece of terribly hot something, but survived. Jonuta and Yanger did not.

"Gone, Captain Janja, gone!" Suko exulted.

Janja sat staring at the screen. "A shame, really. Death must have been instantaneous. What was that lurch? Did he hit us with something?"

"Forget it. Nothing worth thinking about. Nothing we can't rub out with a nailfile when we get back." That was Mulkraj, and he grinned his hideous grin.

Janja glanced up at a tilted screen. "And here comes

Coronet back. Without its captain! I hate to harm Kenowa, damn it. . . ."

"That ship came directly here from Jarpi," Mulkraj said. "This is a slave run. That means he's got Jarps in the cargo hold. Besides—one of ours is onboard."

"What?"

The hairless dome nodded as Mulkraj, not waiting for instructions, keyed in hot evasion and fast redshift.

"Firm. We've had constant reports on Jonuta for months. That's how we were able to be here when he arrived—you don't believe in this kind of coincidence do you? No no—Yanger joined his crew on Qalara, and we are not going to fire on a ship with one of ours onboard."

Janja noticed that he wasn't bothering to call her "captain" now, and he was *telling* her what they were and were not going to do. She firmed her mouth. But it didn't matter. TGO or not, she was not about to go after or fire on a ship with "walking cargo" onboard. Nor did she think that *Coronet* would pay much attention to a command to shut down and stand by for a Red Rover.

Acceleration hit her hard then, and a moment later it was worse, as Mulkraj took them "up" ten and "over" six and dead ahead and "up" and. . . .

"They're not trying for us," she murmured, staring at the screen. "They're going down."

"They can't believe it," Mulkraj told her. "They scanned and found the whole sector clear and clean. As far as they know we appeared out of nowhere and did the impossible. Look—not a piece of anything of that spaceboat—or anything or anyone in it—was bigger than my torso. And that was plasteel. It's done, Captain. How do you feel?"

"Sated," Janja breathed. "No—the opposite. But don't you get any ideas, little fellow! How do I feel. A lot better than the last time—the time I only *thought* I'd killed the slaving swine!" She smiled. "This time I feel very, very good. Exulted and exalted—heroic! Pos, a hero, Mulkraj.

We're heroes, the three of us. Thousands will thank us without ever having heard of us! Those are words another spacefarer said to me once, Mulkraj; another former slave. And *this* time I won't be feeling any let-down . . . I know what I'm going to do next! Jonuta's life wasn't my life and the end of his doesn't end mine or my purpose. *This* time I'm full of purpose up to here!''

The nameless ship shot away from *Coronet* and Aglaya and then Aglaya's sun. Mulkraj nodded, leaned back.

"Tachyon Trail at first opportunity," he told the computer. "Give us all warning possible."

"Acknowledged," the vocally interactive computer said, because it had been programmed that way, because humans liked to know they'd been heard and noted.

"And what is your purpose now, Captain Janjaglaya? What will you do now?" Mulkraj asked, gazing at the woman beside him. His brows were up in a travesty of Ratran Yao's wide-open expression, which was a travesty to begin with.

"You know, little fellow, you know. Back we go, and I start training for the next mission. Rat says I'm *needed* on this one. Take us back to the Rat's nest, Mulkraj."

Behind her in the doorway of the con-cabin where she had silently moved, Suko let her breath out with a smile, and holstered her stopper.

Captain Janja streaked out along the spaceways.